THE ARCHITECT

THE

ARCHITECT

KEITH ABLOW

ST. MARTIN'S PRESS ⚹ NEW YORK

www.stmartins.com

ISBN 0-312-32392-1
EAN 978-0-312-32392-9

First Edition: July 2005

10 9 8 7 6 5 4 3 2 1

For three who treated every page as their own:

Marilyn Firth, researcher
Charles Spicer, editor
Beth Vesel, agent

ACKNOWLEDGMENTS

I am grateful to my publishers, Matthew Shear and Sally Richardson, for believing in my work and continuing to support it. For investing sweat equity, my thanks also to Michael Homler, assistant to my artist-editor, Charles Spicer.

My research benefited from the perspectives of many people, including Brad Garrett of the FBI, former United States Secretary of Transportation Drew Lewis, Sargeant John "Buck" Goodwin of the Revere Police, Joshua Resnek of the Independent News Group, Todd Morley of the Guggenheim Group, J. Christopher Burch, and attorney Anthony Traini.

For their unique and valued perspectives on architecture, I thank Tom Wolfe and Christopher Alexander.

For early reads of my work, I thank Jeanne Geiger, Jeanette Ablow, Allan Ablow, Karen Ablow, James F. X. Doherty, and Alison Jones.

And for their support and the example of their creativity, I am indebted to Catherine Crier, James Patterson, Anne Perry, Ann Rule, Jonathan Kellerman, Janet Evanovich, Robert Parker, Tess Gerritsen, Michael Palmer, James Hall, and Dennis Lehane.

Finally, for being the brightest lights in my life, I thank my family, Debbie, Devin, and Cole.

THE ARCHITECT

PROLOGUE

• AUGUST 3, 2005, 3:33 A.M.

He was barefoot, in a white linen tunic and nothing else, as pre-
scribed by Scripture. His hands were ungloved. Rays of colored
light fell upon the body on the dissecting table before him. Steril-
ized stainless steel instruments were perfectly aligned on a sterling
silver tray at his side.

He picked up the scalpel and ran it smoothly along the skin over
the spine, laying open the flesh, revealing glorious fans of muscle
with equally glorious names: trapezius, splenius, cervicus. He fastened retractors to hold back the severed tissues, then cut deeper,
through fascia and ligament, to bone.

His operatory was built entirely of stone, according to the
golden section, a rectangle sixty-two percent longer than it was
wide, the same proportions used in the design of the pyramids, the
Parthenon, the Venetian Church of St. Mark, even the paragraphs
of Virgil's Aeneid. The hipped roof was built to the same ideal: each
face sixty-two percent longer than its height. Every wall held a
gothic, stained-glass window of precisely the same proportions,
each depicting a pitched battle between forces of good and evil:
God and Leviathan, Zeus and the Titan, Pandava and an army of
demons, and Krishna and Kauravas.

1

Handel's *Messiah* drifted from speakers hidden in the walls. The scent of myrtle filled the air.

He exposed several vertebrae at shoulder level, paused, and took a dreamy breath. This was his reward. Entry to the inner sanctum. A window on God's great design. He loved the spine's perfect marriage of structure and function, rigid enough to protect the cord coursing through it, supple enough for a man to gaze at the stars, to spoon against a lover, to crouch, to spring.

Were he a more humble servant, he would have become a surgeon, dedicated to repairing the body when warped by illness or injury or age. But he needed to create beauty, not simply restore it.

He moved the blade lower, hungry to lay eyes on the cauda equina, the waterfall of nerves pouring from the base of the spine to power the legs.

He felt no more remorse for the blood on his hands than a sculptor would for chips of stone scattered on the ground. Destruction was simply a part of creation, a sweeping aside to reveal something more perfect.

He used a surgical saw to remove the backs of three vertebrae near the tailbone, dissected down to the sheath surrounding the spinal cord, coaxed it open with forceps. Then, trembling with excitement, he ran a fingertip along the moist, white bundle inside. He could almost feel the waves of charged ions that had once surged inside it. And he felt certain that he had indeed been chosen, that his greatest challenge would soon be at hand.

He looked over at a series of silver-framed photographs on the wall: an aerial view of the White House, a shot of President Warren Buckley strolling in the Rose Garden, a family portrait of the president with his wife, his two sons and his daughter, a close-up of the girl—the freak, the accident. His eyes stayed on her, his pupils dilating, his lungs expanding, his heart pumping. And when he looked back at the family portrait, she was gone.

ONE

A map of the United States glowed on the flat-panel monitor at the front of the room.

"You'll remember the first two bodies were found in Darien and Greenwich," FBI analyst Bob White, a forty-something former street cop, said.

Two stars glowed over Connecticut.

"August and October, 2003. Both deep in the woods. The bizarre condition of the corpses got headlines, but things quieted down within a couple months." He cleared his throat, but his gravelly voice didn't change. "Until last year," he said. "The third body. A twelve-year-old boy in Big Timber, Montana."

Another star.

"He crossed state lines, we got involved. Now, two more in the last six months: Southampton, New York . . ."

A fourth star.

"Ironwood, Michigan."

A fifth.

"The press is all over us."

Forensic psychiatrist Frank Clevenger, forty-nine, looked over at Ken Hiramatsu, the agency's chief pathologist. "Tell me about the bodies."

Hiramatsu motioned the control room for the next series of images.

The screen filled with what looked like a photo from *Gray's Anatomy*.

"His dissection is beyond competent," Hiramatsu said, with what sounded like admiration. "In each victim, a different organ or vessel or joint is masterfully exposed. In Darien, it was the heart of a twenty-seven-year-old woman."

Clevenger could see the sternum and rib cage of the victim had been neatly cut away, the muscles and fascia beneath them held back by silver nails, giving a full view of the heart, freed even from the fibrous, pericardial sac that normally clings to it like a glove.

"He goes deep," Hiramatsu said, motioning the control room again. "He wants to see everything."

The image on screen changed to a close-up of forceps holding open a window cut into the left ventricle, revealing the aortic and mitral valves. It changed again to show a second window onto the tricuspid valve, inside the right ventricle.

"You get the idea," Hiramatsu said. He twirled a finger in the air. The slides began cycling.

Clevenger watched one image of meticulous carnage after another. A section of abdominal wall excised to reveal the kidney of a teenage boy, the renal artery and ureter brought into view by threads tied around them, pulled tight and anchored by silver nails. The right hip of a middle-aged woman open to show the neck and head of the femur, with the gluteus medius, quadratus femoris, and iliopsoas muscles stripped clean. The jugular veins and carotid arteries of a beautiful, thirty-something woman. The spine of a man face down in a bed of leaves.

"The spine is the one from Michigan," Hiramatsu said. "His most accomplished work."

Clevenger glanced at him.

"In its attention to detail," Hiramatsu said quickly. "Each and every spinal nerve tied off. The vertebral arteries pristinely dissected. Not one of them torn. Not even a nick."

"Any evidence of sexual abuse?" Clevenger asked.

"None," Hiramatsu said.

"Cause of death?" Clevenger asked.

"Poisoning." Hiramatsu said. "We found traces of chloroform and succinylcholine in every body."

Chloroform was a sedative-hypnotic agent. Succinylcholine was a potent paralytic. Just three milligrams would freeze every muscle in the body, including the heart.

"We've thought about a surgeon," Dorothy Campbell, an older, elegant woman who ran the PROFILER computer system, said. "The blade is consistent with a scalpel."

"You'd think he'd get enough in the O.R.," Clevenger said.

"Maybe some hotshot fired for drugs or malpractice," White said. "Out to show everyone just how competent he is."

"Possible," Clevenger said.

"What we know for sure," White said, "is that he's got a ticket. All five victims are from serious money, even the kid."

"He can't meet these people by chance," Campbell said. "They know him. They trust him."

"Do they know each other?" Clevenger asked.

"The husband of one victim and the father of another served on the board of National Petroleum together," White said. "We could never make anything of it."

"Other leads?" Clevenger asked, looking around the table.

A few seconds passed in silence before White cleared his throat again. He winked. "If we were making a lot of headway, you wouldn't be here."

TWO

Dr. Whitney McCormick, director of the FBI's Behavioral Sciences Unit, had left instructions with her secretary to let Clevenger wait in her office.

He took the armchair opposite her grand mahogany desk and looked at a picture of himself on her credenza, beside others of her with her ex-U.S. congressman father, her mother and sister, her black Lab, her Nantucket cottage.

He focused on McCormick. She was just a teenager in the photo, with a girlish smile and hair down to her waist. Yet even then he could see the rare combination of wisdom and vulnerability in her eyes that attracted him so powerfully to her.

It was no secret that McCormick and he were on again, off-again lovers, though no one at the agency could ever guess whether they were on or off on any given day. He wasn't always sure himself.

He knew they couldn't go a month without seeing one another, at least for a couple of hours in bed. He knew they couldn't go a whole season playing house, shuttling back and forth between his Chelsea loft outside Boston and her apartment in D.C. And he knew some of the reasons why.

They were extraordinarily well-matched intellectually, equally fascinated by the human psyche and its pathologies, with equally stubborn minds that worked problems ceaselessly until they were solved. And they were extraordinarily well-matched sexually. Lock and key. Clevenger liked taking control in the bedroom; McCormick liked yielding it.

They could talk for hours and they could make love for hours and they knew what a rare thing that is in this world. But, somehow, knowing it didn't trump the stuff that kept splitting them apart—this time for a little over three weeks.

"Get what you needed?" McCormick asked, walking in.

He turned to her, kept looking at her as she took a seat behind her desk. She was thirty-seven now, hair just off her shoulders, wearing black silk pants and a simple black camisole shirt under a black blazer. He noticed she'd taken off the diamond crescent moon necklace he'd given her for her birthday two years before. "I'm up to speed," he said. "Take any heat for bringing me on board?"

"I'd bring bin Laden on board if it meant catching this guy."

That put him in rare company. "Listen, I'm sorry," he said, leaning forward. "We should talk about—"

"The case. Let's talk about the case."

He settled back in his chair.

"Obviously, we're dealing with someone organized. He knows exactly who he wants to kill and exactly how."

"Beyond organized," Clevenger said. "Obsessive. Maybe, literally, OCD." He was getting lost in McCormick's deep brown eyes. "This is hard," he said.

"You can handle it." She waited a few seconds. "OCD . . ."

He forced himself to focus. "I don't know about you, but my cadaver in med school didn't look like any of the photos I just saw. I was always in a rush to get where the dissection guide said to go. Things got messy. Not with this guy. He takes his sweet time. He's a perfectionist."

"Which goes with the way he disposes of the bodies—shallow graves, arms folded over their chests, wrapped in plastic sheets."

"Mummies. Clean, protected from the elements," Clevenger said. "He's not angry at these people. No overkill here. He puts them to sleep with chloroform first. He wants them dead, but he doesn't want them to suffer."

"How kind," McCormick said, smiling for the first time since she'd walked in the room. "And he only dissects one area of the body. Nice and neat."

"He loves human anatomy the way some people love fine wine. Savors every drop. He doesn't let himself get drunk on it."

"A connoisseur." She tilted her head, squinted at him.

"What?"

"You haven't been drinking, have you?"

"Not lately," he said.

She kept looking at him, diagnosing.

"If you want to play doctor, I'll get undressed for you."

" 'Not lately,' as in hours, or years?"

"I thought we were gonna stick to the case."

She stared at him.

He looked away, then back at her. "I miss you."

Her eyes went ice-cold. "Let me tell you something: If you're drinking and saying I'm to blame, you can get out right now. We could really use the help, but—"

"Don't flatter yourself," he shot back. "Two years sober. I don't miss you enough to blow that."

She didn't look convinced. "This isn't any easier for me than it is for you. But this time I'm sticking with what I said: I need things you can't give me. If you love me, you'll respect that."

"I do," Clevenger said. He paused, took a breath. "And I will."

"Thank you." She paused. "What do you need to get started?"

"Everything. All crime scene evidence back to 2003—every fiber and drop of fluid, every photo. All police reports and agent field reports, including internal memos. Direct access to the bodies, if they haven't been buried. Maybe even if they have."

"No problem. For starters, you can go through the file before you leave. Order copies of whatever you want."

"And North Anderson comes aboard."

North Anderson, a former Baltimore cop and the first black chief of police on Nantucket, was Clevenger's partner in Boston Forensics—and one of his few friends.

"That's fine," McCormick said. She looked like she had something else to say.

"What?"

"This can't leave the room. Two people at the agency know: me, and the director."

"I don't keep secrets from North."

"We're trying to keep this—"

"Ever," Clevenger said. "You know that."

She hesitated. "North, no one else," she said, finally. "Your word."

He nodded.

A few seconds passed in silence.

"He sent the president a note," she said.

"The president?" He leaned forward again. "Of the United States?"

"It was opened by a staffer at the White House five days after the first body."

"How do they know it was from him?" Clevenger asked.

"The victim's driver's license was enclosed."

Not subtle. "What did it say?"

"I guess the president has his support." She unlocked a drawer at the side of her desk and took out a sheet of paper. She handed it to Clevenger.

It was a photocopy of the card, words typed in the center, a simple cross drawn over them:

> *Keep faith. One country at a time or one family at a time,*
> *Our work serves one God.*

THREE

West Crosse rang the bell at 11204 Beach Drive in Miami, then turned to the horizon, shielding his eyes from the sun, peering at the thick blue line of the Atlantic Ocean, broken only by crests of foam over distant sands bars. A wave of disgust washed over him. Everything was wrong, and he felt it at the core of his being. The roof over the doorway was a slab of white cantilevered concrete, too short to block the glare, yet weighty enough to fill him with the vague anxiety that he might be crushed to death. The marble under his feet was too white and too highly polished, suggesting that his very presence, the fact that he had lived life, that his shoes were *used,* their leather soles *worn,* would stain the premises. The walkway that stretched thirty yards to the street was straight and narrow, bordered on either side by a low-cut, square hedge that warned against strolling or gazing or chatting or thinking. Come and go, if you must. Do not linger.

"May I help you?" a woman with a Hispanic accent asked through the intercom.

He turned around, faced a set of nine-foot glass doors, tall enough for a knight on horseback, too tall to welcome anyone else. "West Crosse to see Mr. and Mrs. Rawlings." He held up a rolled sheet of architectural paper.

"One moment."

Half a minute later the door opened, and a woman about twenty-two, with long, platinum-blond hair, wearing a short white skirt and ribbed, white T-shirt smiled at him. "They're in the library."

"The library," Crosse said. That sounded hopeful. Maybe a touch of walnut or pine to feed his soul.

"I'm Maritza, Mr. Rawlings's assistant." She extended her hand.

Crosse took it, noting her long pink nails, her diamond tennis bracelet, a pavé diamond peace sign dangling from it. He looked into her eyes, much less sparkly. Then he looked down and watched her neck start to flush.

He knew women were moved by him. He was thirty-eight, six feet tall, with a sturdy frame, olive skin, jet black hair, gray-blue eyes, full lips. His features would have been, in fact, too perfect—making him unapproachable—were it not for a jagged scar that began over his left cheekbone and ran halfway to the corner of his lip. The effect was an irresistible combination of refinement and recklessness, strength and fragility. Women wanted to take care of him and be taken by him at the very same time.

He was no less moved by them, and he had designed his scar specifically with them in mind. At twenty, standing in front of a gilded, full-length mirror in his bedroom, realizing that God had given him too much of a good thing, he had cut himself with a straight razor, turning his head quickly to create the jagged line of the wound.

So intense was his determination to re-create himself, so certain his vision of what he had to do, that he had felt no pain.

"I'd be happy to show you in," Maritza said, sounding taken aback by what she was feeling. She slowly let go of his hand.

"After you, then," Crosse said.

He followed her into a low-ceilinged foyer dominated by a wall of glass, then down a long, cramped white corridor that dumped them into a sun-drenched, nondescript concrete box of a room. He glanced up at three massive, cylindrical skylights jutting six feet into the air like smokestacks.

"Mr. Crosse for you," Maritza announced. She turned and headed back toward the foyer.

Ken Rawlings and his wife, Heather, late forties, in designer jeans and matching, white Prada nylon jerseys stood up from their seats at a glass conference table in the center of the room. He was about five-foot-eight, powerfully built, with silver hair and a deep tan. She was a full-figured, bleached blonde, an inch or so taller than he.

The money was hers, from Abicus, a diamond mining company she had inherited from her father. Ken Rawlings was an investment banker on the Morgan Stanley team that had taken it public. They had just purchased five thousand acres in Montana and were interviewing architects to design a main house and three guest houses, a total of more than twenty thousand square feet. Design fees alone would run close to a million dollars.

"Please, join us," Ken Rawlings said.

Crosse looked around the room. No walnut. No pine. A few thousand books, all of them nearly the same height, all of their bindings flush to one another, filled recessed shelves lined with varnished plywood. In front of them were eight pavillion chairs of black leather and tubular steel, designed by legendary architect Mies van der Rohe.

Ten, fifteen seconds passed.

"Mr. Crosse?" Ken Rawlings said.

Another few seconds. "I'm sorry," Crosse said, trying to focus on him. "I was taking in the space."

"We'd love your thoughts," Heather Rawlings said.

He looked at her. "I can be honest to a fault."

"So we've heard," Ken Rawlings said. "Fire away."

"Fair enough," Crosse told him. "It's dead space. Every inch of it."

Heather Rawlings's face went blank.

Ken Rawlings worked to keep his irritation from showing. "It's a particular thing, of course," he said. "But I guess you could say that about the whole international style. Our architect studied with Gropius himself. He stayed true to form."

Crosse smirked. He considered "international style" an oxymoron. German and French architects including Walter Gropius, Mies van der Rohe, and Le Corbusier had spearheaded the movement during the first half of the twentieth century, proclaiming "less is more" and "form follows function." Fueled by a socialistic, antibourgeois vision of the world, they saw no reason for creature comforts, no place for indulgences like vaulted roofs, crown moldings, columns, cornices, bay windows, casings, plants, or draperies. No need even for color. As Le Corbusier put it, "The house is a machine for living in."

"You find something funny," Ken Rawlings said coldly.

"Tragic funny," Crosse said. The smile left his face. He knew Rawlings had been a marine, so he knew the question he was about to ask might cost him the job he had come to get—and a million in fees. But that didn't matter to him. Only the truth mattered. "What are you so afraid of?"

"Excuse me?"

"May I sit down?"

Rawlings didn't respond, but his wife motioned toward the brushed nickel chair across from them. "Please," she said. She took a seat herself, looked up at her husband, who reluctantly did the same.

Crosse sat down. The chair felt stiff and cold. He placed his rolled drawing on the table, laid a hand on the glass. Then he looked Ken Rawlings directly in the eyes. "You're living—or trying to live—in someone else's house. Because it feels safe. But it isn't."

"I'm not following you," Rawlings said.

"This is Walter Gropius's house," Crosse said. He glanced at Heather Rawlings. "It has nothing to do with you, nothing to do with your wife." He felt his own passion beginning to stir, the passion to liberate people from the tombs of fear that kept them from expressing the truest parts of themselves, kept them from feeling completely, exquisitely alive. "Gropius was fond of telling his students in Germany to 'start from zero.' He insisted they throw out every convention, every nuance that spoke to the past. Nothing was worthy unless it was utterly new, pristine. A blank slate. And why? Germany had been destroyed, the German people humiliated. He wanted the past to die. That was his truth."

"I know the history," Rawlings said flatly.

"But that's not the history that matters," Crosse said, speaking quietly. "Where you live and how you live should be about *your* history. And your wife's."

Heather Rawlings grinned slightly, the first emotion she had shown. "I'm afraid that would mean living in a fair amount of chaos."

That stirred Crosse even more. He looked at her. "You don't need to be afraid. Chaos is the best place to start." He gripped the table with both hands. "Ask yourselves, 'What is it we yearn to do in our home? Who do we yearn to be inside it?' Is it about walking through gardens together, getting to know one another even better? Or is it about private time to read on a terrace built for a single chair? Will you feel most yourselves entertaining in a home with two thousand feet of deck, or in a refuge behind stone walls? Or must it be both—a grand reception hall with a sweeping semicircular drive, entirely separate from a main house deep in the woods?

Maybe one of you has a hidden desire to become a painter, but no studio where you can start working—start *awakening*. Living." He could barely contain himself. "Maybe you've fantasized about making love in a secret garden. On a rooftop deck under—?"

"Let's see if we can get back on track," Ken Rawlings said. He crossed his arms. "I'm sure you received the photographs of our parcel in Montana. You brought drawings?"

Crosse saw that Heather Rawlings's neck had turned a splotchy red. "Only one," he said.

Rawlings nodded at it.

Crosse picked up the drawing, slowly pushed the elastic band off. "I always do my homework," he said.

"Your references were impeccable," Ken Rawlings said grudgingly.

"Truly extraordinary," Heather Rawlings said. "The Binghams and Fishers couldn't have been more complimentary."

Crosse knew that was the only reason Ken Rawlings hadn't thrown him out. His clients didn't just appreciate what he did for them, they loved him for it. He changed their lives forever.

He stood up and unrolled the drawing on the table, never taking his eyes off Ken Rawlings's face. He saw disbelief, then anger tinged with sadness.

"What the hell?" Rawlings whispered.

The drawing was of stables, grander, but clearly inspired by those where Rawlings had ridden as a boy in Pennsylvania, on his grandparents' farm. Post-and-beam construction, curved corner brackets, mortised and tenoned joinery, a gambrel roof, board and batten siding front and back, arched windows loft-height at either end. And just under the roofline, in the center of the facade, Crosse had drawn a circular insert of repeating cut-glass triangles, a kaleidoscope to catch the sun or the moon. "October 18, 1971. You were sneaking a cigarette in the stables. The hay caught fire. Three horses died. It made the *West Chester Gazette*. The local library keeps it on microfiche back to 1932."

"You've been to West Chester?" Rawlings asked, still looking at the drawing.

"I said I do my homework."

"I had no idea you rode horses," Heather Rawlings said, looking at her husband.

He didn't look up, didn't say a word.

"More than 'rode.' He was county jumping champion, headed to Nationals," Crosse said. He paused. "I found a dozen articles about competitions you won before the fire, none afterward. You gave it up."

Ken Rawlings touched the edge of the drawing. His sadness had already eclipsed his anger. "Maybe by way of apologizing."

"It was an accident. You loved those horses. You loved the sport."

"I grew up. Sometimes, you leave things you love behind, even things that are part of you," Rawlings said. He finally looked up at Crosse.

"By mistake," Crosse said. "Not by design. At least, not by mine."

FOUR

Clevenger caught the shuttle out of D.C. and landed in Boston at
8:40 P.M. He thought of stopping by his office to put things in order
for the next day, but knew he would just be avoiding whatever
mess his son Billy had gotten himself into *that* day. So he headed
straight for his loft in Chelsea.

He didn't see Billy's car anywhere on the street and was relieved to find the loft empty. But feeling that way about Billy bothered him. He walked into the kitchen and reached high into a
cabinet for a sealed bottle of Absolut vodka that had sat there for
over two years—a symbol of his resolve to stay sober. Now, having
snuck a few glasses of merlot in the last few days, all it symbolized
was his hypocrisy.

Billy had been in trouble almost constantly since becoming a father himself, at nineteen. He started walking out of classes at
Chelsea High, then stopped showing up at all. Chelsea superintendant of schools Brian Coughlin, who happened to be a friend of
Clevenger's, cut Billy plenty of slack. After all, Billy had never gotten very good at taking care of himself. All of a sudden he was supposed to help care for a newborn. How was he supposed to focus on
calculus with his head wrapped around that kind of equation?

Clevenger had adopted Billy Bishop at age sixteen, after clearing his name in the murder of his infant sister on Nantucket. The case had ended with Billy's brutal father sentenced to twenty years, and his equally destructive mother declared unfit to parent.

No one had predicted anything but calamity when Clevenger first came up with the adoption idea. Billy already had his own history of drug abuse and violence, which explained his being the lead suspect in his sister's murder to begin with. Clevenger had just gotten sober. But Clevenger couldn't walk away from the kid, probably because it felt like walking away from something broken inside himself.

They had honeymoon successes. Billy put down the drugs. He walked away from fights. He started to talk to Clevenger about his painful childhood, instead of trying to drink it away or smoke it away or give it away to anyone foolish enough to miss the predatory gleam in his eye and take a swing at him. He started to *feel* for himself, which is the only way to start feeling for others.

But all those gains evaporated on September 11, 2004, when Jake Bishop was just twenty days old. That was the day three members of a gang called the Royals decided there was enough safety in numbers to ignore that gleam in Billy's eye, ignore his broad shoulders and lightning-fast reflexes, ignore even the fact that he was Golden Gloves out of Somerville Boxing Club. They figured none of that mattered more than his having seriously dissed them by stealing Casey Simms away from Mario Probasco, their jailed leader.

The problem for Billy was that only one of the three Royals who blocked his path that day got to throw a punch before all of them hit the pavement. And all of them were bleeding.

Even that overwhelming response might not have outweighed Superintendant Coughlin's goodwill toward Clevenger, but Billy hadn't stopped. He had to *be* stopped. It took eight students and two teachers to hold him back.

"I talked the police out of charging him," Coughlin told Clevenger. "They know what the Royals are. But the truth is, he easily could have killed somebody. You're the shrink, but I think he was trying to tell us something by walking out of class. He can't hold it together."

Clevenger watched the label give way as he twisted the top off the bottle of Absolut. He poured some into a glass, stood there looking down into it. He felt like he deserved a drink, which made him shake his head. Alcohol had nearly killed him. Feeling entitled to it was like feeling entitled to hemlock. But maybe that was the point. Maybe he was trying to kill the part of himself that was feeling all the pain—the part that knew Whitney McCormick was right to be asking for a child of her own, or the part that knew Billy Bishop wasn't even close to being father material, or the part that wondered whether he was any closer.

He threw his head back, poured the poison down, put the bottle back up in the cabinet.

He walked over to an old library table he used as a desk and looked out a row of Palladian windows at the green steel spine of the Tobin Bridge arching into Boston. Beneath it, an LNG tanker under Coast Guard escort moved slowly toward one of the fuel depots that dotted Chelsea's shore.

He had chosen to live this side of the bridge even though he could have afforded the Back Bay or Beacon Hill. He loved Chelsea, a two-square-mile jumble of brick row houses, converted factories, storefront, and triple-deckers that had played host to wave after wave of immigrants—the Irish speaking Gaelic, Russian Jews escaping anti-Semitism, Italians, Poles, Puerto Ricans, Vietnamese, Cambodians, Salvadorans, Guatemalans, Serbs. The raw energy of their struggle to survive was everywhere. The streets had absorbed it, and, twice, in 1908 and 1973, the city had burned nearly to the ground. It seemed to Clevenger the kind of place that would forever remind him that people live in pain most of their lives. But sometimes—like tonight—he still couldn't bear his own.

The warm feeling in his gut was spreading into his head. He sat down and picked up an August 5 *USA Today* article he had printed out the night before, headlined, "Bizarre Killer Claims Another Victim." He reread it:

Pacific Heights, California
Special to USA Today

Opening another front in the terror that has struck four prominent American families across the nation, police yesterday discovered the body of colorful real estate developer Jeffrey Groupmann, 46, in Ironwood, Michigan, not far from a hotel and office complex he was developing there. Mr. Groupmann, builder of San Francisco's Cloud Marina and Big Sky Mall during the late 1990s, was also a philanthropist who endowed theaters and concert halls on the West Coast and in his native state of Illinois. He leaves a wife, Shauna, son, Loren, and daughter, Lexi.

Ironwood Chief of Police Richard Owens had no comment on cause of death, but issued a statement confirming that Mr. Groupmann had been murdered and that his injuries included "multiple lacerations consistent with a dissection of the body postmortem." He also confirmed that Michigan State Police and the FBI are working with local detectives and consider Mr. Groupmann the fifth victim of a bizarre killer who has taken lives in Connecticut, Montana, and New York.

He put down the printout and dialed American Airlines to book a flight to San Francisco for the next morning.

While he waited on hold, he turned on his desktop to search for more articles on Groupmann. Google came up with 11,234 entries. He scrolled through them. Most were from the *San Francisco Chronicle, Los Angeles Times, Chicago Tribune*, and local newspapers around them, with headlines heralding Groupmann's real estate deals and donations to charity. But a few hundred entries down was a *GQ* article from July 2004, "California's Jeffrey Groupmann: Bankruptcy by Design." He clicked on it:

San Franciso-based entrepreneur Jeffrey Groupmann has always believed good business and good design go hand-in-hand. He is, after all, the maverick, jeans-and-T-shirt-clad patron of the arts who gave San Francisco its Cloud Marina, a breathtaking residential fantasy of fifty oversized boathouses and docks. Shoppers still wait in line for twenty glass elevators to rocket them 250 feet to his Big Sky Mall, carved into the side of Mount Rafael. But Groupmann's uncompromising passion for beauty in business, the trademark that propelled him to star status, may also be his Achilles' heel.

The story starts with a meeting at Starbuck's between Groupmann and architect David Johnson. Order: Two caramel lattes, two blueberry scones. Topic: The ultimate skyscraper. A gauntlet thrown down to Frank Gehry and Daniel Libeskind, reigning kings of Deconstructivism. Projected costs: $2.5 billion. Who knows what the tab might have run to if they'd been drinking espresso?

A photograph showed a titanium model of the skyscraper, a twisted rectangle cleaved partway down the middle, each half bent away from the other, leaving it open like a divining rod at the top. The windows were asymmetrical sizes and shapes, giving the whole building the appearance of having tumbled to earth, partly melting on reentry and fracturing on impact.

The American Airlines representative finally came on the line. "May I ask when and where you're traveling?" he asked.

"Tomorrow morning, Boston to San Francisco, with an open return." He heard the iron door to the loft slide open and swiveled around in his chair.

Billy walked in. He was wearing baggy jeans torn at both knees and a tight, ribbed white tank top. His long, dirty blond hair, done up in dreadlocks, looked like it belonged to an exotic breed of dog overdue for a shampoo. A tattoo of a Roman cross in flames covered his biceps. But none of that was enough to overshadow his brilliant blue eyes, chiseled features, or perfectly sculpted body, let alone his infectious smile. And that was a big part of Billy's problem: He looked too good to be so troubled. Friends, especially girlfriends, followed his lead, instead of running in the opposite direction or leading him to a better place.

Clevenger covered the mouthpiece. "Hey, buddy."

Billy barely nodded, disappeared into his room.

Not good. Clevenger swiveled back around and finished booking his reservation. He hung up.

He wanted to give Billy a little time to himself. He focused on the *Esquire* piece. The article detailed Jeffrey Groupmann's failed attempt to build the skyscraper, a combination of retail shops, a hundred luxury apartments, and a performing arts center, originally planned for downtown San Francisco.

Costs spiraled out of control. David Johnson, the architect, demanded he be free to rework his design—again and again. He successfully lobbied to move the site of the building to the waterfront to give it unobstructed ocean views. Then he changed his mind about the exact orientation of the tower relative to the shore and ordered the cassions ripped out and reinstalled. Even with the frame half-built, he still wasn't satisfied. He wanted to rip the cassions out again. When Groupmann refused, he complained to the mayor and the press that he was being forced to compromise his artistic vision, in violation of his contract. Groupmann sued him. He countersued. Investors sued them both.

In the end, the aborted structure was torn down and the land sold at a staggering loss. Groupmann returned what was left of the investors' money, which wasn't much.

Clevenger got up and started toward Billy's room, but his door opened, and he walked out, headed for the kitchen. Clevenger followed him, pulled a bar stool from underneath the center island, took a seat.

Billy opened the refrigerator.

"How was your day?" Clevenger asked.

"Fucked," he said, without turning around. He took out a loaf of bread and a package of turkey, tossed them on the counter in front of Clevenger, then started rummaging through the refrigerator again.

" 'Fucked,' in what way?"

Billy shrugged.

"Jake all right?"

He shrugged again.

"Did you see him?"

He pulled out a jar of mayo and a head of lettuce, finally turned around, but still didn't look at Clevenger. "Casey wouldn't stop bitching on the phone, so . . ."

Clevenger felt his pulse rate start to rise. "They live in Newburyport, Billy. It's forty minutes from here. You haven't seen him in four days."

He started putting his sandwich together. "He's eleven months old. He doesn't care if I see him or not."

"That's not true."

Billy looked up, probably because he had been looking to blow off steam and finally saw a chance. "According to which textbook?"

Clevenger heard him loud and clear: He hadn't fathered children himself. But that message wasn't all that reached him. He also smelled booze on Billy's breath. He saw that his eyes were bloodshot. And right about then, he really wished he hadn't had those merlots, and certainly not the vodka, because he couldn't say what he wanted to say—that Jake Bishop sure as hell needed his dad, that at eleven months he might not look like much to Billy, but he was powerful enough to have him running scared, and that booze wouldn't change any of that. "Did you drink before or after you looked for a job?" he asked him.

Billy took a bite of his sandwich. "I'm on that first thing tomorrow," he said with his mouth full.

Clevenger nodded. "Tomorrow."

Billy had been out of work six months, ever since Peter Fitzgerald, who owned the shipyard down the street, had stopped ignoring the fact that Billy was spending more time talking about the Red Sox with the guys who ran tugboats out of the place than he was helping to build the new dock. And some of those guys had started wandering by on their days off, which might mean they enjoyed Billy's company, but probably meant they enjoyed the grass he always had on him.

"I'm not going to pay your child support forever," Clevenger told him, hating the fact that he sounded like a typical, codependent parent.

"You shouldn't," Billy said, turning back to the refrigerator. "He's not your blood."

"If you have something to say about being adopted, say it."

Billy reached way back in the refrigerator, pulled out a beer.

As far as Clevenger had known, the only alcohol in the house was the symbolic bottle of vodka he had just opened. Billy and he had made that commitment to one another. "You brought beer into the house?"

Billy laughed. "Dude, it's been there two days. You had to see it."

"No, I didn't," Clevenger said. He could feel his pulse in his temples. "Throw it out."

"Lighten up," Billy said. "It's one beer. I'm not driving anywhere. It helps me sleep." He flipped open the can.

Clevenger was off his stool before Billy could get the can to his lips. He pushed him against the counter. "I said, throw it out."

The predatory gleam flashed in Billy's eyes. Then it was gone, or hidden. "You smell like vodka," he said. "And you're on *my* case?" He winked, brought the can to his mouth, took a sip.

The psychiatrist in Clevenger could have pointed out to another father that his son was drinking right in front of him when it would be easy to hide it, that he was picking a fight with him when it would be easy to avoid one, that he must be pleading for help. But this time Clevenger *was* the father. He was in this story, not listening to it. And the most his training could offer him was a kind of split personality, so that he was able to note the mistake he was making as he smacked the can of beer out of Billy's hand, grabbed him by his T-shirt, dragged him toward the front door, and pinned him against it. And he was able to stop himself before he opened it and threw him out. He looked at his clenched hands. They reminded him of his father's fists during the beatings he had taken, beatings that never seemed to end, maybe never had. He let go. "Listen, we've got to—"

"*We* don't have to do shit," Billy said. He turned, slid open the door, and walked out.

FIVE

• AUGUST 10, 2005, 11:10 P.M.

By 9:00 P.M. West Crosse had heard from two of the three people he had met at 11204 Beach Drive.

Ken Rawlings had called to tell Crosse that he and his wife wanted him to design their Montana home. They hoped he could start immediately.

Rawlings's assistant Maritza had called to find out whether he was too tired to meet for a drink at the Delano Hotel on South Beach, where the Rawlings had put him up.

He was never too tired to serve a client. He met Maritza at the hotel's Blue Door restaurant, a whitewashed art deco nightmare with round plaster columns blasting fifteen feet into flat ceilings, sheer draperies over walls of glass, white tablecloths, white chairs, a white candelabra holding white candles. It made him feel like a plastic figurine on an egomaniac's wedding cake, and he would have liked nothing more than to have used one of the candles to set fire to the white shades of the white standing lamps, just to give the place a little color and heat and life.

Instead, he focused on Maritza—her full lips, light brown skin, platinum-blond hair, long nails. In just seconds, he imagined her with more naturally blond, straighter hair, a better complement to her chestnut-brown eyes and slightly rounded face. He trimmed her nails, wiped away her pink nail polish in favor of a more subtle French manicure. He pulled off her tight, scoop neck T-shirt and covered her in a looser, rose-colored camisole that showed less cleavage. He helped her out of her hip-hugger jeans, redressed her in black cigarette pants. He changed even the pressured way she was trying to explain why she had called him, made her speak more softly and slowly.

"Which is," she summed up, "a long way of saying, I don't know why I called, exactly."

"Of course you do," Crosse said. He leaned toward her. "Would it be easier if I said it?"

"Maybe."

"You called because you know you can be more with me than you can without me." He saw her stiffen, mistaking his honesty for arrogance. "I feel exactly the same way about you. You can add something to my life. I'm certain of it. Otherwise, I would never have accepted your invitation."

That put the two of them on an equal footing. She relaxed.

"What we can't know is what we ultimately have to give one another. It could be as simple as your teaching me about growing up in Cuba, what you loved about it and what you hated about it. The way the light changes during the day. The ideal plants and flowers for a garden. The most beautiful beach and street and archway you remember. The piece of land where you dreamed of having a house as a little girl. What that house would look like, smell like, feel like." He paused. "Or you may have even more to teach me, about what makes you feel most alive, about your passion."

Her neck began to redden, as it had at the Rawlings's house. "What do you have to teach me?" she asked.

"For starters, that you're more captivating than you believe. You worry someone might miss your beauty. That's why you grow your nails a bit too long." He took her hand, ran his thumb down her slender fingers. "You dye your hair a dramatic shade. You wear tight clothing." He looked into her eyes. "But your beauty is unmistakable." He saw her eyes start to sparkle. "When you see it as I do, so will every man you meet."

She looked down, fiddled with her silverware. "How do I know you don't say this to every woman you meet?" She looked back up at him.

"Because the truth is all I have. I wouldn't trade it for anything. Certainly not for sex." He gazed even more deeply into her eyes. "Not even for love."

She believed him. And why not? He sounded like he meant everything he said with every fiber of his being. And she believed him even more as she lay naked on his white bed in his white room looking over the whitecapped waves of Miami Beach. Because no one could fake the tenderness with which he ran his fingers through her hair as he kissed her mouth. No one could invent the hungry, yet unhurried way he caressed her neck and breasts and stomach. No fraud would have noticed when she lifted her hips half an inch, inviting him between her knees. No liar could lead their dance precisely where she hoped to go, sense the moment when nature was about to take control, and suddenly stop, leaving her trembling at that velvet edge where her body and soul were fading into one another. No one but a lover of truth—*her* truth— could give her back all that control—what she so feared and craved—by simply rolling onto his back and crossing his wrists over his head.

A minute later they lay together, spent, her head on his chest. "How did you get your scar?" she asked.

"I cut myself shaving," he said.

"Try again."

"Let's just say there was a straight razor involved and leave it at that."

She kissed his chest, rested her head on it again. "I don't want to lie to you," she said.

He listened to her breathing.

"Ken can't know about us," she said.

Ken, not Mr. Rawlings. "Why is that?" he asked.

"He's a jealous person."

He let a few seconds pass.

She took a deep breath, slowly let it out. "We haven't always been . . . professional with one another."

"I appreciate your telling me," he said. He paused. "Do you love him?"

"I'm not sure what love is."

She loved him. "Is he a good person?"

She shrugged.

"You're worrying about my feelings," he said. "You don't need to."

"Yes," she said, reluctantly. "He's a good person."

"And he's generous?"

"Mmm. Hmm."

"Strong?"

She nodded.

"Then why are you here?"

"I don't know," she said quietly.

That was an honest answer. "Because he's with his wife?"

"Maybe."

A very honest answer. "You've met him at this hotel."

"Don't . . ."

He touched her bracelet with the pavé diamond peace sign. "He gave you this," he said.

"I won't wear it if it bothers you."

"It doesn't."

She looked up, worried.

"It's a spectacular gift."

"Shhh." She laid her head back down on his chest.

He took her hand in his. "It's the truth. His, and yours. You've needed one another. That has nothing to do with you and me. The bracelet says something wonderful."

"That he shops at Barney's?"

They laughed together. "Not only that," he said. "It says that his wife's fortune—her diamonds—can't do what you do for him. You give him inner peace."

She pressed her finger to his lips. "I don't want to talk about him anymore," she said. "I'm with you now."

He knew that was a lie and that she would have to do something to hide it.

As if on cue, she slid under the sheet, kissing his chest, his abdomen, moving lower.

SIX

Clevenger had had Whitney McCormick's office arrange a meeting for him with Groupmann's widow, Shauna, at the family estate in Pacific Heights. He landed at San Francisco International and grabbed a cab.

En route, he tried Billy's cell phone. No answer. No surprise. Billy hadn't come home the night before, which meant he'd either crashed at a friend's place, hooked up with a girl, or slept on one of the tugs docked at the Fitzgerald Shipyard. Unless he'd taken a girl with him to the shipyard. It was a lot easier for him to pull off that kind of rendezvous than get himself on a train to Newburyport to see his son.

Clevenger had woken three times during the night, walked to Billy's room, and found it empty. He had thought about heading down to the shipyard himself. But he didn't think anything good could come of that. Billy usually needed a few days to cool off when things between them heated up. And this time, Clevenger had to admit he needed a day or two himself—to put down the booze and put away any hopes he had for a quick fix for his trouble with Whitney McCormick. Because his hopes weren't lining up with reality, and his mood kept falling into the gap.

He knew he should have taken a later flight and kept his ap-

39

pointment with his psychiatrist Ted Pearson, knew when he left him a message at 4:10 A.M., canceling their 7:00 A.M., that he was avoiding him, which amounted to avoiding himself. But thinking about that had just made him feel worse, so he had swallowed another couple of ounces of vodka to make the feeling go away.

That's how it works—until it doesn't anymore.

He dialed Billy's cell phone again. Voice mail, again. He hung up and dialed his partner, North Anderson.

"Smooth sailing?" Anderson asked.

"Right on time." It felt good to hear Anderson's voice. They had been partners seven years, long enough to visit hundreds of crime scenes and morgues together, interview dozens upon dozens of murderers, rapists, bereaved parents, sisters, brothers, children, then watch each other try to live seminormal lives, in spite of it all.

Anderson had always seemed to manage that better. He'd kept his marriage together twenty-one years, kept his two kids out of trouble. And those were no small things for a man who still limped from the bullet he had taken during a bank robbery in Baltimore, who still couldn't sleep half the time, replaying the single shot he had fired back, through the heart of the masked robber, who turned out to be a fifteen-year-old boy.

On his way to the airport, Clevenger had stopped at the office and left Anderson his notes on the FBI meeting, together with a packet of printouts on Groupmann and the killer's four other victims. "Did you find the folder I left on your desk?" Clevenger asked him.

"Already read through it," Anderson said.

"There's something else. I'll tell you in person. But what do you think so far?"

"I think there's a connection between the victims that the Feds haven't dug up yet. This guy's going out of his way to target the

high and mighty. Why? Their internal organs look exactly like anyone else's. He's got to have another reason."

"You're reading my mind."

"There's a frightening thought."

"Horror show," Clevenger said. It was an offhand remark, but it
carried some of Clevenger's pain with it.

A pregnant pause, then: "You didn't sound so good on your message about heading to San Francisco."

"I'm fine," Clevenger said. He knew Anderson could hear that
he wasn't. He squinted out the window of the cab. "Billy and I got
into it."

"About?"

"Jake."

"Ah."

"And some other stuff."

"How bad?"

"He slept out last night." He pictured himself pinning Billy
against the door, remembered the rage he had felt surging inside
him. "Bad."

"Want me to check on him?"

"If you could."

"Done. When are you back?"

"Unless something comes up, I'm on a flight home tonight and in
the office first thing tomorrow morning."

"I'll call you later."

"Thanks for—"

"No need. Got to do what it takes to keep my brother sober,
right?"

He knew, Clevenger thought. He always knew. "One day at a
time," he said.

"One day at a time."

They hung up.

The driver was taking the turn onto Broadway, the Fifth Avenue of Pacific Heights, one of the most prestigious neighborhoods in the world. Between palatial homes, Clevenger caught glimpses of the breathtaking expanse of the Golden Gate Bridge over San Francisco Bay, its waters dotted with sailboats gliding past Alcatraz Island, Angel Island, the hills of Marin.

The taxi slowed, turned between a set of fieldstone columns marked 2910, then headed up a twenty-foot-wide, oak-lined driveway shaded by a canopy of branches. It ran at least a hundred yards, ending in a figure eight in front of one of the most beautiful homes Clevenger had ever seen.

He paid the fare, stepped out, and stood there looking at the place. It was a shingled Victorian with woven corners and deep green trim and window sashes that seemed to drift into the hills around it. Its roof was a series of gables and dormers, with a brick chimney at either end. It had to be ten or twelve thousand square feet, yet it looked warm and inviting, with ten-foot-deep wraparound porches and a covered entryway with a porch swing on either side.

Clevenger took the wide steps to the front door and looked through its panes of beveled glass. He could see through a central great room to the back of the house, where giant, boxed-out windows let his eyes keep going, past an acre of green lawn that seemed to roll into the sky, a blue-gray canvas for the glistening Golden Gate Bridge.

He rang the doorbell.

"One moment," a woman's voice called out.

A few seconds later a slender, very pretty woman, about thirty-five, with straight, dirty-blond hair tied back in a ponytail, wearing

Levi's and a white, little boy's V-neck T-shirt, opened the door. "You must be Dr. Clevenger."

She spoke in a formal way that made him take her for the Groupmanns' personal assistant. "I'm a little early," he said.

"Not to worry." She held out her hand. No jewelry. Neat, unpolished fingernails. "I'm Shauna Groupmann."

He shook her hand. "I'm very sorry about your loss."

"I appreciate your saying so. We can't quite believe this is happening."

Maybe not, but he heard calm, not disbelief in her voice. And he saw no sadness in her emerald eyes.

"Please, come in," she said.

He followed her through the great room with its fir wainscoting, maple floors with inlaid walnut borders, exposed beams and rafters and those magical windows on the bridge. It was pristine, timeless space that could have been built six months before or a hundred years before.

He heard voices, then laughter, and looked through an elliptical archway into the dining room. A man with his back to the doorway, a teenage girl, and a ten- or eleven-year-old boy were eating lunch. The boy looked at the man and broke into laughter again. The girl smirked, shook her head.

"My son and daughter," Groupmann said, looking back at him. "You're welcome to talk with them later."

"Thank you," Clevenger said. "I'd like that." He already had a few reasons. First, Groupmann's children seemed to be grieving the loss of their father about as much as their mother was. Second, they looked very comfortable with the man in the room—and Groupmann hadn't mentioned him.

Still, Clevenger had seen every kind of grief reaction: A mother who insisted her child had been abducted by aliens rather than face

43

the fact he had been strangled for his New England Patriots jacket. A newlywed who lost all memory of his young bride rather than recall the final hour they spent together, with him tied up and her at the mercy of three men who had no mercy. When grasping reality feels like holding hot coals, the human mind will sometimes grasp for straws.

Groupmann took him into a library as big as his loft, with three walls of floor-to-ceiling walnut bookcases accessed by three moving staircases on rails. You could climb one of the staircases, take a volume off the top shelf, sit down and read a few pages. The fourth wall held another fireplace, this one bracketed by soaring Gothic-style windows that looked out on a bluestone patio surrounded by gardens.

She motioned him toward a pair of roomy leather club chairs in front of the fireplace and took a seat on a green suede couch across from them.

Clevenger sat down. Looking at her, he realized she was more than pretty. Her features were nearly perfect—large eyes, a small nose, high cheekbones, full lips, a strong jaw. Bright white Chiclets for teeth. She looked like a model on a day off, even more beautiful because she wasn't trying. "I understand this may be difficult," he said. "But I need to know as much as possible about your husband."

"I think I've told the FBI everything. There really wasn't anything out of the ordinary that night. He said he was staying late at the office in Ironwood, which wasn't unusual. I tried him around midnight and didn't get a call back, so I went to bed. When I woke up just after eight, I still couldn't get him. I called the superintendent at the construction site, who said Jeffrey had missed a seven A.M. meeting with him. That's when I called the police."

Clevenger leaned forward. "I'm less interested in those details than in learning about your husband as a person." He paused. "What was he like?"

"As a person?" A hint of a smile. "He was amazing."

"Amazing, in what way?"

"He was . . . charming. Beyond charming. He could sell anything to anyone."

Not exactly tombstone material, Clevenger thought. "A born salesman," he said.

"Definitely."

"Rather than, say, a great artist." Or a great husband, or a great father.

"An artist . . ." She pondered that. "In the commercial sense, I suppose. Maybe that's the better way to put it. He was an absolute genius at getting people to sign on with his creative vision, to *join* him in it—a little like one of those Sirens from Greek mythology."

The Sirens were beautiful creatures—part woman, part bird—who lived on an island and lured sailors to their doom with their irresistible singing. "You're saying people were charmed into joining him when they shouldn't have."

"I'm sure you've done your homework," Groupmann said. "Jeffrey took us to the brink financially more than once. We always came out fine, even on the David Johnson project."

"The skyscraper."

She nodded. "Some people weren't so lucky." She grew more serious. "That was the problem with my husband: He was easy to follow; it was harder to know where you would end up."

For the first time, Groupmann sounded bitter, as though she had been one of her husband's bankrupt investors. Maybe she was—emotionally. "Was he as persuasive with you?" Clevenger asked.

She smiled a wider smile that lasted longer. "None of the police or FBI agents asked these kinds of questions."

"They're not psychiatrists."

"I could have used you a long time ago." She chuckled to herself, then grew serious again. "Let's just say I bought a set of plans from Jeffrey."

"Plans . . ."

"You don't quit."

Never. "Should I?"

She took a deep breath, let it out. "Plans for a life together, a family. He had an incredibly poetic and powerful way of describing how it would be to travel, to raise children."

"You couldn't resist him."

"Him, his plans . . . whatever." She folded her hands on her lap, looked down.

"The two of you didn't get to build what he had in mind."

She looked up. "Not even close."

"Why?"

Her eyes filled up. "Christ. What does this have to do with his murder?"

"Maybe nothing," Clevenger said. "But we are talking about it. So maybe it does."

A tear started down her cheek. She wiped it away. "Or maybe you just like causing people pain."

He knew he was causing her pain. For a psychiatrist to be any good, he has to be willing to corner you, close off the easy exits, even when it hurts. It's supposed to.

They stared at each other for several seconds.

"I really don't care if you know," Groupmann said, finally. "I don't care if the whole goddamn world knows." Her lip began to quiver. "My husband was gay." She looked down, hugged herself. "That was definitely not part of the plan."

Clevenger waited until Groupmann seemed to be in control. "When did you find out?" he asked her.

"Around the time we moved here from Carmel." She looked at Clevenger. "A little over four years ago."

"How?"

"He sat me down one night and told me. He pulled out all the old clichés: How he'd been 'living a lie.' He 'didn't want to pretend anymore.' It 'had nothing to do with me.'"

"Did he have a . . . partner?"

She cringed. "I didn't ask. He didn't tell. But I doubt he would have confessed he was gay if all he'd done was fantasize about it. I don't think we ended up in San Francisco by accident."

"That was your husband's idea?"

"He said he 'fell in love' with this property. I've never wanted to know what he really fell in love with here."

"Did you think about leaving him?" Clevenger said.

"Sure," Groupmann said.

"But . . ."

"The kids were younger, in new schools, with new friends. We didn't want them to have to deal with a divorce, headlines in the papers, whatever. And I . . ." She shook her head.

"You . . . ?"

"I really could have used you back then."

Clevenger stayed silent.

She shrugged. "I already had my own life. Jeff and I hadn't been good together—in *that* way—for a couple years before he told me what was going on. I had pretty much moved on."

"To another relationship."

"Yes," she said, her voice warmer, as though thinking of her lover.

Clevenger put two and two together. "The man in the kitchen with your children?"

"That's right. David."

He heard real tenderness in her voice. "So you and your husband decided to live together, separately," he said. "You had David. He had . . . whoever."

"That's putting a very positive spin on it," she said. "We lived a lie."

The bitterness was back in her tone. "It wore on you," Clevenger said.

"It basically wore us out."

"How so?"

"We had chosen new partners. Jeff had a whole new lifestyle. We tried the friendship routine, but it's hard to be friends when you feel abandoned or tricked or whatever."

"Who had a harder time of it?"

"I think we were about equal on that. Neither of us did well with it."

That didn't add up. Groupmann's husband had radically altered the family structure by declaring his sexual orientation. Why should he resent his wife expressing hers? "What problem did your husband have with your new relationship?" Clevenger asked.

"He thought I could have chosen someone else."

"He didn't like David."

"It was much worse than that," she said.

Clevenger looked at her askance, urging her to say more.

"He loved him." She paused. "David was Jeffrey's favorite brother. They were twins."

SEVEN

Looking at David Groupmann took a little getting used to. Clevenger had seen photos of his identical twin—dissected—before leaving Quantico. Here was a living, breathing copy.

They were sitting in the leather club chairs in the library. Shauna Groupmann had gone for a walk with the children. Clevenger could see them strolling hand-in-hand in the gardens beyond the patio.

"It was incredibly complicated, or incredibly simple, depending on how you looked at it," Groupmann told Clevenger, in a smooth, deep voice. He was a willowy man, more elegant than masculine, with deeply tanned skin and a full head of brown hair, combed straight back. His eyes were much darker, nearly black. He wore a sky-blue Lacoste jersey, chinos, and deck shoes.

"Which way did you look at it?" Clevenger asked him.

"Before Jeff came out of the closet, I felt pretty much disgusted with myself," he said. "If anyone had ever told me I'd be having an affair with my brother's wife, I would have told them they were crazy. It tore me up. I couldn't sleep. I lost fifteen, twenty pounds. I mean, we were very close. The whole twin thing . . . talking over one another, finishing each other's sentences." He shook his head. "I loved Jeff. We only had each other—no brothers or sisters. I felt like the worst person on earth."

"Then why?"

Groupmann looked down. "They were already having serious problems. Jeff wasn't involved with the kids as much as Shauna expected—work was everything to him—but that was just part of it. There was no passion there. Zero. Not that that's a green light, I know." He looked back at Clevenger. "I don't have a decent answer. If I had to guess, I'd say that deep down I've known most of my life what Jeff finally admitted to himself—and Shauna. I noticed things even when we were kids. I'd turn around to look at a girl; he wouldn't. He was popular, played football at Andover and Yale—you know, the whole package—but he didn't date much. The few girls he took out told me they liked him because he didn't push them. Maybe a little kissing. Maybe. That was it." He smirked. "I actually convinced myself at one point that he was alright with me and Shauna, that he kind of wanted it to happen, to let him off the hook."

"When was that?"

"When it started, about six years ago. I was living a couple of miles away from them in Carmel. There were times when Jeff was out of the country raising capital or whatever, and he'd send me to look at a piece of land or a building in Chicago, Philly, Boston, to get my take on it. Sometimes he'd want Shauna's opinion, too. So he'd charter a jet and fly us out together, put us up in the same hotel. The energy between us was . . . phenomenal. I don't see how he could have missed it."

"You were working for him at the time?"

"Just helping out. I'm an artist. The little I know about real estate I learned from my brother."

Helping out was one way to look at it. "What kind of artist are you?"

"Bullshit artist, can't you tell?" He rolled his eyes. "I'm a painter."

The one-liner convinced Clevenger that David Groupmann wasn't grieving any more than Shauna Groupmann—at least, not in any usual way. "You've been able to make a success of it?" he asked him.

"I think a number of my paintings have been successful," he said. "That's the only kind of success I care about."

Meaning he hadn't made much money. All well and good. But it also meant that his brother had been the financial success in the family. And the famous one. Until now. Now David Groupmann had it all—his brother's wife, full access to his multimillion-dollar house, maybe even access to his fortune. "What happened to your relationship with your brother once he knew about you and Shauna?" Clevenger asked.

"We went from being inseparable to being cordial." He stopped, pressed his lips together, rubbed his eyes. "That really is bullshit. He barely put up with me. He could hardly look at me."

Groupmann was finally showing some emotion. Clevenger wanted to push him, to see how much anger might have brewed beneath the surface of his strained relationship with his brother. "You were trading your relationship with Jeff for the love of a woman, who happened to be his wife. Putting up with you could be seen as heroic."

"There's no excuse for what I did," Groupmann said plainly. "None. Maybe we just were too much alike. Maybe that explains it. Like I said, I don't know."

"Say more."

"We both loved her," he said. "He loved her enough to betray his nature, have kids with her, stay with her almost fifteen years. And I loved her enough to betray him. Bottom line: I'm straight; he was gay. So maybe in some terrible way, what happened made some kind of sense."

"And now that he's dead . . ." Clevenger pushed.

"I never wished for that," Groupmann shot back. "Never." He looked away, shook his head. "But I have to believe he would have wanted his family taken care of."

"Are you two planning to move in together?" Clevenger asked him.

"Not right away."

"I see."

He looked Clevenger in the eyes. "There's no sense pretending anymore. Shauna and I were meant for each other. She and my brother weren't. So who gets the blame? God?"

EIGHT

Loren and Lexi Groupmann hugged their uncle David as he left the library, then took seats on the couch across from Clevenger. Loren hadn't wanted to be interviewed without his older sister present, which seemed entirely normal for a ten-year-old, especially one who had just lost his father.

"Mom said you're a psychiatrist?" Lexi asked Clevenger.

She had her mother's sense of decorum, but her features were all Groupmann—the thick, brown hair, the brown-black, impenetrable eyes. "That's right," Clevenger said.

"But you work for the FBI," she said.

"I help them understand violent people. Sometimes I help them find violent people."

"Like whoever . . . hurt Dad," she said. "And the others."

"Yes," Clevenger said.

Loren started to tap his foot on the floor. He was a gaunt, pale boy with his mother's dirty-blond hair, green eyes, and fine features. "A profiler," he whispered.

"Are you okay?" Lexi asked him, laying a hand on his thigh.

Loren glanced at Clevenger, shrugged.

"Do you have something to say, Loren?" Clevenger asked gently.

The boy half-squinted at him. "Are any of us in trouble?"

Lexi smiled a nervous smile. "No one's in trouble, Lore. Mom said he needs to know more about Daddy to—"

Clevenger held up a hand. "Why would you think that, Loren?" he asked. "Are you worried someone here could be in trouble?"

"I've just seen stuff on TV," Loren said.

"He watches way too many crime shows," Lexi told Clevenger.

"They always think it's somebody in the family," Loren said. "Then, half the time, they find out they were wrong. But it's too late, because the person already committed suicide or got executed or killed by the real killer or—"

"This isn't TV," his sister said. She grinned at Clevenger. "He's such a weirdo, sometimes." She mussed up Loren's hair. "You're so weird."

Lexi was displaying the same odd sense of detachment from tragedy that Clevenger had seen in her mother and uncle. There was certainly no shortage of unusual grief reactions in the family. "Are you scared of anyone here?" Clevenger asked Loren.

The boy started tapping his foot again. "Kind of," he said.

"Who?" Clevenger asked.

He shrugged. "You, I guess."

"He works with the police," Lexi said. "He's like the guy they call in to—"

"Why are you afraid of me?" Clevenger asked him.

He looked at Clevenger, but said nothing.

Clevenger stayed silent, waiting.

Loren's eyes began to fill up.

Clevenger slowly leaned forward. "It's alright, buddy. Whatever it is, it's alright. You can tell me anything."

"I don't want you to ruin anything," Loren said. "I just want to be happy. I want everything to be good now."

Talk about unusual grief reactions.

NINE

West Crosse stood looking out the plate glass window of Ken Rawlings's thirtieth-floor office at Abicus, the diamond mining company his wife had inherited from her father. He could see most of Miami, a concrete, stucco, and glass statement against imagination, against beauty, against life itself. No wonder people moved there to die.

"Two-hundred-fifty-thousand dollars," Ken Rawlings said, signing Crosse's retainer check. He stood up from his desk, walked over, and handed it to him. "I know we're making a great investment. And I like making it in another Bonesman."

Crosse slipped the check into his shirt pocket. He never brought up the fact that he had been one of fifteen classmen tapped for the Order of Skull and Bones during his third year at Yale. He never had to. Every one of his clients for the past seven years had been part of that secret society, the ultimate referral network, twenty-five hundred of the most powerful families in the world, including the first family. "This is really an investment in yourself," he said. "Every one of us has the innate capacity to create a slice of the universe. I know you have the resources. Now the question is whether you have the courage."

"Courage?"

"To create something authentic, something liberating that tells the truth about who you are."

"Like building the stables," Rawlings said.

"For example," Crosse said.

Rawlings nodded. "Well, we're committed now." He held out his hand.

Crosse shook it. As he let go he gestured at Rawlings's wedding band. "How long have you been married, by the way?" He walked over to a credenza at the side of the office that held a dozen or more framed photographs of the Rawlingses together—sailing, hiking, skiing, seated at a formal dinner, dancing.

Rawlings glanced at his wedding band. He forced a smile. "Eighteen years, this May."

Crosse picked up the photo of the Rawlingses dancing. "No children," he said.

"That's right."

"Why not?" Crosse asked, still looking at the photo.

"Why should it matter?" Rawlings asked, his voice suddenly cold.

Crosse slowly put down the photo. He took Rawlings's check out of his pocket, walked over, and laid it on his desk. He started to walk out.

"What in God's name are you doing?" Rawlings asked.

In God's name. That turned him around. "I have plenty of money. I won't steal yours."

"I don't understand."

"You handed me a quarter of a million dollars to start helping you create something extraordinary. By the time we had broken ground you would have paid me at least four times that much. The reason you think I'm worth it is because you've seen buildings I've designed for other clients. They moved you. But here's the problem: You still think I did it alone. You think I'm an artist, like Gropius or Mies or Gehry."

Rawlings didn't respond.

"I promise you, you're wrong," Crosse said, a combination of excitement and faith and fear in his voice. Fear, more than the others. Fear of the inexplicable, immeasurable creative power that coursed through his mind. "Don't you see? You're the artist. I'm just the medium. To make me worth anything, never mind a million dollars, you have to stop thinking of me as entirely separate from you, as someone to hide from. Because, in the end, you're just hiding from yourself. And what you create will have no soul, no life. You'll build another maze and get lost inside it." He paused. "I won't be part of that." He turned, took the few steps to the door, reached for the handle.

"Wait," Rawlings said.

He stopped, faced him, again.

Rawlings studied him, nodded once. "Jimmy Bingham told me you were . . . unorthodox, to put it mildly. He said you asked him and Andrea questions no reporter ever has. Frankly, they found it more than a little uncomfortable."

"Of course they did," Crosse said. "People are trained from childhood to pretend to be something other than what they really are. When someone asks you to drop the mask, it feels as risky as it would for any creature coaxed out of its shell. I understand that. I simply chose not to work with people who won't take the risk."

Several seconds passed.

"Alright," Rawlings said, finally. He sat on the edge of his desk. "Ask me anything you like."

"I have," Crosse said.

Rawlings gestured at the couch at the side of his office.

Crosse walked over, sat down.

Rawlings took an armchair catty-corner to the opposite end of the couch. He was still keeping some distance. "I would have loved children. Heather wasn't able to have any."

"I see."

"I think we just waited too long. She was thirty-nine when we finally tried. We went through all the things people go through. Tests. Fertility drugs. In vitro. Nothing worked."

"You tested fine, then?" Crosse asked.

Rawlings stared at him. "You need to know whether I'm potent in order to be my architect?"

"I need to know you."

Rawlings smiled, shook his head. "Maybe we aren't a match."

Crosse knew his questions were no more intimate than ones asked of Rawlings during the initiation ceremony for Skull and Bones. Both men had received the same secret message, tied with black ribbon, sealed with black wax. Both had been taken to the Tomb on the Yale campus, a vine-covered, windowless, brownstone hall on High Street with a roof that doubles as the landing pad for the society's private helicopter. Both had been naked during much of the ritual, covered in mud, placed in a coffin. Both had visited room 322, the inner sanctum of the Tomb. And, there, both had revealed all the secrets of their young lives.

It was not rare for Bonesmen to unburden themselves to their Bones Brothers throughout life, sharing their innermost thoughts and feelings, especially their sexual experiences and fantasies.

"I guess brotherhood only goes so far," Crosse said.

Their eyes locked. Several seconds passed.

"It was a great pleasure meeting you," Crosse said. He extended his hand.

Rawlings didn't take it. A few more seconds passed. "I tested normal," he said. "Not that it matters much who had the problem."

Of course it mattered, Crosse thought. Rawlings had made that clear when he had said his wife "wasn't able" to have children, that he would have loved to. And the fact was, he still could. "Why did you wait so long to try?" Crosse asked him.

"Why does anyone? We were enjoying one another. We love to travel. The years got away from us."

That didn't ring true. Not for a couple like the Rawlingses. Middle-class families, upper middle class, even millionaires might feel that children would invade their time and limit their options, but the vastly wealthy—with tens or hundreds of millions of dollars or more—don't usually think in those terms. They can "staff up" to handle the burdens of parenthood. Nannies. Housekeepers. Personal assistants. They can parent from a distance, keeping busy social schedules, out three or four nights a week, continuing to travel the world, even with babies and toddlers. "Did your wife want children as much as you did?" Crosse asked.

"I wouldn't say it was a major priority for her, no."

"Do you have any idea why not?"

Rawlings looked as though he was still unsure how much of the truth to reveal.

"Whatever you tell me stays with me," Crosse said. "I give you my word."

"You're like a priest. Is that the idea?"

"More than that. I'm your brother."

Rawlings took a deep breath, let it out. "She had a very painful childhood," Rawlings said. "I don't think she cared to relive it. And I'm not sure she believed she could be a good enough mother, not having had a decent one herself."

"So adoption was out of the question as well."

"It wouldn't have been any easier for her. The same issues would have been there."

Crosse was satisfied with the story line now. He could believe it because it had internal consistency. It explained the facts, rather than obscuring them. He had met other childless men and women who had remained so for similar reasons. And rarely was there complete agreement on the issue between husband and wife. Almost always one of them secretly wished for a son or daughter, secretly yearned to create life. Ultimately, the keeping of that secret killed any love between them.

For Crosse, understanding a family was really no different from understanding the building they would call their home. It either told a truth or it told a lie. It either liberated the energy of those within it or it stifled that energy. It was either good at its foundation, or evil.

The paradigm held for every building and every family, without exception. He was certain of it, and that gave him the courage, determination, and *patience* to do whatever needed to be done in service to it—cosmetics, a gut rehab, or new construction. The final design could take a month, a year, or five years.

"I appreciate your openness," Crosse told Rawlings.

"Are we done for now?" Rawlings asked.

Crosse smiled. "For now."

"Fair enough."

The two of them stood up.

Rawlings walked over to his desk, picked up the retainer check, and carried it over to Crosse. "We have a deal then?"

Crosse took the check. "We have a deal."

TEN

Clevenger left the Groupmann estate at 4:50 P.M., PST. Shauna Groupmann had called a car service to take him to the Cloud Marina, where the president of her husband's construction company was waiting to be interviewed by him. He got in. The car pulled away.

He checked his cell phone. He'd gotten fourteen new calls, including seven from North Anderson and three from his assistant, Amy Moffitt, at the Boston Forensics office. He checked text messages. The first was from Anderson. He'd never gotten one from him before. He clicked on it:

F— Call me re Billy —N

Clevenger's mind raced. Had Billy been hurt, hurt himself, overdosed? He dialed Anderson.

"Frank," Anderson answered.

"What's up?"

"It's about Billy."

It's about Billy. Even that much beating around the bush was rare for Anderson. "Just tell me."

"He got drunk, drove up to Newburyport this morning."

"Is anyone hurt? The baby . . ."

"Jake's fine. He got into it with Casey. I guess she laced into him about not being around—"

Now Clevenger's head was spinning. "Tell me he didn't . . ."

"He didn't hit her, but he punched a pretty good hole in her bedroom wall. She says he kept screaming about her setting him up, trapping him, whatever. She tried to get out of there, but he wouldn't let her leave. Sounds like he was mixing it up—booze and marijuana, maybe more."

Clevenger looked out at the Golden Gate Bridge, shimmering in the late afternoon sun. Its timeless beauty made what he was hearing sound that much uglier. "Is she alright?"

"Shaken up. She called 911 when he finally stormed out. Half the Newburyport Police Department responded. Rob Vacher, Keith Carter, the whole crew."

"Did she file?" Clevenger asked.

"Better believe it."

"209A. Domestic assault."

"And kidnapping. He kept her there five or ten minutes, but that's enough to trigger the statute. Then he took off in his car and got pulled over for blowing through a stop sign."

"DWI," Clevenger said.

"And resisting arrest."

"He ran?"

"No." Anderson paused. "He took on four cops."

The bottom fell out of Clevenger's stomach. Where was this story going to end? Was Billy dead? "North, if you're trying to let me down easy . . ."

"Let you down . . ."

"Just tell me?" His voice cracked. "Is he alive?"

"*Alive?* Of course, he's alive. What the . . . ? He's at the Middleton jail. They set bail at twenty grand."

Clevenger closed his eyes, hung his head. He was always waiting to hear the worst about Billy. It had been that way for years—the constant feeling of impending doom, the constant battle to bring light to a life that seemed to tend, almost inexorably, toward darkness. That's what you're up against when you try to turn a story built on early chapters full of suffering. Kids are less resilient than people think. "Have you seen him?" he asked Anderson.

"He's not taking visitors," Anderson said. "I wouldn't even know what happened if Carter hadn't called me."

"I'm on the next flight back."

"If you need anything . . ."

"Thanks."

They hung up.

"Excuse me," Clevenger called out to the driver.

The driver turned around. He looked close to seventy, with gray hair combed over his bald head, his face gaunt and tired, deep crow's-feet around his pale blue eyes.

"Change of plans. I need to get to the airport right away."

"Not a problem." He slowed down, moved into the turning lane. "Trouble at home, huh? Couldn't help overhearing."

"My son."

He glanced at Clevenger in the rearview mirror. "Three boys and a girl. All grown. You do the best you can, then you pray."

"How do you know if you're doing that?" Clevenger asked.

"What?"

"The best you can."

He glanced at Clevenger, again. "They tell you," he said. "Might take 'em thirty, forty years, but they tell you."

Clevenger looked out at the bridge. And real doubt crept into his mind for the first time since the day Billy had come to live with him—doubt about whether he had done the right thing adopting him, whether he knew what to do next. And for some reason, that doubt made him want to talk to Whitney McCormick, maybe because he knew without a doubt that they loved one another, even if that didn't mean they would ever have a life together. He dialed her office, got put through to her.

"How's San Francisco?" she asked.

"It was fine, until North called to tell me Billy got arrested."

"For what?"

Clevenger told her the whole story. "He's at the Middleton Jail."

"Are you okay?"

Hearing her ask that question, her voice warm and steady, steadied something deep inside him. "I'm fine," he said. "I wish I could say the same for him."

"If you need to put the case on hold . . ."

"No, I—"

"I would understand. Really."

Clevenger had put his work on hold more than once for Billy. In some ways, he had put his whole life on hold. Maybe that was the only thing to do, or maybe it was only codependence, preventing either one of them from really jump-starting his existence. "I'm not making bail for him, so he's staying put. No reason I should stop working."

"Your call."

"I appreciate that."

"Let me know when you can talk more about what you found out at the Groupmanns'."

"I'll call you tomorrow, at the latest."

"No rush."

"Thanks, again, Whitney." He was about to hang up.

"Frank?"

"Yup."

"I hope this is the end of it. I mean, maybe this is bottom for him. Maybe he turns it around from here."

Clevenger's throat tightened, partly because he shared the same hope, partly because he knew McCormick was trying to help him survive parenting Billy, when what she wanted more than anything else was to be a parent herself. "Maybe," he said.

"Take care."

"You, too."

"Can I get you anything?" a female flight attendant asked Clevenger.

On a good night, that question ran about 52 to 48 against, a slim victory for sobriety. On a night like tonight, with Clevenger thirsty for sleep, locked inside the suspended reality of an airplane in flight, sobriety went down in a landslide. "Vodka, rocks, please," he said.

She poured it, placed it on the cup holder beside him. "Enjoy."

"You don't know how much."

She smiled, moved on.

He sipped the vodka, half-thinking he'd leave most of it, call the flight attendant back to clear it away. But then he took a long swallow. He was going to be alone with his thoughts for the next six hours or so. That was a little more company than he could stand.

ELEVEN

The call West Crosse had been waiting for, planning for, dreaming about, came on his cell phone, just as he was leaving his suite at the Delano Hotel to meet Maritza at her apartment.

"Mr. Crosse, this is Virginia Blakely at the White House. Would you be able to hold for the president?"

A thousand icy fingers tightened around his spine. "I would," he said.

Ten seconds passed.

"Are we calling too late?" President Warren Buckley asked, his voice pure self-assurance.

"No, Mr. President."

"We're past titles, you and I."

"I appreciate your saying so," Crosse said.

"I don't think this could come as a surprise, given your drawings, not to mention the time you spent with Elizabeth and me, but we'd like to hire you on, if you're still willing."

With those words, a crown of shivers ringed Crosse's scalp. He was being asked to follow in footsteps reaching back to 1792, when Thomas Jefferson placed an ad in leading newspapers across the country announcing a competition to design the president's house. He was following James Hoban, the architect who had won that competition and worked directly with George Washington on the building's original design, then worked to rebuild it after the British set it ablaze in 1814. He was following the likes of Andrew Jackson Downing, President Thomas Jefferson, Louis Comfort Tiffany, Charles F. McKim, and Beatrix Farrand—artist-architects who had left indelible imprints on one of the greatest symbols of freedom in the world.

Ten months before, Crosse, like hundreds of architects across the country, had submitted his plans in a new competition to design the first addition to the White House since the Truman administration.

The idea was the first lady's: a majestic expansion of her East Wing offices into a Museum of Liberty showcasing paintings and sculpture by leading artists from new democracies around the globe—nations freed from oppression by the United States and its allies.

The project had precedent. In 1961, Jacqueline Bouvier Kennedy spearheaded legislation that placed the White House under the National Parks Service and established it as a public museum with a permanent art collection.

Crosse was one of a dozen architects—and only two men— selected for a series of interviews with the first lady and the president, interviews during which Crosse complemented his exhaustive knowledge of their home with a deep understanding of the workings of their family. He asked question after question about President Buckley's courtship of Elizabeth Cunningham, the births of their two sons, now in their late twenties, the accidental birth of their youngest child, now seventeen. He studied the first lady's work habits and management style, what helped her focus and what distracted her, how she communicated with her staff and children and husband during the day, her preferred colors, lighting, attitudes about design, the White House rooms she liked most and liked least, buildings she admired, the art and books and films and chapters of history and animals and hobbies and causes she cared most about.

But he learned much more. The president was a Bonesman, Yale '73, and he, like the others, had taken Crosse into his confidence, speaking at length of his wild youth, his coming of age, his sense of destiny, the personal and political hurdles still in his way, his love for his wife, the joys of raising his two sons, the pain of learning that his daughter had been born with mental retardation.

Why reveal so much? Could being Bones brothers fully explain it? Did being recommended by America's most powerful families truly recommend Crosse for instant intimacy with the leader of the free world? Was it some combination of Crosse's boundless curiosity and physical presence—the magnificent gray-blue of his eyes juxtaposed with the jagged scar down his cheek? Or was there something more subtle and far more powerful at work?

Crosse believed there was. He believed the families who came to him for help were directed his way by God. He believed they unconsciously knew the architecture of their lives was faulty and that they needed an agent of the Truth to help them rebuild.

President Buckley was no different. He intuited, at a level beyond words or thought, that Crosse had the power and the will to help perfect his existence. Why else confess that his marriage and his political future were both being threatened by his damaged daughter?

A month before, Crosse and Buckley had sat together in the Red Room, the antechamber for the Oval Office and the President's Library. Buckley had seemed truly impressed by Crosse's early conceptual sketches of the Museum of Liberty, yet distant and burdened. More than once he apologized for having trouble concentrating.

"Perhaps another time would be better," Crosse said.

Buckley nodded. "Maybe so."

Crosse began rolling up his drawings.

"Blaire is pregnant," Buckley said, just above a whisper, like a prayer. He pressed his lips tightly together.

Crosse was suddenly aware of dozens of eyes upon him—the eyes of the carved, wooden lions and sphinxes around the room. He slowly slipped an elastic band around his drawings, then looked directly at Buckley.

"Seventeen, special needs and having a child," Buckley said. "Not a pretty picture."

"How many months is she?" Crosse asked.

"Two, give or take." He let out a long breath. "The boy who did this is in the same situation as she is, even more impaired." He shook his head. "Elizabeth dreamed last night that she terminated the pregnancy."

"Is that something you would . . . ?"

"The whole country knows where I stand on that."

That didn't answer the more personal question, and Crosse and Buckley both knew it.

"The *Times* will run this front-page every chance they get," Buckley said.

"Do they know about it?"

He shook his head. "Her mother and I, her doctor—and you."

Her mother, her father, her doctor, and Crosse himself. Could there be any doubt he was again being called upon to heal? "I would never violate your trust."

The president stared into Crosse's eyes for a split second, let him see through the shiny veneer of statesmanship to the unbridled ferocity and pain and love churning inside him. "I know that," he said. Then his gaze drifted.

Crosse had stayed true to his word. He had taken the knowledge he received that day as a sacred trust, held it close, meditated on it, and waited patiently for the call that would give him permission to act upon it.

This call.

"I'm honored," Crosse told the President.

"Don't waste a lot of time on that. Get to work. Do the nation proud."

"You have my word."

He was still tingling, still in the grip of God's greatness, when he arrived at Maritza's apartment.

She opened the door.

For an instant, Crosse could not have said whether he was looking at the real Maritza or his idealized vision of her. She had abandoned her platinum-blond hair for light brown with subtle blond highlights. Her makeup was nearly undetectable—no rosy cheeks or red lips. Her nails were long but not nearly as long as before, coated in clear polish rather than pink. In place of her tight jeans and top she wore an aubergine cotton and velvet tunic over black silk, wide-leg, cuffed pants. Only when she blushed was he certain she was no illusion.

"Do I look different?" she asked.

"You look magnificent," he said. He checked her wrist for her gift from Ken Rawlings—the bracelet with the diamond peace sign. Gone. "Why did you take off your bracelet?"

"It didn't feel . . ."

"You should wear it. It's beautiful." He walked inside, closed the door behind him and gently pushed her against the wall. "I won't be angry that another man loves you. What man wouldn't?"

He kissed her forehead, her cheek, her neck, the skin at the V of her tunic. When she started to breathe faster, he ran a hand down her abdomen, inside her pants, pressed his finger against the soft, moist cloth between her legs.

They kissed deeply.

She unzipped his fly and reached for him.

He took a step back. As she watched, he undressed completely, let her eyes drink in his perfect body, every muscle as if etched in stone, the whole of him a work of art, maintained by purity of diet, five-mile runs each day before sunrise, an hour of tai chi each evening.

They made love—for Crosse, an act of God. He was over-whelmed by the wondrous design of feminine beauty and by the absolute rightness of his being drawn to it, the miraculous fact that his body could literally harden and enter a woman's, and that that perfect union of structure and function had the potential to create a human being, the ultimate expression of the Lord's undying hope for man.

For an instant, he thought of the president's daughter, a perversion of that hope, a broken promise of nature, now threatening the health not only of the first family, but the nation.

"Do you want children?" he asked Maritza.

"Of course."

"How many?"

"Four. Two boys. Two girls."

He smiled. "I guess you've thought about this."

"For as long as I can remember."

He held her close, thinking what a wonderful mother she would be for the Rawlings children. "You deserve to have them," he said.

TWELVE

• AUGUST 12, 2005, 6:55 A.M. E.S.T.

Clevenger landed back at Logan just after 6:00 A.M. and headed straight to the Middleton Jail. His third and last vodka had been at midnight. He felt pretty rough and figured he looked at least as bad.

He had visited prisoners at Middleton many times. The three officers behind the huge plate glass window in the lobby, cashiers of humanity, knew him well. He slipped his driver's license and medical license under the window.

Chuck Valentine, stocky, late twenties, leaned toward the intercom. "Here to see Billy?"

"Right," Clevenger said.

Valentine dropped Clevenger's credentials into a metal, hanging file on the wall beside him, grabbed a locker key off a hook and started writing out a visitor's pass.

That was a lot less back-and-forth than Clevenger usually got from Valentine. He looked at the other two officers, Pete Simms and Dave Leone, caught them looking at him. Simms looked down, pretended to be absorbed in paperwork. Leone got up and headed toward the back of the office. "What's going on here, Chuck?" Clevenger asked Valentine.

Valentine slid Clevenger's visitor's pass and locker key under the window, turned to add his name to the visitor's log. "Huh?"

"I can't get anyone to look me in the eye."

Valentine shrugged. "Weird situation, I guess."

"Weird, how?"

He shrugged, again.

"Weird *how,* Chuck?"

"Frank," Dave Leone called out, from behind him.

Clevenger turned around.

Leone had walked out of the security booth and was gesturing for Clevenger to meet him at the steel door that led to the interior of the jail.

Clevenger left his things in a locker and walked over to Leone.

"You look well rested," Leone said.

"I just flew back from L.A."

He nodded. "You might not have heard the whole story here."

"I doubt it," Clevenger said.

"Not everyone knew Billy was your kid."

Clevenger's pulse started to race. "What happened?"

"He's gonna be all right. He got into it with one of the guards in processing. He wouldn't consent to the strip search. This guy's a fuckin' hothead."

Clevenger stared at him, waiting.

"Billy ended up with a couple of facial fractures and a concussion."

"You've got to be . . . That's why he wasn't taking visitors when North called?"

"He was at Mass General getting worked up. Everybody did the right thing for him once we realized . . ."

"I want to see him."

"No problem. I just wanted to give you the heads-up, you know? It looks worse than—"

"I want to see him."

Leone nodded, motioned to a guard perched behind another plate glass window over the steel door. The door slid open.

Clevenger walked inside.

"Follow me," Leone said, moving past him.

"I haven't needed an escort for about ten years, Dave," Clevenger said.

Leone kept walking. He took Clevenger down a wide gray corridor that ended at the door to the One East cell block. Another guard under glass flipped a switch, and it opened.

One East looked like a high school cafeteria surrounded by cages. Prisoners in orange jumpsuits milled about tables and benches bolted to the floor of the common area, playing cards, reading magazines, talking trash, or just staring off into space.

Clevenger didn't see Billy anywhere.

"He hasn't earned any time out yet," Leone said. He pointed toward the far corner, the last cell on the right.

Clevenger started toward it.

He saw Billy before Billy saw him, sitting on his cot, legs up, back against the cinder block wall. His left eye was covered with a heavy gauze patch. His upper lip was badly cut and swollen and seemed to be held together by two lines of sutures. A blue-black streak ran down his forehead, over the bridge of his nose and onto his right cheekbone.

Billy turned, saw Clevenger, and hung his head.

It was all Clevenger could do to keep from crying for him—the part of him that was still the beaten child, the core innocent cowering under all the tattoos and bravado, perhaps minuscule now, perhaps all but unreachable, half memory, half ghost, yet still alive enough to grab Clevenger by the heart and not let go.

Dave Leone had caught up with him. "They don't know whether maybe he lost some sight in that eye," he said quietly. "Maybe all of it."

Clevenger cleared his throat, kept walking.

"The guy's on paid leave," Leone went on. "Like I said, nobody knew until afterward that he was your kid." He stopped and let Clevenger walk the last few feet by himself.

Clevenger stood just in front of the bars. "Hey," he said.

"Hey," Billy said, without looking up.

"We're in a jam, huh?"

Billy closed his eyes.

"Mind if I come in?"

He shrugged.

Clevenger looked back at Leone, who unlocked the door, let him in, and locked it behind him.

Clevenger wasn't sure what to do next—to sit beside Billy or not, touch him or not, scream at him or not. The father in him was paralyzing the psychiatrist in him, and vice versa. So he backed up against the wall and waited, trying to picture what his son's eye looked like under all that gauze, wishing he had been there when the doctor told Billy he might never see out of it again.

Nearly half a minute passed before Billy broke the silence. "I'm gonna need a lawyer," he said, glancing at Clevenger.

"They'll give you one," Clevenger said. He knew that wasn't what Billy wanted to hear. He wanted to hear Clevenger would hire Tony Traini or Joe Balliro or John Haggerty or one of the other high-powered criminal attorneys he counted as friends.

"What about bail?"

A lawyer and bail. He sounded like a thug. Clevenger felt himself getting angry, but tried to stay in control. Billy was more comfortable with confrontation than anything else. Transmuting sadness into rage was his game. Clevenger didn't want to play it. He forced himself to picture Billy as a six-year-old, cowering on his bed, bruised and bleeding, waiting for the next lash from his father's strap. "C'mon, Billy," he said. "Why don't you tell me what happened?"

"She set me up to lose it. That's what happened."

The six-year-old evaporated. Clevenger felt his anger rising again.

"She kept coming at me about why wasn't I doing this and that—yelling, making Jake cry," Billy said. He shook his head. "I just wanted her to shut up. I told her, 'Shut up. Please. Just shut up.' But she wouldn't. She kept going on and on and on."

"It might have been easier to hear her out without the alcohol on board—not to mention whatever else you were using."

"I didn't *want* to hear it. I don't want to hear it now. I gave her Jake, and now she wants . . . I don't know what the hell she wants."

That sounded like an echo of the truth. Maybe Billy really didn't know how to deliver what Casey was asking him for—to be a real father to his son. Maybe the best he thought he could do was help bring a child into the world. Maybe the rest was too scary for him, treading too close to the scorched earth of his own childhood. "She wants Jake to have better memories of you than you have of your father," Clevenger said. He paused. "That's going to be harder to deliver now. We have a lot to deal with here."

Billy turned toward the wall. "Then get me out, or at least get me a lawyer."

"I need time to set up drug testing through the probation office, psychotherapy at the court clinic, AA, the whole nine yards. You might as well get in a few meetings with your lawyer while you're here."

Billy chewed his lower lip. "How long?"

"I don't know. A couple of weeks, anyhow."

He shook his head. "No fucking way."

"You don't have a lot of choices right now, partner."

No response.

"What did they tell you at Mass General about your eye?" Clevenger asked.

Billy shrugged.

Clevenger walked over to him, sat at the edge of the bed. He wanted to hold him, but nothing about Billy's body language or expression suggested he was welcome to. He put a hand on his arm. "We'll figure everything out, okay?"

Billy's lip began to quiver. He yanked his arm away. "I can figure things out for myself," he said.

"I don't know if you can," Clevenger said. "But I know you don't need to."

"Can I please be alone?"

"Billy . . ."

His jaw tightened. "Please?"

Clevenger felt a lump rising in his throat. He stood up and motioned Dave Leone to unlock the door.

Leone walked over, opened it.

"Why don't I come by tomorrow?" Clevenger said to Billy. When he got nothing back, he turned and walked out.

THIRTEEN

"I've never seen anything quite like it," Clevenger told Mc-Cormick. He had called her from his office at Boston Forensics, quickly filled her in on Billy, then moved on to the murder case. He wanted her to know he wasn't going to stop working. And he wanted to remind himself. "David Groupmann has taken the driver's seat of that family like his brother was just keeping it warm for him. Shauna and the kids haven't skipped a beat. She's in love with David. The kids have cozied up to him—probably more than they did to their dad. It's like Jeff never existed."

"Denial?"

"Or acceptance. The way David tells it, Jeff and Shauna never made sense. A gay man and workaholic, married to a beautiful woman all about raising children. With Jeff gone, the pieces of the puzzle fit together better. It feels more natural to everyone."

"Except someone died of very unnatural causes," McCormick said. "Sounds like the brother had motive."

Clevenger took a nip of vodka out of his pocket, a souvenir from the plane. "For this one, maybe." He twisted it open, poured it into the cup of coffee on his desk. "But that leaves four more."

"Unless you make him for a copycat."

"What do we know about him?"

"Super smart. Graduated Yale, 1983, summa cum laude, same class as his brother. Got into Harvard Law, but never went. He studied music at Juilliard, then art history at Oxford. Works as a painter, but doesn't seem to have gotten very far with it. No criminal record. Politically conservative, but not politically active. A practicing Catholic. Never married, no children."

"Since when does the director of Behavioral Sciences keep tabs on people's politics and religion?"

"Since J. Edgar Hoover, or 9/11, depending on how you see it."

Clevenger sipped his brew. "I need to know anything from his past that might have crushed him narcissistically, extinguished his sense of self enough to make him willing to kill in order to live his brother's life. I need to know if he was ever around a dissecting table—anatomy lessons in art school, anything. And, obviously, any connection to another victim would be key."

"We'll get right on it. What else can I do for you?"

"That a trick question?"

She laughed.

An unexpected break in the ice. "Why don't you come see me?"

"And then what?"

He didn't have a good answer.

McCormick was merciful enough to leave him tongue-tied only three or four seconds. "Let's face it," she said, "our relationship would be even harder to solve than this case." She paused. "Tell me what else you need from the FBI."

Maybe he would have felt better if she sounded angry, but she sounded resigned to his speechlessness, even sympathetic to it, and that made him feel as empty as he had leaving Billy's cell. Even emptier. "I want to interview the families of the other victims," he managed, "starting with the man from Southampton."

"Ron Hadley."

"And working backward—the twelve-year-old in Montana, the two victims in Connecticut." He heard the front door open, saw North Anderson walk in.

Anderson headed toward Clevenger's office.

Clevenger motioned him in.

He took a seat opposite Clevenger's desk. He was nearly six feet tall, the same height as Clevenger, with a nearly shaved head like his. The two of them also shared an intensity of gaze—at once understanding and unrelenting—that could occasionally elicit a confession from the most hardened of criminals. If Anderson hadn't been black, the two of them would have looked like brothers, instead of just feeling that way.

"If you have the time, I can schedule all of them over the next four to five days," McCormick said. "I may even be able to set up Southampton for later today. But I know you've got Billy to think about."

"Schedule them," he told her.

"I'll call you."

"Thanks." He hung up.

"You look like hell," Anderson said.

"Thank you, too."

"Did you see Billy?"

Clevenger nodded, reached for his coffee, took a long swallow. "They roughed him up pretty good when he got there. He didn't like the idea of being strip-searched."

"Who the fuck . . . ? That's why they didn't let me in to see him."

"He was at Mass General getting worked up. It was some new recruit with a bad temper." He saw Anderson's mind starting to work at the same time as his jaw—always a sign of trouble. "The guy's been suspended," Clevenger said. "Nothing to do about it. It had to be at least half Billy's fault."

"Is he alright?"

"He may have lost some or all of the vision in one eye. I don't know yet. I've got to get him over to Mass Eye and Ear for follow-up."

"Shit. I'm sorry."

"His eye is just the beginning. He could end up doing two to five on this."

"Who are you getting to represent him? Haggerty?"

Clevenger shook his head. "He can use a public defender this time."

"Right," Anderson said. He didn't sound convinced.

"All he wanted from me was bail and a lawyer. He needs some time to think."

Anderson smiled.

"What?"

"You're the shrink. But I've hung around you enough to know there was no way on earth he was gonna tell you what he really needed."

"And what was that?"

"His dad."

"You know something? I'm not sure about that anymore. I'm not sure he even thinks of me in those terms. Maybe we never got there. Maybe we never will."

"Sure, he does. And so do you. Otherwise, you wouldn't be suffering through this discussion. You wouldn't look like shit." He nodded at the wastepaper basket beside Clevenger's desk. "And you wouldn't be sneaking vodka in your coffee."

Clevenger glanced at the basket, saw the empty nip. He'd meant to bury it. "Let's move on to the case, leave me and Billy for later," he said. "I've got to fill you in on something."

"Whatever you say, partner." He seemed to know, as a real

friend can, that there would be a time to push the issue, and that this wasn't it. "Fill me in. Then I've got something for you."

Clevenger told him about the note the killer had sent President Buckley.

"A serial killer inspired by the president," Anderson said. "The administration can't let that see print."

"Whitney didn't want it to leave her office. I promised her it wouldn't leave ours."

"Got it."

"What have you got for me?" Clevenger asked.

"I'm starting to connect dots," Anderson said. "When Jeffrey Groupmann's skyscraper project collapsed, the biggest loser turns out to be a hedge fund called Next Millennium Capital Partners, out of Manhattan. One of their board members is Sidney Stimson."

"Who is he?"

"*She.* Among other things, her nephew was Gary Hastings, the twelve-year-old victim from Montana."

"How did you find that out?"

"I still speak Nantucket."

Anderson's stint as chief of police on Nantucket Island was the gift that kept on giving. He was still in touch with the rich and famous families who summered there. "Can you track down the other investors?"

"I'm already on it."

"How did I know you were going to say that?"

FOURTEEN

West Crosse had been trying to sketch the main residence of the Rawlingses' Montana estate since leaving Maritza, just after midnight. He was surrounded by a sea of paper. He had not eaten, or slept.

Time was running out. His greatest and, almost certainly, final work was at hand: rebuilding the first family. It mattered not at all to him whether he lived after achieving God's plan for them. He wanted only to finish each of the projects he had started.

His challenge in Montana was to design something true to Ken Rawlings's roots in Pennsylvania and the rugged simplicity of his Quaker upbringing, yet also true to Maritza's childhood in Cuba, where Moorish and Spanish colonial influences resulted in staggeringly extravagant baroque buildings. To do so, he had to marry the clean lines that would appeal to Rawlings with the wide windows and balconies, arches, elaborate wooden ceilings, window grates, and stained glass that would speak to his true love.

He knew what it felt like to close in on the right plan—the growing excitement inside him, the steady building of confidence. All loose ends tied. The way clear.

He thirsted for that clarity. Then he got down on his knees and prayed for it.

The Rawlingses were a lie. Ken Rawlings had married his wife Heather out of insecurity, because he worried he would never achieve enough success in his own right. Now he had Abicus, her father's diamond mining company, but he had no peace, and no children. And why should he? Should God smile upon a lie any more than gravity upon a weak foundation?

When inspiration finally struck, it was a tidal wave that lifted Crosse up. He sketched one rectangle inside another, creating a central courtyard, typical of a Cuban colonial dwelling. To keep the courtyard alive to the world outside he drew four massive arches clear through the house, one centered on each wall. Across the facade he added the same arched windows that had graced Ken Rawlings's grandfather's barn. He covered the gabled roof with cedar shakes, to be stained red to match the half-round roof tiles of Old Havana.

The result was stunning—a Spanish-American fortress in the mountains, built around a Zen center, pregnant with possibilities.

He worked feverishly, roughing out floor plans. He drew the master bedroom, a Cinderella suite with every luxury for the new lady of the house, once the hired help. He placed two window seats, each deep enough to make love in while gazing at snowcapped mountains. Across the cathedral ceiling he drew trusses to be cut from a majestic Pennsylvania oak that had fallen on Ken Rawlings's grandfather's farm during a thunderstorm a month before.

The main house would have six bedrooms—one for Ken and Maritza, four more for their two sons and two daughters, one for a nanny.

He raced on to the nursery, three interconnected rooms down the hall from the master bedroom, allowing for multiple births and space for a nurse. He added tall windows, inspired by the rotunda of Cuba's Museum of the Revolution, fitted them with wooden grates to filter the light. Then he sketched a series of stained-glass skylights in each room, in the shape of shooting stars.

He worked until the minute he left his room and checked out of the Delano, barely in time to catch a noontime flight to Chicago, where he had another plan to complete.

He boarded the plane, leaned back in his seat. He felt magnificently exhausted—well used. And as he fell off to sleep he heard the voices of girls and boys calling to one another, saw them playing tag in the courtyard he had just designed, laughing as they ran out through one archway, in through another, weaving perfect childhood memories.

FIFTEEN

"*What are you afraid* of?" Ted Pearson, Clevenger's psychiatrist, asked.

"Maybe that I found someone who can't be helped," Clevenger said. "Maybe that I made a mistake."

They were sitting in Pearson's study, in deep, worn leather armchairs, facing one another. Clevenger guessed they had sat that way at least a couple of hundred hours over the past seven years, trying to hone in on whatever kept him going back to the bottle, probably the same thing that kept him from letting himself fall completely in love, commit completely to a woman, start a complete family.

Pearson turned his head slightly to the right and squinted at Clevenger, as though he were trying very hard to hear faint music. "A mistake . . ." He rubbed his thumb back and forth over his sterling and turquoise ring.

"Adopting him in the first place."

"Ah." He nodded. "I understand." He was eighty-two years old, barely five feet tall. His hair had gone white, his skin had wrinkled, and his blue eyes had paled. But his mind had only sharpened. He had listened to thousands of patients, tens of thousands of stories. He knew most of the ways people tie themselves in knots, and he never tired of helping them get free. "You're that arrogant. You think you're that good."

Clevenger shook his head. "I said I *didn't* think I could help him."

"I heard you. You waltz into this young man's life, put in three years, figure if he hasn't turned around, he's a lost cause."

"He's not getting better. He's getting worse. He's headed for jail."

"Is that when you'll stop loving him?"

Silence.

"Or have you already?" He turned away before Clevenger could answer, stared out the window at a flowering boxwood he had planted forty-four years before, the day he opened his practice. "Some father."

That landed like a grappling hook in Clevenger's soul. "Why are you . . . ?"

Pearson looked back at him. "Who have you really given up on, Frank—Billy or yourself?"

Clevenger didn't respond.

"Neither one of you had anything but pain as a child. Maybe you can't bear to sit with his any longer. You can't keep your eyes open to that much darkness." He paused. "I forgive you that. I'm not judging you. But I won't pretend someone else might not find light inside that young man."

Clevenger sat there several seconds. When he tried to speak, his throat was too tight, so he sat there a little longer. "I'm not sure where to look anymore," he said finally. "I guess we're both lost."

Pearson leaned forward. "How about looking at that? Where did you get lost?"

Clevenger shrugged. "Trying to be a father to him, trying to do better for him than my father did for me."

"Scary?"

"Yes."

"Hopeless?"

"Sure seems that way."

"Did it ever occur to you," Pearson asked, "that Billy is experiencing the same things you are—fear and hopelessness? Have you ever wondered whether he's making you feel those things as a way of telling you how *he* feels?"

"Transference."

"Like they teach you in residency."

Clevenger kept listening.

"He's lost where you are—trying to be a father," Pearson said. "He'd rather go to jail. He thinks he'll fail that miserably at it."

That felt like the truth. It explained what was happening. And Clevenger was ashamed he had missed it. "And here I am agreeing with him," he said.

"In more ways than one."

"What do you mean?"

"You'd rather drink than get a clear verdict on whether you can be a better father to Billy than your father was to you. Billy would rather get locked up than find out whether he can do it for Jake. Pick your poison, isn't that what they say?"

"That's what they say."

"You want Billy to have courage? You want him to try to be something to that baby that no one ever was to him? Show some courage yourself. Put down the booze, once and for all."

Clevenger's eyes filled up.

"Tell me what you're thinking," Pearson said.

Clevenger looked out at the boxwood tree.

"C'mon, Frank. I'm an old man. Don't make me work so damn hard."

Clevenger smiled. Several seconds passed. "I was just thinking how different it would have been for me, how different I might have turned out, if I'd had . . ." He stopped himself, shook his head.

"If you'd had . . ." Pearson pushed.

He shrugged. "A decent father," Clevenger said. "Maybe someone like . . ." He glanced at Pearson. "I'm not making any sense."

"Someone like me?"

"Talk about transference," Clevenger said, with a chuckle. "I don't know what the hell I'm saying right now."

"Sure, you do," Pearson said. "And there's nothing funny about it."

Their eyes met.

"I wish you'd had a father like the one you *imagine* me to be," Pearson said. His tone grew especially warm. "I wish I could have been that good a father to my own kids."

SIXTEEN

Clevenger flew into Islip Airport, rented a car, and drove out to Southampton, on the tip of Long Island. Whitney McCormick had arranged a 5:00 P.M. meeting for him with the family of Ron Hadley, whose body had been found nine weeks before, buried in a shallow grave on the beach near his oceanfront estate, wrapped in a plastic sheet, his heart exposed and neatly dissected.

Southampton is the summer playground for Manhattan's rich and famous. Steven Spielberg, Billy Joel, Lauren Bacall, fashion phenoms Calvin Klein and Tory Burch, and former Time Warner chief Steve Burns all have second or third homes there. Many properties are valued in the tens of millions.

Clevenger had researched Hadley on the Web before leaving the Boston Forensics offices.

When he died at sixty-one, Hadley was chief executive officer of National News Corporation, which operated newspapers and radio and television stations across the country. In his forties he had served two terms in Congress, representing New York's Fourteenth District, including most of the Upper East Side. He left his wife, Patrice, a former model, and two adult daughters, Nicole and Amy.

Clevenger was prepared for splendor when McCormick told

him the Hadley estate was located on Meadow Lane, the premier street in Southampton, bordering the ocean. But he was taken aback when he drove onto the property.

By Southampton standards, the house itself was not enormous—about eight or nine thousand square feet, not the twenty thousand allowed by town zoning. What made it remarkable was that it sat on at least six acres of rolling lawn, with hundreds of feet of beach front and dramatic views of the Atlantic Ocean and the Great Peconic Bay.

It was also striking for its design. The facade comprised three gray, shingled rectangles, separated by two round towers of slightly darker gray stone. Four chimneys of the same stone pierced the charcoal gray slate roof. The windows were trimmed in lead-coated copper, yet a fourth shade of gray.

The house looked like a charcoal drawing of itself, a work of art on display under the clouds.

Clevenger rang the bell at the front door.

A pregnant woman with auburn hair, about thirty-five, wearing a black one-piece bathing suit, a black pareo, and black Gucci sunglasses answered it a minute later. "Dr. Clevenger?"

"That's right."

"I'm Nicole," she said, with a smile. She extended her hand.

He shook it.

"Everyone's by the pool."

He followed her through the house, no less gracious on the inside, with beachwood floors and ceilings and gray granite fireplaces. A row of six-by-six-inch windows ran along the top of every wall, like a transparent crown molding, allowing sunlight to flow through the entire structure. "This way," Nicole said. She opened a glass door and walked outside.

Acres of lawn, bordered by beach plum and dwarf juniper trees and tall, deep English gardens, rolled toward the ocean. Clevenger could hear waves crashing onto the beach.

He walked with Nicole along a curved bluestone path that gradually widened until it embraced an infinity pool and a pool house shaded by wind-bent jack pines and finished with the same gray shingles, gray stone, and lead-coated copper as the main residence. Two women sat at one of three weathered teak tables at poolside, beneath a sky-blue umbrella. In the distance, fields of wheat-colored beach grass swayed in the wind.

"Mom, Amy, this is Dr. Clevenger," Nicole said, as they reached the table.

Patrice Hadley was in her late fifties, a picture of elegance, with longish, graying hair tied in a ponytail, a magnetic smile, and skin that most women half her age would envy. She was dressed in tennis shorts and a pink T-shirt.

Liz Hadley, on the heavy side, with the prettiest face of the three, shared her sister's auburn hair and sunny disposition. She looked like the older of the two, but only by a few years. She was fidgeting with a diamond solitaire engagement ring that had to be five carats. She wore no wedding band.

Clevenger shook hands with each of them. "It's a pleasure to meet you." He noticed they were drinking red wine. His gaze drifted to the bottle.

"Please, join us," Patrice Hadley said.

Clevenger and Nicole sat down.

"May we offer you a glass of wine?" Amy Hadley asked.

Clevenger told himself that accepting the invitation would break the ice, that he could wait until morning to get sober. A new day, a clean start. "Why not?" he answered. "That's very kind of you."

She poured him a glass.

He took a sip, pictured Ted Pearson sitting in his study, heard his words: "Show some courage yourself."

He took another sip.

"How can we help you, Doctor?" Patrice asked.

"I know how difficult this can be to speak about," Clevenger started, addressing himself mostly to her, "but I'd like to know anything about Ron's life you think could be a clue to his murder."

Patrice smiled at her daughter Amy, who smiled back.

Nicole laughed.

Clevenger wouldn't have thought it possible to witness stranger grief reactions than the Groupmanns', but here he was the very next day, sitting with a widow and her two daughters sharing an inside joke about their murdered husband and father. "I must be missing something," he said. He took another sip of wine.

Amy and Nicole deferred to their mother.

She drained her wineglass, refilled it. "I loved Ron very much, but he made life very difficult for almost everyone he met," she said. "I'm sure dozens of people are breathing easier now."

"Difficult, in what way?" Clevenger asked.

"He was a very powerful personality," she said.

"Overpowering," Clevenger said.

"I know our partners in News Corp. found it very hard to challenge the direction the company was headed," she said. "My husband was vindictive when anyone disagreed with him. He felt attacked. I think that's the dynamic that ended his political career. He made it impossible for the people closest to him to tell him when he was wrong."

Clevenger was struck by Patrice Hadley's seeming lack of emotion—no sadness, no anger. She sounded like her husband's biographer, not his widow. Just like Shauna Groupmann. "Was he as difficult to live with?" he asked, looking around the table.

"At least," Patrice said. She folded her hands in front of her.

Nicole laid her hand atop her mother's.

Clevenger glanced at Amy, saw her twisting her engagement ring round and round.

"We didn't know any different," Nicole said. "But it wasn't a normal situation." She checked to make sure her comment hadn't injured her mother.

It had.

The three women fell silent. The whole setting—the gray house, the wind, the crashing waves—seemed to change from peaceful to foreboding.

"Abnormal, in what way?" Clevenger asked Nicole.

She shrugged.

Clevenger looked at Amy, who reached for her wineglass and took a sip.

Several more seconds passed.

Patrice finally broke the silence. "He ran our lives," she said. "It was my fault, no one else's. Not even his. Ron was a force of nature. It was my responsibility to get the girls out of his way. I didn't."

Out of his way. Where was this headed? "What did that cost them, exactly?" Clevenger asked her.

"Their lives," Patrice said.

"Mom," Amy said, shaking her head.

"It's not like . . ." Nicole started.

"Yes, it is," Patrice interrupted. She looked warmly at Nicole, then back at Clevenger. "They could have started living much sooner than they did."

"It's not the end of the world. I caught up," Nicole said, running her hand down her stomach.

"How many weeks are you?" Clevenger asked Nicole.

"Seventeen," Nicole said. "I got pregnant two weeks after Dad died."

"Any connection?" Clevenger asked her.

"He hated my husband," Nicole said. She shook her head. "I know it sounds stupid, but that's why I waited. I've been married three years. He made it obvious he had no use for Saul from day one. And that bothered me. I cared what he thought. I didn't respect it, but I couldn't get past it and start a family. Saul almost divorced me over it."

"But now that he's gone," Clevenger said, nodding at her stomach, "you're free."

"I feel guilty about that, but that's how it feels."

"You have nothing to feel guilty about," Patrice said.

"Neither do you," Amy said to her mother.

"That's not true," Patrice said. "I knew it wasn't healthy, the way he controlled all of us, for so many years. I should have left."

Clevenger looked at Amy, his gaze settling on her engagement ring. "Did you get engaged recently?" he asked her.

She nodded.

"How long after the murder?" Clevenger asked.

"Seven weeks."

"Your father disapproved of your fiancé?" Clevenger asked.

"He disapproved of every boyfriend I ever had," Amy said flatly. "Jack isn't the first man who asked to marry me."

"No one was good enough," Clevenger said.

"No one was ever *any* good. They were the 'stupidest,' the 'laziest,' the 'ugliest.' He literally wouldn't speak to half the boys who took me out."

Clevenger was sitting with three traumatized women, seemingly liberated only by the death of Ron Hadley. Each of them had a psychological motive for murder.

"Ron would never have gone for help," Patrice said, "but I should have. I was weak. Zero self-esteem. But do you want to know the really . . . ?" She stopped, suddenly choked up.

Now it was Amy who put her hand on her mother's.

Nicole's eyes filled up.

Patrice cleared her throat. "The really strange thing," she went on, "is that sometimes I do miss him . . . quite a lot, which is . . . sick." She bit her lip. "Because we really are much better off without him."

SEVENTEEN

A knock.

West Crosse walked to the door of his suite in the Palmer House Hotel in Chicago, a nineteenth-century Beaux Arts dream with a three-story Louis Pierre Rigal lobby frequently compared with the Sistine Chapel. It made him feel profoundly at peace, even in a city now partly defined by its Millennium Park, home to a sixty-six-foot-long, thirty-three-foot-high sculpture of a bean and to Frank Gehry's monstrous, stainless steel Pritzker Pavilion.

"It's me." A woman's voice.

He opened the door.

Chase Van Myer, twenty-two, stunning in a white baby T and black leather miniskirt, stood outside. "May I come in?"

He nodded.

She walked in. The room glowed with light from dozens of candles. "All for me?" she asked, looking into his eyes.

"Yes."

"It's been so long."

He pushed the door closed and pulled her to him, stroked her long, black hair. "I couldn't wait any longer."

They kissed deeply.

He could taste the bitter residue of cocaine on her teeth and gums. He grabbed hold of her wrists and pushed her against the wall, pinned her hands over her head. He kissed the scars that crisscrossed the undersides of her forearms, lingered on the freshest ones. He ripped open her T-shirt, kissed her naked, pierced breasts. Then he turned her around, roughly pulled her hair away from the back of her neck, and bit the delicate rose tattooed there.

She groaned. "I need to be fucked so bad."

He kicked her feet apart, ran his hand up between her legs. No panties. Wet.

"Please," she said.

He knew she wanted him to make her beg, to humiliate her, to agree she was worthless, not an heiress, ugly, not beautiful. He yanked up her skirt, spanked her until she was red.

She arched her back for more.

"You know what I want to see," he whispered in her ear. He pulled her away from the wall, pushed her toward the bedroom.

He had arranged more candles inside, surrounded the four-poster with white rose petals and myrtle. Handel's *Messiah* played softly on the bedside stereo. Four lengths of gold silk rope lay on the bedspread.

She stood beside the bed, facing him, and pulled off her top. She unzipped her skirt, let it fall to the ground, stepped out of it.

He watched her, stone-faced.

She never looked away from him as she climbed onto the bed, lay down, then spread her legs wide.

His gaze traveled from her breasts, down her lithe torso, her pierced belly button, her smooth crotch, stopped on her right inner thigh, tattooed with the word "FUCKED." That was new in the six months since they had been together. If, in his quietest moments, he had wondered whether her soul could be salvaged, those six letters inked into her skin convinced him once and for all that it could not.

Crosse had met Chase Van Myer a little over two years before, while redesigning the interior of her parents' $20 million, 1922 mansion on Astor Street, in Chicago's prized Gold Coast. Her father, Scout, a venture capitalist, city councilman, and Bonesman, had confided in him that Chase suffered with borderline personality disorder. "She cuts herself," he had said, looking nauseated. "Says it doesn't even hurt. She's in and out of rehab for booze and cocaine. Can't control herself with men. It's all part of the syndrome."

"Men take advantage of her?" Crosse asked.

"She's constantly in a tailspin over one guy or another. Ready to kill herself. Hates him, never wants to see him, then can't live without him, ready to elope, have his baby. She's a mess."

"Has she gotten pregnant?" Crosse asked.

Van Myer looked down. He had just turned fifty, but looked much older. Part of it was the gray at his temples, the crow's-feet beside his piercing blue eyes. But part of it was emotional exhaustion. "She's had three abortions," he said.

Crosse nodded solemnly.

"It's notoriously hard to treat—this borderline thing. Her doctor says she may never snap out of it. It could get worse."

It had gotten worse. In the eleven months Crosse worked on the Van Myer project, Chase's cocaine addiction blossomed into addictions to cocaine and heroin. She became pregnant with her drug dealer's baby, had her fourth abortion.

"You know what I think? We're part of the problem," her father told Crosse one night.

"How so?" he asked.

"Supporting her, for one thing. Making it easy for her to be sick while she lives here. It's time for some tough love. We've got two younger kids to think about. It's affecting them. They worry about her constantly, can't concentrate on school or work. They half-hate her, half-love her. She's tearing everyone apart."

Crosse was all for banishing her. When you have a malignancy, you remove it, as early as possible. Otherwise, it devours everything around it.

The paradigm held for a cancerous cell in the body, a cancerous person in a family, or a cancerous nation on the face of the earth.

He was already sleeping with Chase, already knew how damaged she was. He suspected her father might be the cause, that Scout Van Myer might have had sex with his daughter when she was a child. But her history didn't matter anymore. Because he had no hope for her. The rest of the family was prospering. *She* was the problem now. "I think getting her her own place makes sense," he told her father. "If she has to keep up an apartment, support herself, she might snap out of it."

And so it was decided in the last weeks of the design phase of the Van Myer mansion that Chase's bedroom, still decorated with pink walls and stuffed animals and trophies from summer camp, would become a library and billiards room. No trace would be left of her. She would be relocated to a one-bedroom apartment several blocks away, given six months' rent and her parents' best wishes.

That was the plan. But shortly after her room was gutted, Chase spiraled out of control, overdosed, and was arrested for prostitution. She overdosed again, sliced up her arms, and landed in intensive care.

"We have to take her back," her father told Crosse.

"You're being tested," Crosse told him.

"And if she dies? How am I supposed to live with that?"

"By knowing you tried to save her."

"There are things that happened to her . . . as a child," Van Myer said.

"She isn't a child anymore," Crosse said flatly.

But the Van Myers' will was broken. Whatever demons terrorized Chase now had them terrorized, too. They let her retreat back into their home, emptied the library of books and filled it again with her childhood memories and bed and increasingly rageful art—a clay sculpture of a woman's head with nails for teeth, another of four babies broken into pieces, a painting of a young girl nailed to a cross.

They let the devil into the sacred space Crosse had created, violating God's great design. And the malignancy spread. Life turned out no better for Chase, and far worse for the rest of the family.

The Van Myers began to fight constantly. Their other children began competing with Chase for attention. Her sister Gabriela landed in the emergency room twice, with cocaine overdoses. The youngest sibling, a sixteen-year-old boy, dropped out of school.

Over the last month, Scout Van Myer had called Crosse, his Bones brother, panicked, watching his life unravel, unable to see any way out of the maze he had helped to build.

Now, there was only one way out.

Crosse walked over to the bed. He picked up one of the lengths of gold silk rope.

Chase smiled.

He fastened her right wrist securely to the bedpost.

She stretched her left hand toward the opposite bedpost.

He fastened her left wrist, then her left ankle, then her right.

"Try to get out," he told her, with no emotion. He was a surgeon now. A soldier for the Lord. He felt no excitement, no sorrow, no fear, no pity.

She pulled hard against her tethers, flexing her arms and legs the little she could.

"Good," he said. "Lie still."

She obeyed.

He unbuttoned his shirt, took it off, unfastened his belt, removed his pants, then his underwear.

She stared at him wide-eyed.

He walked to the bedside table, opened the drawer, and removed a white silk scarf. He folded it into a blindfold.

She lifted her head off the pillow.

He tied the blindfold around her head. "Can you see?" he asked her.

"No."

He reached back into the drawer, took out a bottle of chloroform and another white scarf. He poured the liquid over the cloth, then held it over her nose and mouth.

She struggled only weakly before falling asleep.

Crosse was certain he knew why she didn't fight harder: Chase Van Myer understood better than anyone that her life was bringing her and her family more pain than pleasure. And she knew there was no end in sight. Why else would she try to commit suicide again and again?

He reached into the drawer, removed a tourniquet and a syringe filled with the paralytic agent succinylcholine. He tied the tourniquet around Chase's arm, and injected one milligram. Within fifteen seconds he saw Chase's arms and legs, then her face and neck, begin to twitch with disorganized contractions as the succinylcholine relentlessly stimulated each and every one of her muscles.

He knew that even her heart and diaphragm were tightening in on themselves over and over again, unable to stop squeezing. Her body had itself in a death grip and would not let go.

Crosse was not moved. He was certain that what he was doing was in service to liberty, and that freed him to do whatever was necessary with a firm hand and a clear conscience.

Within one minute, Chase's muscles were so fatigued, her system so poisoned with the metabolic waste products of physical exertion, that she lay completely still, paralyzed. Her heart might occasionally shudder, but would no longer pump any blood. Her lungs would move no air. Her respiratory and circulatory systems had collapsed. She was suffocating in silence.

Crosse untied her arms and legs, removed her blindfold, and pulled the bedspread out from under her, leaving her naked on a plastic sheet he had placed there before she arrived. He unfolded the sides of the sheet so that it covered the entire bed and several feet of the carpet on either side of it.

He rolled his vintage Louis Vuitton steamer trunk to the bedside, pulled open one of its drawers, revealing a scalpel, surgical saw, retractors, and surgical clamps.

From another drawer he took a perfectly pressed white linen tunic and pulled it on. He knelt beside the bed, closed his eyes, and prayed:

Lord God, King of the Universe
May you steady my mind and heart and hand.
Your resolve is mine,
As I liberate this family from evil.
I once was lost, but now am found.
Was blind, but now, I see.

He stood up. He watched and listened to make absolutely certain Chase was not breathing. He checked her wrist to make sure she had no pulse. He did not want to cause suffering in the world. He wanted to end suffering.

She was gone.

All that remained for him was to leave a symbol of his love of beauty and truth. He knew it would be one of his last chances to do so.

He pushed Chase's legs together, spread her arms out to the sides, replicating Leonardo da Vinci's famous illustration of the divine proportions of the human body.

He turned up the volume on the stereo, allowed the grace of *The Messiah* to fill him.

He picked up the scalpel.

Behind the eyelids, deep to the bony orbits and orbital septum, lay a world of perfect structure and function. Bands of rectus, levator, and oblique muscles, enervated by three separate cranial nerves, embraced the eyeball, allowing the brain miraculous control over eye movement. The ophthalmic artery branched a dozen times, a tree of life feeding not only the eye muscles, but retina, lacrimal gland, iris, and cornea.

Crosse's first incision bisected Chase's right upper lid. He took two handmade sterling silver nails out of the steamer trunk and pinned back each flap, revealing the delicate axons of the supraorbital nerve. Waves of excitement began to course through him. He thought to himself how little other people were willing to see, how terrified they were to look toward the light, to imagine where freedom might take them and then summon the courage and faith to get there.

He worked more than three hours, placing his last sterling silver nail through Chase's right optic nerve at 3:05 A.M.

He stood back in awe, not of the work he had done, but the perfection he had exposed. In this, as in everything, he was no more than God's messenger.

He made deep, curved incisions under Chase's hips, slicing into the muscles and fascia connecting her legs and pelvis. He wrapped the plastic sheet around her, emptied the steamer trunk of its drawers, and placed her inside, with her knees tucked tight against her chin.

He called the parking attendant and told him to have his black Range Rover waiting, cargo door open. He took the elevator down to the lobby, calmly checked out of the hotel, and then strolled toward the front doors, pulling the steamer trunk behind him. As he walked, he reveled in the travertine marble walls, the rare Irish wool carpeting under his feet. But he was moved especially, as he always was, by the Rigal mural overhead, composed of twenty-one individual paintings, each a tribute to Greek mythology. He felt completely at peace, reassured that great art endures and that his greatest work was almost at hand.

EIGHTEEN

Clevenger had gotten a call from Whitney McCormick just before 7:00 A.M. and had managed to grab an 8:35A.M. flight from Boston to Chicago.

He stood with her in front of Chase Van Myer's naked body, sitting upright, wrists bound to the armrests of the center seat in the front row of the Jay Pritzker Pavilion, a billowing, stainless steel band shell designed by Frank Gehry, the centerpiece of Chicago's $475 million Millennium Park. Her eye sockets had been meticulously dissected, revealing the muscles, nerves, and blood vessels that once controlled and nourished her eyes. The result was a grotesque audience of one, staring up at the 120-foot-high edifice, as though the sight of it had been enough to peel back her flesh.

Despite a makeshift tent of tarps placed around the body, word had leaked out that Scout Van Myer's daughter lay behind it. Dozens of onlookers, including television and newspaper reporters, were being kept away by a wall of police officers, cruisers, and ambulances.

A CSI team was combing the area, snapping photos, dusting for fingerprints, casting footprints.

Clevenger motioned toward the word "FUCKED" on Van Myer's thigh. "Looks pretty new."

"Yeah. But most of the scars on her arms aren't. Neither are most of the needle marks."

"Troubled kid."

"Black sheep of the family. She's been arrested for prostitution, shoplifting, drug possession, drunk and disorderly conduct."

"Have her parents been notified?" Clevenger asked McCormick.

"They're on their way."

Clevenger and McCormick both knew they could never comprehend the horror of a mother or father looking upon a daughter's mutilated body. They knew it was beyond all commiseration. And that was enough to make them want to hold each other close, to hold the line against death and destruction. Because they felt more alive together than they did apart. And they knew that that itself was a kind of miracle.

"How did they ID her?" Clevenger asked.

McCormick nodded toward a folding table closer to the stage, where evidence was being tagged. "He left her wallet, license, credit cards—the whole deal, just like the others."

Clevenger gazed out at the trellis of crisscrossing steel pipes that stretched over the lawn around the pavilion, shimmering under a blazing August sun. He looked back at the stage. "This one's different."

McCormick looked at him.

"The other victims were just as prominent," Clevenger said. "And he didn't try to hide their identities, either. But he covered up their bodies. He buried them close to home—a cozy neighborhood park, the beach." He looked at the crowd around the pavilion. "He's going public in a big way here."

"And going faster and faster," McCormick said. "Three in seven months."

"He wants attention and he wants it now."

"Well, he's got it. National news tonight, every network. If you have anything I can hand up the food chain at the office, let me know. I'll be getting a call."

"North says he's close on financial connections between some of the victims' families. But he needs more time."

"We tried to run down a few of those leads, too. The trouble is, when you're talking about families at this level, you get a lot of cross-pollination. They marry each other. They do business together. It's hard to know whether the connections mean anything, in terms of the murders."

"Something else connects at least two of the victims."

"What's that?"

"What I told you I noticed at the Groupmanns, I noticed again yesterday with the Hadleys. The absence of grief. They've moved right on with their lives. In some ways, both families seem to be doing better than ever."

"I guess if it is some kind of extreme denial, you could understand it better after sudden deaths, especially murders. Too much shock and horror to bear. Maybe both families were desperate to put it all behind them."

"That doesn't square with other survivors I've met."

"These people are unusual. They have the money to cover up a lot of their pain. They have family histories that outlive any individual family member—legacies to worry about. It could even be that Groupmann and Hadley were so focused on growing their family's wealth that they never grew close with their wives or children. The unusual grief reactions could be a side effect of that."

"I'm not so sure. I think people are people when it comes to death."

McCormick looked over at Chase Van Myer's body. "All right. But there has to be an explanation. What are you thinking?"

"I don't know. But neither man was exactly beloved. Groupmann was a gay man married to a straight woman. He wasn't much of a father. Hadley was a control freak. He did a major job on his wife and daughters, in terms of their self-esteem."

"So someone in each of their families could have had motive. But we've got *seven* dissected bodies. If you're pitching two copycat killers, it sounds like a huge stretch."

A thought crystallized in Clevenger's mind. "Maybe that's the point."

"Huh?"

"It is a stretch. But what if I've got the motives right, but the killer comes from outside either family? Their motives become his." He paused to put his thoughts together. "These guys were in the way. Problems. Their families were stifled by them."

"So our perp did them a favor and cleaned house? Why? What does he get out of it?"

"It's what he's talking about in his note to the president—some sick version of 'family values.' "

"You just lost me."

"He said, 'One country at a time or one family at a time, our work serves one God.' Maybe he thinks he's liberating them."

"By killing."

"It's in style right now," Clevenger said. "Especially in the White House."

"Spoken like a true Bostonian."

"I'll take that as a compliment."

There was a flurry of activity among the reporters and onlookers at the perimeter line set up by the police. The crowd parted and

Scout Van Myer and his wife Carolyn walked through, escorted by four uniformed officers and John Jameson, Chicago's chief of police.

Jameson, a bear of a man, six-foot-four, stopped the couple about fifteen yards away from their daughter's body. He seemed to be prepping them for what they were about to see.

Clevenger saw Carolyn Van Myer, late forties, anorexia thin, with short brown hair, bury her face against her husband's chest. He brushed his hand against McCormick's.

She reached out, squeezed his hand, then walked over to the Van Myers.

He followed her.

Jameson introduced the Van Myers to them. "They know the . . . condition we found Chase in," he said. "They would still like to see her."

"You understand there's no need to make a positive identification on the scene," McCormick told them. "You could see her . . ."

"At the morgue?" Carolyn Van Myer asked.

Scout Van Myer, handsome and regal, in a starched white dress shirt and khakis, stayed silent.

"I want to see her now," Carolyn Van Myer said.

"Of course," McCormick said. She looked down.

McCormick, Clevenger, and Jameson followed a few feet behind the Van Myers as they walked to the makeshift tent surrounding Chase's body, then moved to where one of the tarps had been tied back to let Clevenger and McCormick see in.

Carolyn Van Myer gasped. She didn't so much sit, as collapse into the seat next to Chase. Then she reached out and held Chase's lifeless hand, leaned, and kissed the top of her head. "It's okay, Baby Doll," she said, in a clear, strong voice, without a hint of sorrow. "You can rest now." Her voice grew quiet. "We can all rest."

Clevenger and McCormick exchanged glances.

Scout Van Myer made the sign of the cross, then knelt in front of his wife and daughter. "She's finally found her peace, Carrie," he said. "She's in God's hands."

NINETEEN

"*I want to interview* one or both of them while I'm here," Clevenger told McCormick, watching the Van Myers walk away with Chief Jameson. "They're holding together too well."

"They sounded like they were saying good-bye to some great-aunt after a five-year battle with cancer," McCormick said. "I'll make a call and set it up for you. They should be at the station a couple of hours, but it's probably better to catch up with them later at home. They'll be more open."

"That gives us a little time," Clevenger said. "Want to get coffee, go over things?"

"Sure. Where?"

"Room service at the Palmer House is the best espresso in town."

McCormick smiled. "You never give up."

"Not on a great idea."

"I'm not sure we're such a great idea."

Not sure was progress. "Why don't you make that call on our way to the Four Seasons."

She shook her head. "No chance."

She sounded angry. He tried to regroup. "I know I shouldn't be pressuring—"

"Make it the Ritz, and you got a deal," she said.

They took a cab to the hotel. Clevenger chose a suite on the twenty-second floor. But they couldn't wait until they were inside it. As soon as the elevator doors closed, they were in each other's arms, kissing and biting each other's lips, neck, ears, reaching for parts of one another that had been out of reach for months.

"I love you," Clevenger whispered in her ear.

"I love you," she said.

"I can put us first."

She gently pushed him away. "Don't promise something you—"

He kissed her deeply, then held his finger to his lips.

She grabbed his wrist, slid his finger into her mouth.

The doors opened. They walked, pushed, danced one another to their suite.

When they made love, it was new again, yet familiar. The combination was intoxicating. McCormick knew to resist. Clevenger knew not to overpower her too quickly. They had been right for each other for a long time. And if an undercurrent of sadness seeped into their passion, it was only because they shared the unspoken knowledge that their timing never had been.

Later, they lay together in soft, polished cotton robes, fifteen floors above the reality that they were the best defense against a killer who was ramping up his carnage, that Clevenger was still Billy Bishop's best chance to get out of jail and stay alive, that McCormick still needed things from him that he might or might not ever be able to give her.

"It would be nice to be able to stop time outside this room, and just stay here a couple days," McCormick said.

Clevenger ran his hand over her check. "A couple of years."

She pulled away, squinted at his hand, then touched it. "You're shaking."

He hadn't had anything to drink for about ten hours. "I didn't eat a thing today," he said.

She looked at him. "You're in withdrawal?"

"I'm fine."

"Jesus Christ." She got up, started to get dressed.

"Look, I haven't let it get out of control. A couple of drinks a day, for a month, on and off. I'm done with it, as of right now."

"Give me a break," she said, buttoning her blouse.

He sat up. "How about giving me one? I came out here when you called. I made it to California and the Hamptons, no problem. It hasn't gotten the best of me."

She pulled on her shoes. "You had the balls to tell me you could put us first?"

He stood up, walked over to her. "I meant it."

She looked away.

"When I'm done here, let's fly back to D.C. together. We can talk about it over a late dinner. A couple of steaks and a couple of Diet Cokes."

No response.

"I'm not touching it, from here on out. Period."

She looked at him.

"C'mon," he said. "Book us a flight."

A few precious seconds passed. "Alright. If that's what you want. But one more drink, and I don't take your calls. I don't get dinner with you. I don't hire you. It's called a 'last chance,' in case you never heard of it. You sure you want to take it right now?"

"I'm good with now."

"I mean it, Frank. If you need six months to get your act in gear, take them."

He stared into her eyes. "Now is good," he said.

"I'll book the flight," she deadpanned. "There's a five-forty-five. That should give us enough time to get things done here."

He pulled on his jeans as she gathered her things.

She started to head out, stopped, and turned around. "One other thing, on a completely different note: What you said before, about the killer having some sick take on 'family values'?"

"Yeah?"

"And about killing 'being in style' in D.C.?"

He nodded.

"Let's keep that sort of thing between us. It's political dynamite. Someone could use it against the administration. We're out to stop a killer, not hurt the president."

"Spoken like a true politician."

"I'll take that as a compliment."

TWENTY

Clevenger stood a full minute in front of the Van Myers' Astor Street mansion, taken aback by its beauty. The building was majestic: an ivy-covered, brick double bowfront behind a tall, wrought-iron fence with square granite piers every twenty feet. But the real magic started at the entryway, framed by a towering bronze sculpture of two nearly bare trees whose branches formed an arch over bronze gates fitted with security cameras. Behind the gates, a limestone walk inlaid with bronze leaves, as if they had blown off the trees, stretched toward a cut granite staircase leading to front doors of bronze and beveled glass, etched with more leaves. The effect was to turn a classic, early-twentieth-century building into a mystical work of art.

Clevenger was about to press the intercom button at the gate when his cell phone rang. North Anderson. He answered it. "What's up?"

"I may have something."

"Talk to me."

"Jeff Groupmann's skyscraper is looking like one-stop shopping. Besides Sidney Stimson, the aunt of the twelve-year-old victim from Montana, another investor was Ron Hadley. He lost five million dollars he invested through a limited partnership with Bruce Grimes."

"*The* Bruce Grimes?" Clevenger asked.

"Energy secretary under President Buckley during his first term."

"Hadley served in Congress. That must be the connection to Grimes."

"They also graduated together," Anderson said. "Yale, class of sixty-three. And there's more. Stimson kept her maiden name. Her father was chairman of the board of Brown Brothers Harriman investment banking. He was a Yale grad, too. And he served as university president for seven years."

"How about Groupmann?"

"Class of seventy-one."

Clevenger looked down Astor Street, lined with brownstone and brick mansions. "Three victims connected to one university."

"At least three," Anderson said. "I'm going down to New Haven to do a little research at the alumni office."

"I'm about to interview the Van Myers. I'll find out if there's a Yale connection here."

"How bad was the scene at Millennium Park?"

"He left their twenty-two-year-old daughter taped into a front-row seat at the Pritzker Pavilion. Another anatomy lesson. Her eyes."

"Jesus."

"Let me know what you find out at Yale."

"Done."

They hung up. Clevenger turned off his cell phone, pressed the intercom button.

"May I help you?" a man's voice answered.

"Frank Clevenger. I'm here for Mr. and Mrs. Van Myer."

The gate buzzed.

Clevenger walked to the front door.

A minute later a striking man of about fifty-five, wearing a deep-blue suit and gold tie, opened the door. He had remarkably kind, light-brown eyes, thinning silver hair, and perfectly tanned skin. "Please, come in," he said.

Clevenger stepped into a foyer that was actually an atrium framed by a grand, four-story staircase that hugged the walls. Cantilevered catwalks provided access to each floor. He could see straight up to the roof of the house, a glass dome, etched with more falling leaves.

The man extended his hand. "Harold Burns," he said, with a wide smile that showcased bright white teeth. "I'm the Van Myers' attorney. It's a pleasure to meet you."

"Frank Clevenger," he said, shaking Burns's hand. He noticed a teenage boy and a young woman in her late teens or early twenties walk onto the second-floor catwalk, carrying two large boxes.

"Right this way, Doctor," Burns said. "We're set up for you in Scout's office."

Clevenger walked with him down a wide, barrel-vaulted hallway with deep red walls and maple wainscoting. Framed black-and-white photographs showed the Van Myers with a host of celebrities and politicians, including former Chicago mayor Harold Washington, Chicago Cub's coach Dusty Baker, country singer Garth Brooks, former astronaut and Ohio senator John Glenn, and former Illinois senator Paul Simon. Set off from the rest were three photos of the Van Myers at a black-tie event with President Buckley and the first lady.

"I didn't know Mr. Van Myer was a friend of the president," Clevenger said.

"They could be better friends," Burns said, with a smile. "Scout ran Illinois for President Buckley in the last election. You might remember, he lost by nine points."

Scout and Carolyn Van Meyer were seated on a couch at one side of the office when Burns and Clevenger walked in. They stood up.

"I believe you've already been introduced," Burns said.

"We have," Clevenger said. He shook hands with the Van Myers.

Burns took one of two tapestried armchairs in front of the couch and motioned for Clevenger to take the other.

Clevenger sat down. He glanced around the room, which had to be six or seven hundred square feet. The wall over his shoulder, behind Scout Van Myer's desk, held a window seat looking out on a manicured lawn and gardens. A large telescope was permanently mounted in front of it, pointing skyward. Each of the other three walls had an alcove built into it, with floor-to-ceiling recessed shelves filled with books. One alcove held a half-finished canvas atop an easel. In another were two wing chairs on either side of an elaborate silver chess set. The third held a small puppet theater, with velvet drapes and marionettes suspended over a high-gloss black wooden stage.

"Interesting space," Clevenger said.

"My interests," Scout Van Myer said. "It was designed to keep me in touch with some of the things I love to do."

"Painting, obviously. You're also a puppeteer?"

"It's a lot easier than controlling people," Van Myer said with a grin. "Chess I loved as a boy, then forgot all about it when my mother passed away. I picked it up again about a year ago. Same with astronomy."

Van Myer's little joke about controlling people, along with his ability to talk about his pastimes when his daughter had just been killed, were in the same league as the peculiar grief reactions of the Groupmanns and Hadleys.

"I hope you don't mind Mr. Burns sitting in," Van Myer said.

Clevenger knew that prominent families were often represented in any discussion involving the law. "Not at all," he said. He paused. "And I want to say how sorry I am for your loss."

"Thank you," Van Myer said.

Carolyn Van Myer nodded solemnly.

"What is it we can help you with?" Van Myer asked. "If I understand correctly, you'll be preparing a psychological profile of Chase's killer?"

Clevenger was struck by the way the words "Chase's killer" rolled off Van Myer's tongue. Most parents fresh from losing a child to murder can barely stand to think of it, let alone speak of it. "That's right," he said. "And to do that, I need to know as much as possible about your daughter."

"We've already given the police a list of the men she's been involved with—at least the ones we know about," Carolyn Van Myer said.

"Drug dealers, some of them," Van Myer said. "Who knows what other garbage?"

"Criminal records, the whole nine yards," Burns added.

Clevenger had invited the Van Myers to speak about their daughter, and her mother and father had begun with her sexual history, not her talents or dreams or how much they had loved her. "Was that a problem of hers?" he asked, as sensitively as he could. "She lacked control in that area?"

"To say the least," Carolyn Van Myer said. "And now . . ." She looked away, shook her head.

Van Myer laid his hand on his wife's leg.

"Why was that, do you think?" Clevenger asked.

"Why was what?" Van Myer asked.

"Why was she acting out that way?" Clevenger asked.

"The drugs," Carolyn Van Myer said, looking back at Clevenger.

"But it was more than that," Van Myer said. "Chase suffered with borderline personality disorder. I'm told the drugs and . . . indiscretions are typical."

Clevenger nodded. "Borderline personality disorder is a diagnosis, a label," he said. "Many people with that diagnosis do use illicit drugs. They get lost in highly charged relationships. But they do both to escape waves of depression and anxiety." He leaned forward. "My question is whether either of you know *why* your daughter would have had trouble controlling her emotions."

"Our other children had no trouble," Carolyn Van Myer said. "Until they saw what Chase was getting away with."

If it was unusual for Chase's father to speak of his daughter's *killer*, it was extraordinary for her mother to be blaming her for whatever else might be going wrong in the family. Parents of murder victims usually idealize them, describing them as "angels," "too good for this world."

Burns leaned forward. "I think we're getting a little off track," he said to Clevenger. "Would it be helpful if the Van Myers shared their list of the men Chase was involved with? I wonder whether you'll find any of them fits the profile of a serial killer."

Burns was trying to direct the discussion away from the Van Myers themselves. That didn't mean they were guilty of anything, but it did mean that Burns was feeling that he should protect them.

Clevenger pushed a little farther. "The list will be important," he said. "But I'm trying to get at something else." He looked at the Van Myers. "Do either of you have any sense why Chase might have been drawn to the kind of men she was, or why she had a low enough opinion of herself to tattoo a slur on her thigh?"

"I'm sure we don't," Van Myer said. Something new and predatory came into his eyes. "I take it you're a Freudian."

Clevenger didn't confine himself to any one school of thought in psychiatry. But that wasn't the point. Van Myer was invoking the name of Freud to discredit him, to suggest that he was lost in psychological theories about the past, unable to see the truth of the moment. "I think the roots of suffering like your daughter's can go very deep," he said. "I believe to turn her around someone would have had to dig down that far. I suppose Freud would have said the same thing." He looked into Scout Van Myer's eyes, saw a flash of guilt and worry. He didn't want to lose him completely. "But I see your point. No sense getting bogged down in ancient history now. So, please tell me more about these men Chase spent time with."

The Van Myers ran through a list of unsavory characters.

Clevenger took notes, asked questions. Now and then, he glanced up at the wall beside him, covered with framed photographs, letters, degrees, awards. It took him about fifteen minutes to find what he was looking for. Nearly lost amidst the rest was a small black-and-white photograph of Harkness Tower, Yale University's most recognizable building, a Gothic tower with four copper clock faces. The tower appeared on the *Yale Herald* masthead. It contained a famous fifty-four-bell carillon, played daily by members of a university club founded just for that purpose.

When the Van Myers were through downloading their list of Chase's lovers, Burns moved to shut down the meeting. "Does anything jump out at you immediately, Doctor, or would you like to reconvene at some point?"

"I'll need a little time," Clevenger said. "I think I have plenty to get started on."

Scout Van Myer nodded.

Burns stood up.

Clevenger stood, shook hands with Burns and the Van Myers. He nodded at the photograph of the tower. "Is that Harkness, by the way?" he asked.

"Well, yes," Van Myer said.

"You went to Yale?" Clevenger asked.

"My father."

"I took a few public health courses there one summer," Clevenger said. "Quite a place."

"We support it aggressively," Van Myer said. "It was a big part of my father's life. Captain of the football team, Skull and Bones. The friends he kept were the ones he made in college."

"He loved the tower especially?" Clevenger asked.

"He helped raise funds to renovate it."

"A worthy cause," Clevenger said. "I've heard the bells."

"Dad adopted a number of prominent buildings to restore," Van Myer said. "Churches, mostly. He was passionate about architecture. We had that in common."

"I gathered as much, from your home," Clevenger said.

"Thank you for saying so."

"Please call us if you need anything at all," Carolyn Van Myer said.

Except, Clevenger thought to himself, if I need any information about Chase's childhood or insight into her emotional life. "I will," he said.

Burns escorted Clevenger to the foyer. Three boxes packed with stuffed animals, trophies, and what looked like art projects were lined up near the front door.

Clevenger heard footsteps upstairs and looked up. The teenage boy he had seen before was carrying another box out of the room on the second floor. He placed it in the hallway.

"Someone moving?" Clevenger asked.

"Tristan and Gabriela are trying to help their mom and dad get over this," Burns said.

"Chase's brother and sister?" Clevenger asked.

"That's right."

"How are they helping?"

"Packing Chase's things," Burns said, unable to utter the words as matter-of-factly as he probably had hoped.

"Packing," Clevenger said, stunned. "No sense keeping bad memories around, I guess." He reached into one of the boxes, pulled out the painting Chase had done of a young girl nailed to a cross, looked at it for several seconds. It told him much more about her than her parents had. He gently put it back in the box. "Her bedroom was up there?" he asked Burns.

"Yes."

"Mind if I take a look?"

Burns hesitated.

"I won't be more than a minute," Clevenger said.

"I suppose . . ."

"Let me know if I'm overstaying my welcome," Clevenger said, moving past him, up the stairs.

Burns followed him.

Chase's brother Tristan was filling yet another box when Clevenger got to Chase's bedroom, a masculine space with fir-paneled walls and a fir-beamed ceiling.

Clevenger introduced himself to the boy, a wiry kid of about fifteen, with a crew cut and two silver hoops through each ear. He reminded Clevenger of Billy. "Pretty unusual room for a girl," he said.

"It was hers, then it wasn't, then it was again," Tristan said. "They just never put it back the way it was."

"Chase moved out to her own apartment when the house was renovated," Burns said. "Her bedroom became the billiards room. She couldn't make it on her own. She wanted her old space back."

Scene of the crime, Clevenger thought. "People get attached to places," he said.

"Where are the boxes going?" Clevenger asked Tristan.

He shrugged. "That's Dad's deal."

A brother who didn't know or seem to care where his murdered sister's art ended up. "I'm sure he'll keep them safe," Clevenger said.

Tristan shrugged, picked up Chase's clay sculpture of a woman with nails for teeth and tossed it into the box.

"Your sister Gabriela got tired of helping out?" Clevenger asked.

"She did a lot," Tristan said. "She's hanging with her friends."

"Young people get support where they can," Burns said quickly. "I found that with my own kids."

"If they're lucky enough to get it at all," Clevenger said.

"Are we all set then?" Burns asked.

Clevenger nodded. "Thank you, Tristan."

"No sweat," the boy said.

"I'm very sorry about your sister."

"Thanks, man." He pulled the pink comforter off his sister's bed and threw it toward the open box.

Clevenger and Burns walked back downstairs.

"Thank you for all your help," Clevenger said. He held out his hand.

Burns shook it.

Clevenger noticed Burns's signet ring, engraved with the distinctive seal of Yale University, carrying the Hebrew text *Urim v'-Tumim* and its Latin translation *Lux et Veritas*. The most common English translation was "Light and Truth," but many scholars insisted a more accurate translation was "Light and Perfection." In the Bible, the words appear on the breastplate worn by the high priest in the temple. "So, you're Yale, too," Clevenger said, nodding at the ring.

"Undergrad and law school," Burns said. "They couldn't get rid of me."

"Get back much?"

"Whenever I can," he said. "In a lot of ways, I never left. Most of what I am, I became when I was there."

TWENTY-ONE

Clevenger stopped at a pharmacy on Michigan Avenue and wrote himself a prescription for a few Ativan tablets to slow his pulse and stop the churning in his gut—both symptoms of withdrawal from alcohol. He was in a taxi on his way to the airport to meet Whitney McCormick for their 5:45 flight to D.C. when he finally thought to check his messages. He turned on his cell phone and dialed his voice mail.

The first message was from from Tony Traini, one of the best criminal attorneys Clevenger had ever worked with. He had heard Billy was in trouble and was offering to help.

Clevenger wondered whether he ought to take him up on his offer. Letting a public defender handle Billy's case would prove a point, but if it cost Billy years in jail, hanging out with hardened criminals, it could also prove to be the end of Clevenger's dreams for him.

The second message was a dinner invitation from Jan Urkevic, one of Boston's leading psychiatrists. Urkevic looked like a rock star and had lived like one until he had gotten married and had his first child, a glistening little girl named Ava. Clevenger liked spending time with him, his wife, Lisa, and their four kids at their estate just south of the city. When Clevenger's hopes for a normal life dimmed, he could sometimes rekindle them just by watching Urkevic shower love on his family, and watching his family love him back.

The third message, from North Anderson, dwarfed the first two. "I've got a little news about Billy you ought to know," he said. "Give me a call as soon as you get a chance."

Clevenger hung up and dialed him.

"Hey, buddy," he answered.

"So, what's up with Billy now?"

"He made bail."

"What? Bail was twenty grand."

"His public defender petitioned the court and got it reduced to five."

"He doesn't have that kind of money."

"He didn't post it himself. Dave Leone called our office from the Middleton Jail to give us the heads-up. A group of those gang-bangers Billy used to tangle with walked in with cash. The Royals. No way the jail could turn them down."

Clevenger's heart sank. "Any idea where he is?"

"Not yet. I'm in New Haven. I meet with the dean of alumni services in ten minutes. I put the word out to our friends at the Chelsea police station to look out for him."

"Thanks." He was about to say he would head home right away, but McCormick was probably already at the airport waiting for him. At some point, he needed to start salvaging his own life, not just Billy's. "Phone's on," he said. "Call me with anything."

"You know I will. Anything else?"

Clevenger could barely focus on what he needed to tell Anderson about the case. "One thing before we hang up," he said. "Scout Van Myer's father was a Yale grad and major contributor. I'll tell you more later. But we're definitely up to four victims with connections there."

"Worth the trip," Anderson said. "Can't wait to hear the rest."

"You will."

"Stay safe, man."

"You, too."

They hung up.

The taxi dropped Clevenger off at the American Airlines terminal. He met McCormick at the gate.

"I thought you were standing me up," she said. "We're about to board."

He kissed her on the cheek. "Not a chance." He heard how forced the words sounded as he spoke them. He looked toward the line of passengers forming at the door to the jetway.

She knew him well enough to know there was something wrong. "What's going on?"

"Nothing," he said, barely glancing at her. "C'mon. Let's go."

She didn't move. "Tell me."

"It's nothing."

"Frank."

He shrugged. "Billy, again. Big surprise, right? I mean, he's fine, so far as I know. But he . . . He made bail. He's out."

The line of passengers started to move.

"You said bail was twenty thousand dollars."

"His public defender got it reduced to five. Then some members of that gang in Chelsea—the Royals—paid it."

"They bailed him out? Where did he go?"

"North has the Chelsea cops out looking for him. If he hears anything . . ."

McCormick squinted at him. "You can't leave it to North. You need to go home."

"He'll be fine for the night." He looked at her, saw that she didn't believe that any more than he did.

She leaned and kissed him on the cheek. "Go home. Call me and let me know if you find him."

Clevenger's throat tightened. He knew she was right. He knew his mind would be in Chelsea with Billy, even if he flew to D.C. with her. But he didn't want it to be that way. He wanted to start giving her the time she deserved.

She saw he was struggling. "I'm not upset," she said.

She didn't sound upset, which, for some reason, made him feel even worse. "I am," he said.

"Call me tomorrow." She leaned and kissed him on the cheek, again. "I have to go." She walked away, headed toward the jetway.

He waited to see if she would turn around after handing over her ticket. She didn't.

TWENTY-TWO

West Crosse waited in his Thunder Bay, Ontario, compound for the *Nightly News* to begin. He had called Heather Rawlings and told her that he wanted to meet her there the next day to show her an early scale model of the Rawlingses' Montana home. He asked her to keep her trip a secret, so he could surprise her husband by learning more about his life to incorporate in a final plan.

He believed she would keep his confidence, but it probably didn't matter if she violated it.

Ken Rawlings would never tell the police.

Crosse had always been careful to avoid suspicion. He was patient, pacing himself, sometimes waiting years after a building was constructed to complete his final design of the family that would occupy it. He cloaked his work in secrecy, serving only his Bones brothers and their extended families.

Nonetheless, any of the men or women he had liberated could have focused on him as a suspect in the death of their "loved" one. None had. They were unconsciously partnered with him. He was expressing their hidden desires. To think of him as a killer would be to think the same of themselves.

Wasn't that, after all, the way most people lived, outsourcing the hardest parts of living? People who ate meat, but would not hunt.

People who would want SWAT teams to rescue them if they were kidnapped, but would never own guns to protect themselves. People who liked premium gas in their SUVs, but would balk at going to war for it. People who liked their homeland safe, but didn't have the stomach to torture terrorists plotting to destroy it.

Was that not the lesson of Christ? Did he not die alone on a cross for doing God's work alone?

Ken Rawlings might know that his wife had met West Crosse the night she died, but he would keep that from the police, even if it meant forgetting what he knew. He would protect his friend, even grow closer to him, as close as a hidden chamber of his own heart.

And if Rawlings were Judas and broke faith with Crosse, it would still be too late to stop Crosse's greatest plan from unfolding.

Crosse had called the White House earlier and arranged to visit two days later to begin gathering as-built dimensions from the East Wing and to meet again with the president and first lady.

He heard music heralding the beginning of the *Nightly News*. The NBC logo appeared.

"In Chicago today," the anchor's voice began, over a photograph of the Chicago skyline, "a sixth gruesome slaying of a member of a prominent American family. . . . This time, a twenty-two-year-old woman . . ." A photo of Chase Van Myer. "Her body left at an American landmark designed by renowned architect Frank Gehry." A photo of the Jay Pritzker Pavilion.

Crosse felt a wave of disgust looking at the structure, a 120-foot stainless steel malignancy invading the earth, with unrestrained ribbonlike walls folding in on one another, the whole mess held up by an exposed skeleton of steel tubing. Like so many deconstructionist buildings, Gehry's was based on twisted axes, disjointed forms, curved facades, flowing, melting volumes of space seemingly without boundaries. Cancer.

It was no wonder that Gehry's work had come to symbolize the fragmentation of contemporary life, a social order without restraint. Anarchy.

Gehry's architecture was all about the architect. About self-love. About the radical's empty joy in roiling tradition.

Crosse loved structure, not tearing it down. His work served his clients' needs, not his own. He knew that freeing them to live more complete lives didn't have a thing to do with bending the walls of their homes. It meant finding the structure that reflected their inner truths and then achieving it, at any cost. It meant going to war for an architecture that replicated the stunning marriage of form and function found in human anatomy.

Freedom was about drawing the right boundaries, not living without them.

Scout Van Myer appeared on the television, at a press conference outside the magnificent gates in front of his home, surrounded by his wife Carolyn, son Tristan, daughter Gabriela, and several uniformed officers. "Whoever did this to my daughter will be brought to justice," he said confidently. "Until that time, I want to thank you for being here today and keeping us in your prayers tomorrow."

Crosse smiled. Van Myer looked strong and confident—at peace. And Crosse doubted it was an accident he had gathered his wife and children around him for the cameras. He was presenting the Van Myer family, newly constituted, liberated from the tyranny of his daughter's sickness.

Crosse felt peaceful, too. When you do the right thing, even when it is hard to do, even when the cost is a human life, you can sleep well at night, a happy, tired soldier of the Lord.

He switched to ABC, then CBS, then CNN, all of them focused on Chase Van Myer, on the hand of God.

He turned off the television.

He did not want to die, but he sensed that his life was drawing to a close, that to ask for more time than he needed to complete his masterwork would be to ask too much. He thought of Martin Luther King's speech foreshadowing his own demise. "I've been to the mountaintop," he had said, "Like anybody, I want to live a long life. Longevity has its place. But I'm not concerned about that now. I just want to do God's will."

Crosse, too, had been to the mountaintop. He had seen God's truth and carried it in his heart. And he was ready to die in service to it.

He walked into the bathroom, took a straight razor out of his shaving kit, flicked it open. He looked at himself in the mirror, letting his eyes move slowly across his wide shoulders, down his armor-like pectoralis muscles, his washboard abdomen. He held his arms out to his sides, spread his legs slightly, becoming da Vinci's divine human form. Then he slowly cut himself, shoulder to shoulder, neck to groin, in the pattern of a cross, just deep enough to start his blood flowing.

TWENTY-THREE

Eleven-ten P.M. Clevenger turned on his phone the moment his plane landed at Boston's Logan. It started to ring. North Anderson, again. He answered it. "What's up?"

"Where are you? I've been trying to call you."

"I just landed at Logan."

"I didn't know you were coming back."

"I didn't like the idea of Billy out on bail and me out of town. Did you hear anything?"

"Can you meet me at the old Perkins Box and Paper in, say, twenty minutes?"

"Sure. What's going on?" Clevenger said.

"A buddy of mine on the Chelsea force named John Rosario called me. Word on the street says the Royals are staging 'extreme fights' in a ring they built inside the factory, starting at eleven. Sal Ramirez and a dozen other cops are raiding the place at midnight. He heard Billy's involved."

Clevenger shook his head. "Great."

"He figured we'd want to get him out of there before he gets himself arrested, again."

"I guess . . ." Clevenger said, too angry, disappointed, and worried to say more.

"You don't exactly sound over the top on the idea."

Clevenger started walking off the plane. "Maybe it's better if they pick him up again. This time they'll hold him without bail. We'll get drug testing as a condition of probation when he's convicted."

"Your call," Anderson said. "But he's already looking at kidnapping, assault, a DWI, and resisting arrest. Granted, even a rookie public defender is gonna let some air out of the D.A.'s tires. But if Billy reoffends while he's out on bail, they tack on this illegal fight rap, maybe possession . . . all bets are off. He could pull eight-to-ten at Walpole. Not to mention the fact that he's Golden Gloves. These guys fight bare-fisted, no holds barred. He could end up killing somebody."

Clevenger let out a long breath. "But it's my call, huh?"

"I didn't mean to push."

"Sure. I'll meet you there in fifteen minutes."

"Later."

They hung up.

Fifth Street was the part of Chelsea that had remained immune to gentrification. Rusted, corrugated steel buildings, mountains of scrap metal, and tenement houses patched with plywood clung like barnacles to the cracked pavement. Pay phones outnumbered streetlights. The only store was a packie with iron grates on the doors and windows.

Clevenger drove by Perkins Box and Paper, saw the lot was full of cars, lots of them souped up, lowriders. More cars lined the usually deserted streets nearby.

He pulled his black F-150 pickup into a space two blocks from the factory and started toward the place. He was almost there when North Anderson's midnight blue Porsche Carrera roared into an empty space in front of him.

Anderson stepped out. "I always get a great spot," he said, with the wide grin that made people like him, even when he was leaning on them. "I'm lucky that way, you know?" He reached back into the car, tossed Clevenger a Glock 9mm pistol.

Clevenger caught it.

Anderson tucked another pistol inside the waistband of his jeans, covered it with his black T-shirt.

They started walking toward the factory together.

"Thanks for doing this," Clevenger said.

"Thank me after we get Billy out of there," he said. "Then let's go over what I found out at Yale."

There were two teenage bodybuilder types stationed at the front door of the pale yellow cinder block building. Techno music pounded through its walls, into the night.

Clevenger and Anderson walked up to the teenagers.

"Whazzup?" the smaller of the two, a Hispanic kid about fifteen, with glazed eyes peering out of the hood of his ripped sweatshirt, asked.

"How much?" Anderson asked.

The crowd inside roared over the music.

"Somebody getting his ass *kicked,*" the other kid, black, tougher, a couple of years older, said. He gave Anderson the once-over, his gaze lingering on Anderson's Rolex Yachtmaster watch. "Fifty," he said. He glanced at Clevenger. "Each."

"A C note to watch a couple of pussies take off the gloves," Anderson said, grinning again. "Fucking inflation." He handed the black kid a hundred dollar bill. "Better see somebody bleed, brother."

"Count on it," the black kid said.

Clevenger and Anderson walked inside. At least five hundred people were crowded onto staging around a makeshift ring in the center of the gutted building. The music was nearly deafening. The air was thick with smoke from what smelled like a bonfire of tobacco and marijuana.

They climbed to the second level of staging, caught what looked like the end of a not-very-even fight between a six-foot, twenty-something with scars and tattoos all over his body, and an even taller, much heavier teenager with a shaved head who was slumped against the ropes, blood streaming from his nose and above his left eye. The six-footer kept landing lefts and rights, but the heavy kid stayed on his feet.

Clevenger scanned the room, looking for Billy. He saw adults, high schoolers, even some kids who couldn't possibly be farther along than seventh or eighth grade. They were mostly Hispanic, black, and Asian. They tipped their heads back, drained cans of beer and fifths of scotch and vodka. He didn't see Billy anywhere.

The heavy kid took a front ball kick to his abdomen that doubled him over, then a roundhouse kick to his head that snapped it back and sprayed blood into the air. The crowd cheered wildly as he slid down to the canvas. He tried to get up twice, but couldn't manage more than a slow roll onto his stomach. On his third try, he got to one knee, but was straddled by the tattooed fighter, who wrapped his powerful arms around his neck and, pulling hard, choked him. He collapsed to the canvas and weakly slapped it several times, surrendering.

The crowd erupted as the tattooed fighter climbed the ropes and pumped his bloody fists into the air.

The heavy kid's buddies helped him out of the ring.

Still no sign of Billy.

Suddenly the place went dark. Strobe lights began flashing, fracturing time into frames half-a-second long. Two teenage girls in thong bikinis climbed into the ring and started dancing to rap music.

In the darkness between flashes, cigarettes glowed red, and joints floated like fireflies as they were passed around.

Anderson nudged Clevenger, pointed toward the corner of the

room, where the two fighters who had just been in the ring were disappearing through a door marked MEN. A makeshift wooden sign in front of the door read DRESSING ROOM FIGHTERS ONLY.

They started pushing their way through the crowd, headed for the sign. They were still about twenty feet away when the music stopped, and an announcer bellowed over the P.A. system: "Give it up for our next two gladiators!"

Shouts and whooping from the crowd.

"Fighting out of the Brazilian Boxing Club in Medford," the announcer said, "Manuel 'the Snake' Santiago!"

Music blared as a tanned, handsome young man, about twenty-five, with a body that looked like sculpted steel, jogged out of the men's room, wearing bicycle shorts and a thick, gold rope chain with a six-inch crucifix dangling from it. He headed toward the ring with his entourage, a group of eight men who couldn't have looked more grave if they were fronting a heavyweight title bout in Vegas.

The music stopped again.

"And fighting out of the Middleton Jail," the announcer said, with a laugh, "The kid with the Golden Gloves. Chelsea's own, Billeeeeeee Bishuuuuup!"

The crowd went wild as the music started again. Billy had been a local legend in Chelsea ever since winning Golden Gloves, and people were scrambling higher on the staging, craning their necks, to get a look at him.

Clevenger had pushed to within ten feet of the dressing room when Billy walked out, covered in sweat, in baggy black cutoff jeans and a black hooded sweatshirt. He was surrounded by at least a dozen Royals wearing skullcaps and their trademark jerseys, emblazoned with a skull wearing a crown.

"Billy!" Clevenger called out.

A bunch of people around Clevenger thought he was starting a chant and echoed him. "Billy! Billy!"

Billy just stared straight ahead and kept moving toward the ring.

Even without the music, he probably wouldn't have heard Clevenger. He was always in a different place before a fight, nearly unreachable, getting his mind in touch with the parts of him that were the angriest, like loading bullets into a pistol.

Anderson tried to push his way through to block Billy's path, but everyone was backing up to make way for him, and Anderson couldn't overcome the tide.

Clevenger looked at his watch: 11:47. The cops would be there in thirteen minutes.

Billy pulled himself up into the ring and started to bounce on his feet. The crowd grew even louder. He pulled off his sweatshirt, revealing his dreadlocks and the flaming cross on his biceps and a torso that looked like a drawing from *Gray's Anatomy*.

His opponent stole a few glances, then tried not to look.

Eleven-fifty-three. The referee, a black man about sixty, who looked like he had done legitimate work in the ring, held each fighter's hand as he went over the rules. It took him all of ten seconds. He backed away, motioned someone outside the ring, and a bell sounded.

Santiago came out fast, crouched, and rushed Billy, trying to grab him around the waist and drive him back, maybe trip him up and slam him to the canvas. But Billy danced away and watched him bounce off the ropes instead. By the time he had spun around, Billy was there in front of him, the techno music was cranked louder than thunder, and it was too late.

Billy had always had a rare combination of speed and power, but what he unleashed on Santiago was something greater than the sum of those parts. It was surgically focused rage, a hurricane of lefts and rights that opened gashes over both of Santiago's eyes and his right cheekbone, covering his face with blood.

For almost everyone watching, what happened next would have looked like the beginning of the raid that started thirty seconds later.

Clevenger and Anderson, who had been fighting to get to the ring, got there, climbed inside, and rushed over to Billy, grabbing him from behind and dragging him away from Santiago, who somehow found the strength to take advantage of the moment and rush Billy headfirst, ramming him in the stomach, knocking the wind out of him. He drew back to throw a punch, but Anderson pushed him into the ropes, whisked out his .44 Magnum, and shoved it between his ribs.

Santiago looked down, saw the barrel of the gun.

"You think you're bleeding now . . ." Anderson shouted in his ear.

Just as the Royals started piling into the ring, the faint sound of sirens could be heard. Then the crowd began parting like the Red Sea, and a line of cops in riot gear started pouring into the place.

The music kept playing.

Billy was still winded, and Clevenger still had him in a full Nelson.

"Everyone down on the ground, hands behind your heads," a cop yelled through a bullhorn.

A gunshot rang out, then two more, and one of the Royals who had climbed into the ring fell back against the ropes, with bullets through his right shoulder and neck. He dropped a revolver on the canvas.

"Down! Now! Hands on your heads!" the cop with the bullhorn screamed.

"Come with me, or you're in jail till I'm on social security," Clevenger yelled into Billy's ear. He grabbed his wrist and pulled him out of the ring, toward the door.

Before they could get there, one of the cops directing the raid pointed toward Clevenger and Billy, and two other cops moved toward them.

"Shit," Clevenger said.

"Doesn't matter," Billy said. "I don't give a fuck."

Clevenger looked at him. His pupils were pinpoint. He was high on something, maybe even heroin. But if this was going to be the last time he saw his son outside a jail cell for several years, he wanted to make sure he said what he felt, because maybe the part of Billy's brain that wasn't rage and wasn't wired would somehow hear him and remember. Maybe. "Well, I do care," he said. "No matter what happens."

Billy looked away.

The music stopped.

The cops grabbed Billy, yanked his arms behind his back, and cuffed him.

The father in Clevenger kicked into full gear. "Where's Rosario?" he asked one of them. "I want to talk to John Rosario."

"You're looking at him," the younger of the two cops said. "No need to talk to me, Doc. Thank North for saving my ass a couple years back." He winked. "Meet me in back of Demoulas's Market in five minutes. Mike Tyson here is your problem, not mine."

Clevenger looked over at the kid who had been shot. A paramedic was laying a blanket over him, covering his face. "Do me a bigger favor," he told Rosario. "Let me meet you at the Mass General E.R. If Billy refuses to sign in for a detox on their locked unit, I'm gonna call you and ask you to come back and arrest him. You owe North that much?"

"At least," Rosario said.

TWENTY-FOUR

Billy had already registered at the E.R. when Clevenger got there. He was refusing to let him visit or sign a release of information to let the E.R. doctor talk to him.

"He's nineteen. I shouldn't even confirm or deny whether he's here," Dr. Jane Monroe told Clevenger at the triage desk.

Clevenger didn't know Monroe. More important, she didn't know Billy. "I wouldn't ask you to violate his confidence," Clevenger told her. "But if he's headed back out to the street, he could be headed for real trouble. He's out on bail for assault and battery and kidnapping. And I think he's using more than alcohol, probably opiates. I'll commit him myself if he doesn't sign in voluntarily."

Monroe was in her early thirties, still unsure how to balance what she was learning about practicing medicine with what she had learned in medical school. "Anyone asks," she said, "I didn't tell you a thing."

"You threw me out of your E.R."

She smiled. "He signed in. He goes up to detox after he's medically cleared."

"The locked unit?"

She nodded.

"Good news," Clevenger said.

"He can still sign himself out," she said. "He just has to meet with a psychiatrist and contract for safety before he leaves."

"Better than nothing."

"He says he's never been detoxed before."

"Not true," Clevenger said. "He's been over at North Shore Medical Center. Paul Summergrad has his whole history."

"Let's hope the second one's a charm, huh?"

The second one or the twenty-second one, Clevenger thought to himself. That was the point his psychiatrist Ted Pearson had been making. Healing someone like Billy wasn't a three-month job or a three-year job. It could be three decades. Clevenger had seen men and women turn their lives around after thirty detoxes, or five failed marriages, or abandoning their children, or a dozen DWIs, or fifteen suicide attempts, or homelessness and prostitution, or decades in state prison, or any number of other signs that their lives were hopeless or worthless. It was sometimes hard to believe the human soul was capable of a comeback after so many defeats, but it was. On a good day, it was easy for Clevenger to remember that. On a bad day, it was a lot harder. On his worst days, he just prayed it might be true. But down deep he knew it was, and it was the greatest lesson he had ever learned. Because once you believe it is never time to give up on another human being, then you have the chance to believe it about yourself. "Let's hope," he told Monroe.

"Good luck," she said. "I think there's a sensitive kid somewhere underneath all that muscle."

"I think you're right. Thank you for saying so." He turned to walk away, then turned back. "His eye," he said. His stomach sank with the realization that Billy had climbed into the ring despite his injured eye. "He got hit in the eye the day before yesterday," he said. "If we could have someone come by from ophthalmology and take a look at him, I'd appreciate it."

150

"Not a problem," Monroe said.

"Thank you again." He turned and walked out to the main lobby.

Anderson was waiting there. Clevenger filled him in. "It's a start," he said. "At least he's agreeing to get help."

"It's a start," Clevenger said.

"So, let's move on to Yale, for a minute."

"What did you find out?" Clevenger asked.

"We're batting a thousand," Anderson said. "They're all connected to the university. Of the six victims, two were Yale alumni, two were spouses of alumni, and two were first-degree relatives."

"Six out of six. Maybe we're looking for a Yale grad or staff member."

"There's more. I went on-line to research the family names of the victims. Each of them brings up hundreds of entries about building or banking or investing or whatever, just a handful of articles about Yale. But when you put all the names on one search line together, the first fifty or so references that come up are all about Skull and Bones."

Clevenger remembered Scout Van Myer mentioning his father had been a member. "They're all members?"

"One generation or another."

"I thought it was supposed to be a secret society."

"It is," Anderson said. "But in 1985, someone named Anthony Sutton got his hands on a list of all the members, living and dead. Two volumes. Supposedly, a disgruntled Bonesman turned it over to him. Sutton generated the whole conspiracy theory that these guys run the world for fun and profit—oil, drugs, you name it. He says they use the military like a private army to move the world in the direction they think it should go. I'm not big on that stuff, but I've got to admit, the list does read like a Who's Who of American power brokers: Rockefeller, Payne, Pillsbury, Luce, Harriman, Bundy. We're talking President Taft, Supreme Court justices, senators, congressmen, the founders of the CIA."

"And President Buckley," Clevenger said.

"And Buckley. And our killer sent him a little fan mail."

"So maybe the killer's Skull and Bones, too."

"Or a relative of a Bonesman. Or someone who wishes he was picked for it. One interesting side note: David Groupmann comes up in a special way when you search for him and Skull and Bones. When his twin brother Jeffrey got tapped for Bones, he made a big deal out of not being chosen along with him. He got drunk one night and tried to break into the Tomb on High Street where the club meets. Got the shit beat out of him by a few of the members the next day. The *New Haven Register* covered it front page. He never pressed charges."

"Someone I should talk with again."

"Once you open it up to people like him who don't like those guys, you end up in a very big pond. The conspiracy theorists are everywhere."

"True. But I go back to the killer's vision being *the same* as the president's, not different," Clevenger said. "He's using violence—killing—to reshape families. He thinks the president is using it to reshape the planet in the name of God. 'One country at a time or one family at a time.' That's what he wrote. If David Groupmann isn't our man, I'm betting we're looking for a Bonesman, not an outsider."

"Then if you go with the list Sutton published, and if you figure our man is over, say, forty, the pond is much smaller. We're only talking fifteen new members a year. Going back twenty years, that's only three hundred people."

"We should run criminal background checks on every one of them."

"I'll put a few researchers and P.I.'s on it."

"Great. But let's think for a second. Maybe there's a way to find the sweet spot here. Why is he targeting these *particular* families? They've got to have something in common besides Skull and Bones."

"Maybe. Or maybe it's pure chance. Maybe these are just the families he's come into contact with through business or whatever."

"Possible."

"Any obvious link between the Groupmanns, Hadleys, and Van Myers?" Anderson asked.

"Just the unusual grief reactions, so far as I can tell. But I'm going to have to think more on it."

"What's next?"

Clevenger looked at his watch. One-twenty A.M. "Sleep," he said. "Sleep is next."

"Let's talk in the morning."

"You got it."

They started to walk out.

"What did you do to help John Rosario, anyhow?" Clevenger asked.

Anderson smiled. "John's a compulsive gambler. Mostly the track, but some football, baseball, whatever. He ran up a debt of forty-two grand with Grossett in Revere."

Sam Grossett was a bookie with an even worse temper than most of his colleagues.

"And?" Clevenger asked.

"I took care of it," Anderson said.

"You got Grossett to back off? What did you do, pay the vig for a while?"

"No. I lent Rosario a grand and he bet it on the Red Sox to win the Series. The Yankees were up three games to none. It paid out seventy-to-one."

"What a story," Clevenger said. "I don't know if it does anything to cure his underlying problem, though."

"Call it preventive medicine," Anderson said.

"How do you figure?"

"It prevented Grossett from breaking his arms and legs."

Clevenger laughed. "Good point, Doctor Anderson."

They grabbed their cars out of the Mass General garage and turned onto Storrow Drive, headed for the Tobin Bridge, to Chelsea.

Clevenger was shaking again and a little sweaty. He'd used all his Ativan tablets. He remembered there was still vodka in the loft, which made him relax a few seconds, then made him shake more. He thought again of what Ted Pearson had told him: *Show some courage yourself.*

He drove past the exit for Chelsea, kept driving to an all-night Brooks Pharmacy fifteen minutes down Route 1.

He walked in and headed for the pharmacy.

The pharmacist, a man about forty, with an earring and a couple of days growth of beard, was behind the counter, labeling someone's prescription. "Help you?" he asked, without looking up.

"I'm a doctor," Clevenger said. "If you've got a prescription pad, I'll write one out."

"Will the patient be coming in tonight?"

"I am the patient."

The pharmacist glanced at him. "I have to ask you for your medical license."

Clevenger pulled his wallet out. "No problem."

He glanced at him again. "I can't dispense any controlled substance if you're writing for yourself. Sorry, state law."

"I'm writing the exact opposite," Clevenger said.

That got the pharmacist's full attention. He looked at him. "Huh?"

"Antabuse," Clevenger said. "Do you have any in stock?"

Antabuse blocks the body's metabolism of alcohol midstream, causing a buildup of the extremely toxic metabolite acetaldehyde, a poison that is usually quickly broken down into harmless chemicals in the bloodstream. But in the presence of Antabuse, acetaldehyde levels skyrocket, causing a massive surge in blood pressure, runaway pulse, nausea, vomiting, and, sometimes, death from either cardiac arrhythmia or stroke.

"I've got some," the pharmacist said. "You know how it works, right? You got to tell everyone to keep all liquor out of your food, including desserts. Even aftershave on your skin can get you sick. Obviously, if you drink, you can die."

"I guess I better not drink then," Clevenger said. "Which is kind of the point. I can either be sober or dead. It simplifies things. I pick sober."

The pharmacist grinned, walked over, and handed him a prescription pad.

Clevenger wrote out a prescription for thirty 250-milligram tablets. While he waited for the medicine, he grabbed a Diet Coke from the soda aisle. He walked back to the pharmacy, picked up the vial of Antabuse and paid for it.

"One day at a time," the pharmacist said. "Good luck to you."

"I'll need it," Clevenger said. "Thanks."

He went back out to his truck, climbed into the driver's seat. He unscrewed the caps off the Diet Coke and the prescription vial, poured an Antabuse tablet into his hand, and then just sat there. Writing the prescription was the easy part. Once he swallowed the tablet he would have no escape from whatever feelings visited him. Depression. Anxiety. Anger. He'd have no backdoor out of the chaos of life. And the truth was, that scared the hell out of him. But maybe the fear was good. Maybe being scared and depressed and anxious and angry were the only sane responses to a world in which the son you love could turn up dead or kill somebody the next day, in which building a life with the woman you loved always seemed just beyond where your life plan could take you. A world in which giant waves could wipe out 165,000 people, and a serial killer could find inspiration in an American president. Maybe learning to be human was about learning to live in pain, not trying to figure out how to live pain-free.

That's what he needed courage for.

He sat there several seconds longer. Then he popped the pill into his mouth, took a swig of Diet Coke, and swallowed it down.

TWENTY-FIVE

Clevenger called Whitney McCormick on her cell phone. He wanted to update her on what he knew about Yale and Skull and Bones, but he also wanted to reassure himself that she hadn't written him off for choosing Billy over her the night before.

"How's Billy?" she answered.

She sounded more like a doctor inquiring about a patient than a woman inquiring about her lover's adopted son. "In detox," Clevenger said, and left it at that.

"Great. You did the right thing."

"Listen, I wanted to . . ."

"No need," she said. "You can't walk out of his life when he's in trouble."

Clevenger wanted to say that Billy's troubles were over for now, that he wouldn't be leaving her alone at any more airline gates. But he couldn't know that. "How about if I come down to D.C. for dinner tonight?"

"Sorry. Meetings."

"We could make it late."

"You know what? Let's hold that thought," she said. "We'll definitely do it another time."

"Okay," Clevenger said.

157

"Anything else going on?"

"There's something on the case, if that's what you mean." He half-hoped she would linger a little longer on the personal side of their business together.

"I'm all ears."

So much for that half hope. He told her about Yale and Skull and Bones and David Groupmann. "North is checking criminal records for everyone over forty on the membership list."

"We'll get the list and run them through our system, too," she said. "I think you should visit with Groupmann again, maybe even today. Check whether he has an alibi for one or more of the killings."

"I had the same thought. Let me check flights. I could probably get there by dinnertime, then red-eye it back."

"I'll make the call, see if he's available."

"And if there's any way to get a list of Skull and Bones members that includes men in their twenties and thirties," Clevenger said, "that would be terrific. Sutton's list is dated."

"If anyone can, we can. I'd like to avoid getting the president involved, but if I have to press for that, I will."

"Let me know."

"Of course."

"Alright," Clevenger said. "Take care." He moved his thumb to the End button.

"Frank?"

"Yeah?"

"I'm not trying to be hurtful, about the dinner thing or anything else. I just think we have to admit to ourselves that our timing may not ever be right."

"Whitney—"

"And I want to just leave it at that. Okay? Because, otherwise, I'm not going to get on with my life, and I really need to."

The way she said those last words gave Clevenger pause. "Are you seeing someone?"

"I mean, sort of, but that's not even—."

"I didn't know. I—"

"It's nothing. This has nothing to do with him."

Hearing her utter the word "him" hurt almost as much as if she had used his name.

"It's . . . Just, please. Help me out with this, okay? I've got a lot on my plate. I can't afford to get depressed here."

Clevenger thought about telling her he wanted to talk it over in person, but he knew whatever night he coaxed her to choose could be a night Billy would decide to take on three of the other patients in detox, or to sign himself out of the place, or who knows what. He could deny all that, but probably at her expense. "Okay," he said.

"Thank you," she said quietly. "I'll call you after I talk to Groupmann."

"Right. Talk to you then." He hung up.

TWENTY-SIX

Heather Rawlings's private jet landed at the Thunder Bay airport at 1:55 P.M., in patchy fog and drizzle. West Crosse had sent a car to take her to his compound, fifty acres on a bluff overlooking Lake Superior.

Thunder Bay, sitting at the geographical center of North America, was rich in every way. Its history stretched back to 5000 B.C., when Paleo-Indians mined copper from its hills and valleys. Over thousands of years, the land continued to feed a thriving trade of gemstones, silver, fur, and lumber.

The views of Lake Superior were magnificent, the waters treacherous. Beneath them lay more than a hundred vessels, the only freshwater marine sanctuary of shipwrecks in the world.

But more than anything else, it was the tradition of healing that had drawn Crosse to settle at Thunder Bay. In the 1600s, the Chippewa Indians, facing deadly diseases introduced by European traders, had founded the Grand Medicine Society, a secret religious order of shamans who performed elaborate healing rituals, including the use of potions, bloodletting, and sacrifice. A master healer, having risen through four levels of membership in the society, was given power over life and death. Taken as a whole, their efforts, inexplicable to most, mistrusted by many, were later credited with

161

helping the Chippewa not only survive, but become one of the most powerful tribes on the continent.

Courageous medicine men had done what was necessary, in the name of their gods, thereby achieving the greatest good for the greatest number.

It was a lesson as deeply rooted in the culture of Thunder Bay as it was in Crosse's soul. The first time he visited, he felt immediately at home.

Heather Rawlings was not prepared for what she saw as her driver emerged from the half-mile-long, winding, tree-lined private road leading to Crosse's property. The main building could only be described as a castle, but like none she had seen on her trips to England or France or Ireland.

Three stone arches, each two stories high, dominated the facade of the four-story, gabled, stone structure, which was built into the side of a cliff, so that parts of it literally faded into the earth. Bronze gates across each archway allowed views of stables that held at least a dozen thoroughbred horses. A reflecting pool ran the length of the place, mirroring the three arches, thereby creating the illusion of two figure eights, joined end to end.

Only Crosse and a few of the physicists, geneticists, and chemists he invited to dinner from time to time saw the half-stone, half-water pattern for what it was—a double helix, the structure of DNA, the basic building block of human life. And perhaps Crosse alone saw his lifework reflected in that symbol. Because DNA was constantly rebuilding itself, evolving to defend itself from pathogens intent on commandeering its structure and turning it toward disease. The molecule had the capacity to cut its own amino-acid spine in order to rid itself of contamination. It knew what all of humanity needed to learn—that there is nothing to be gained from allowing the whole of something to be destroyed by one toxic part.

At either end of the main building were two smaller structures, one of stone that looked like a chapel, with luminous stained-glass windows depicting ancient battle scenes, the other a scaled-down replica of the Parthenon, the Athenians' attempt to achieve the appearance of perfection.

Crosse had stayed true to the original in every detail. He had helped build it himself from the same luminescent Pentelic marble, from Mount Pentelicus, eleven miles outside Athens. He had replicated Ictinus's and Callicrates' ingenious design of the facade, widening the columns midway up the shafts to make them appear straight from a distance, lowering the steps at the center to create the appearance that they were level even when viewed from extreme angles. And he had commissioned sculptors to replicate the metopes adorning the east, west, north, and south faces of the structure, each depicting a struggle between order and chaos: mystical battles between the Greeks and Trojans, Lapiths and Centaurs, the gods and giants, the Greeks and Amazons.

The driver let Rawlings out at the beginning of a fifteen-foot-wide, twenty-five-foot-long plate glass walkway over the reflecting pool, leading to an equally wide bluestone path to mahogany front doors, each carved with a double helix.

A minute after Rawlings rang the bell, Crosse himself answered the door. "Welcome," he said. "I'm so pleased you were able to visit."

"This is beyond anything I imagined," she said.

Crosse was unmoved. This was a woman who could not even imagine being a mother, using her own anatomy for its god-given purpose. "Thank you," he said. "I'm anxious to show you what I've come up with so far."

She followed him through a maze of rooms that made her stop and stare, again and again—at a chestnut floor inlaid with life-size, bronze children skipping across the room, at a fireplace fashioned from a single, massive boulder, blasted and carved in place, at a mahogany library behind French doors of beveled glass trimmed with thousands of shimmering amethysts, at a foot-thick crown molding of hundreds of carved crowns, each of them unique.

"You created all this?" she asked.

"Yes," Crosse said.

"How long did it take?"

"If you include creating the stone, millions of years," he said.

She laughed.

He barely smiled. "If you mean moving the pieces around to suit my taste, about seven."

She followed him deep into rooms buried in the cliff, then through an underground passageway to an elevator.

He entered a series of digits on a keypad.

"Where in God's name are we going?" she asked.

In God's name. "My workspace," Crosse said. "The cathedral. You may have seen it from the road. There's no entrance at ground level. This is the only way to access it."

No entrance. No exit.

The elevator doors glided open, revealing interior walls covered in chestnut, a ceiling of stained glass, limestone on the floor.

"After you," Crosse said.

Rawlings walked in.

The doors closed.

The elevator ascended two floors, and the doors opened into Crosse's operatory.

Handel's *Messiah* drifted from the speakers in the walls. The scent of myrtle filled the air.

Crosse waited for Rawlings to leave the elevator, then followed her into the room.

"The windows are so beautiful," she said. "And the music . . .

The Messiah. What a beautiful cross . . ." She walked over to a seven-foot wooden cross in a massive bronze stand. A quote of Ralph Waldo Emerson's from the *Yale Book of American Verse* was carved across the horizontal beam, then down the vertical beam:

'Tis man's perdition to be safe
When for the truth he ought to die.

"I made that myself," Crosse said, "with wood from a Tibetan monastery."

"Magnificent," Rawlings said. "I don't think I've ever seen one as beautiful."

"It's yours."

She turned to him. "Excuse me?"

"My gift to you."

"I couldn't . . ."

"A symbol of our work together. Please."

She hesitated, then nodded. "Thank you so much. I'll treasure it." She spotted the silver-framed photographs on the far wall, walked over to them. "The first family," she said. "Are you part of that competition to design an addition to the White House?"

Crosse walked over to his dissecting table, covered with white canvas. "I won that competition."

She turned back to him. "I didn't hear your name announced, even as a contestant."

"You won't," he said. "I'll work under a pseudonym."

"Why is it you insist on complete privacy?"

"To work in peace," Crosse said. "So I can create plans like I have for you." He gestured toward his plans for the Rawlingses'

Montana retreat, spread out on top of the white canvas. A rudimentary wooden scale model of the property sat beside them. "I think you'll understand my vision immediately."

She joined him at the dissecting table, looked down at the first page of the plans, the exterior elevations of the home to which Ken Rawlings would bring his new bride, Maritza. Confusion registered on her face. She glanced at Crosse, back down at the drawings, over at the scale model. "A red roof . . ."

"Your gut reaction. No editing."

"I don't know. It's unexpected. It feels almost . . . Moorish to me. And the central courtyard . . . May I look at the interiors?"

"Of course," Crosse said. He turned the page.

Rawlings focused first on the master bedroom suite. "I love window seats," she said. "Interior grates on windows . . . I'm not sure. I . . ." Her eyes scanned the page, stopped on the three interconnected rooms labeled Nursery. She leaned back, looked at Crosse, and smiled. "Nursery? That has to be a mistake. Unless you know something I don't."

"I'm sure I do," Crosse said. "I know your husband wants children. I know he would make a fine father."

She squinted at him. "Excuse me?"

"If I'm wrong, please tell me. I assumed he would. I put that into my plans."

She shook her head. "Whether Ken would be a good father or not is ancient history. We're . . . past all that."

Crosse looked down at his plans and nodded. "You are. I know." He looked at her again. "Would he make a good father, though?"

"I suppose. Well, what difference could that possibly . . . ? We're certainly not building any nursery. I can assure you of that."

Crosse reached for a glass container sitting beside the plans. Inside it, a white cloth floated in chloroform. He began to unscrew the top of the container. "Don't worry," he said. "I always remove the things that don't make sense." He paused. "Tell me about Maritza."

Rawlings looked dumbfounded. "Maritza? I have no idea what you're asking.

"Do you think she would make a good mother?"

"Why would I care in the least, what sort of mother she or any other—"

Crosse held up a hand. "She or any other woman would make. You wouldn't. I know that, too. You had too difficult a time with your own mother."

"And who in God's name told you that? Ken?" Her face registered something beyond irritation, some combination of shame and panic. "I think this meeting—"

In God's name. "You're right, we're not getting anywhere," Crosse said. "I'm sorry. It doesn't matter. It's all ancient history, as you said." He finished unscrewing the top of the container, reached in for the white cloth.

"Well, then," she bristled, "more than enough said. We can just call it a—"

"Yes. Let's call it a day. You don't deserve any more time." He walked in back of her, as if headed back to the elevator.

Shocked, she turned to watch him, but he grabbed her from behind, holding the wet cloth over her nose and mouth.

As with Chase Van Myer, the struggle was mercifully brief, no surprise to Crosse. Why should a woman cling fast to life, after all, when she cannot stomach the thought of new life stirring within her? Why should she fight against the grave with every fiber of her being when her mother was no mother, her marriage no marriage, when she is deadwood blocking the growth of the ever-blossoming tree of life?

He uncovered the dissecting table, lifted Rawlings onto it, injected her with succinylcholine, then knelt and prayed as her muscles danced their last chaotic dance. Then he separated her legs and stretched her arms out to her sides, honoring da Vinci.

He rolled his surgical tray over to the table.

A competent dissection of the neck is beyond the skills of most surgeons. But this time—nearly his last—Crosse wanted to linger in a region that required even more of him, to demonstrate the full genius of God's design of man.

He cut through the skin and the sheetlike fan of platysma muscle, connecting the lower mandible and the clavicles, used retractors to hold them back.

The deeper musculature of the neck was architecturally perfect, easily divided into three triangles bounded by the sternomastoid, digastric, and omohyoid muscles. Crosse located them, tied sutures around them, and anchored them with silver nails, all without disturbing the blue, black external jugular vein, the rust-red cervical artery, the delicate, pale yellow accessory nerve trickling down like a stream from the base of the brain to enervate the trapezius muscle. A rainbow of anatomy.

And all this was merely a start. Deeper still were layers of genius that made the Parthenon look like child's play: nerves, arteries, and veins running together, then splitting off into perfect arcs, bringing nourishment and feeling to band upon band of muscle. The glorious fibrous rings of the trachea, not only delivering air to the lungs, but supporting the pillowy thyroid gland clinging to it and protecting the much softer esophagus hiding behind it. On and on and on. The parotid, sublingual, and submandibular glands. The hyoid bone. The subclavian arteries. Miracle after miracle after miracle.

Crosse dissected all the way down to the front of the cervical spine. He had no idea and no concern how much time had passed.

He knew only that there was no longer any light streaming through the stained-glass windows, that his bare hands ached from his journey in search of God's infinite wisdom and that his heart was filled with his love.

TWENTY-SEVEN

Clevenger met with David Groupmann at 7:00 P.M. in what had been Shauna and Jeffrey's home at 2910 Broadway in Pacific Heights. At night, the place was even more magnificent, with low sodium landscape lights making the windowpanes glow orange-yellow and turning the perfect lawn into a magic carpet as it rolled toward the Golden Gate Bridge, a river of headlights in the night sky.

Groupmann and Clevenger sat in a den off the central great room, a small space, but two stories high, with randomly crisscrossing fir beams beginning at a height of about ten feet, then rising at least another ten, like a web or a maze. Above them, a piece of glass, illuminated from above, was etched with more crisscrossing, as if the motif continued infinitely.

"A second visit from you can't be good news," Groupmann said. He ran his fingers lightly over the arm of his leather club chair.

"It can keep me from coming back a third time," Clevenger said. He crossed his left leg over his right thigh, bringing within reach the pistol in an ankle holster under his jeans. Whitney McCormick had arranged for an agent to deliver it to him at a Mobil station outside the San Francisco airport.

Groupmann nodded. "How can I help?"

"Tell me about Skull and Bones."

Groupmann raised an eyebrow. "How would that help?"

"All the victims in this case are connected to that group. Either they belonged themselves or a close relative did. From what I understand, you know a little bit about it."

"Less than I had hoped."

"You weren't tapped for it," Clevenger said.

"And I'm sure you know I took that rather hard," he deadpanned.

"I read the article in the *New Haven Register*. You tried to break into the Tomb on High Street."

"It really shouldn't take a forensic psychiatrist to figure out what that was all about."

Clevenger kept listening.

"When you're a twin, everything that happens to your brother—good and bad—either feels like it's happening to you, or should be. When Jeffrey was tapped, and I wasn't, I assumed he would turn them down."

"But he didn't."

"No. And I didn't want to be left behind. I didn't want him keeping secrets from me. I wanted in. Figuratively, and literally."

"They made you pay for trying."

"They jumped me one night, beat me up pretty badly. Broken arm, ribs, a concussion." He looked down. "I recovered."

"Your brother wasn't there to defend you."

Groupmann didn't look up for a few seconds. When he did, it was with a forced smile. "No. He wasn't there to defend me. Which was a gift, really. I learned I was my own person."

He didn't sound like he appreciated the lesson. He sounded hurt and bitter. Clevenger suddenly had a gut feeling Skull and Bones had come between David and Jeffrey Groupmann in a very dramatic way that night. After all, weren't Bones brothers closer to one another than their own flesh and blood? "You refused to press charges," he said. "Who jumped you? Did you recognize any of them?"

Groupmann's nearly black eyes caught the light and flashed like obsidian. "What's your real question?"

"Was your brother one of them?"

"Yes," he said coldly.

"Did he . . . ?"

"He broke my right arm."

Clevenger felt the weight of that revelation settle somewhere deep inside him. He had to clear his throat to speak. "I'm sorry," he said.

"Let's stay focused," Groupmann said. "You must be wondering how hard I took it."

Clevenger didn't respond.

"You're wondering if I took it hard enough to start killing Bonesmen, including my own brother. Maybe I'm just like they are. Getting into the club is everything."

"Are you?"

Groupmann smiled. "You don't get it," he said.

"Help me out."

"You don't kill your better half."

"Jeffrey."

"I never stopped thinking of him as part of me, and vice versa. His business, his wife, his children—every one of his achievements made *me* feel less like a failure, especially during the years I couldn't sell a painting to save my life." He paused. "Believe me, I thought more than once about killing myself. But I never, ever thought of killing him. Not for an instant. Not even the night he broke my arm. I felt more alive when he was alive. In the long run, I don't know if I'll ever be able to make a go of it on my own."

"Why not? You have what was his."

"I do and I don't," Groupmann said.

"Shauna, the children, this house," Clevenger said.

"She fell in love with him, they were born to him, he built it. I may own the canvas; he painted it. There's a big difference. Jeffrey will always be my big brother."

Clevenger looked up into the web of beams above him, then back at Groupmann. "Where were you the night Jeffrey was killed?"

"In my studio, down the street from here."

Not much of an alibi. "Have you traveled much in the last few years?"

"All over the country. I paint landscapes."

Clevenger glanced at Groupmann's hand, saw he was wearing a Yale ring, just like the Van Myers' lawyer.

"Let me help you out," Groupmann said, with a wink. "Get my medical school transcript from Yale."

"Medical school?"

"I would have been class of eighty-four. I left in the middle of the second semester."

"Why?"

"I failed anatomy—twice. I was hopeless. It's the same trouble I had with sculpture. I just can't do it. No depth perception, whatsoever. I was born that way. Jeffrey and I had that in common, too."

TWENTY-EIGHT

• AUGUST 15, 2005

Clevenger had just boarded the red-eye back to Boston when Whitney McCormick called his cell and told him to get off the plane. He grabbed his things, headed back toward the door. "What's up?" he asked.

"David Groupmann has the perfect alibi," she said.

"What? What's going on?" Clevenger asked, walking back up the ramp to the gate.

"We've got another body, in Michigan. A woman. According to the medical examiner, she was killed hours ago, not days."

"Where in Michigan?"

"Lake Superior."

"The body washed up?"

"Would that be our man's style? She was floating close to shore, strapped to a wooden cross, naked. She had silver nails through her palms, feet, the whole nine yards. And he left us another message."

"What?"

"The cross was carved with an old Emerson quote: ' 'Tis man's perdition to be safe, when for the truth he ought to die.' Guess where it was first published."

"*National Enquirer?* I'd make a lousy *Jeopardy* contestant."

"Close. The *Yale Book of American Verse.*"

175

Where else? "Who found her?" Clevenger asked.

"A young couple walking along the lake."

"Obviously, no ID."

"Wrong. He still wants to make that part easy. Her driver's license was nailed to the cross, too. Heather Rawlings, from Miami. Her husband runs a diamond mining company. He supposedly didn't even know she was out of state."

"Another anatomy lesson?"

"Her neck, from the front all the way back to the spinal column."

Clevenger hung his head. "Are you in Michigan now? You want me to head there?"

"I've got things covered here. I was hoping you might have the steam to head to Miami, visit with the husband."

"Of course."

"Good. You're in luck. There's a delayed flight supposedly getting off the ground in forty minutes. You're booked on it."

"In case I have the steam."

She laughed. "Just in case."

Clevenger finally boarded the flight at 1:37 A.M. By the time it took off, it was four hours and seven minutes late, and the airline had decided to make it up to the passengers by offering free beer, wine, or mixed drinks. Clevenger watched the cart as it slowly headed down the aisle toward his row. Starts and stops. He'd taken one Antabuse tablet about twenty-four hours before, and the effects were supposed to last three days, but he didn't like the fact that he was wondering whether that was really true, that he was actually trying to figure his odds of surviving a gin and tonic. Or two.

He reached into pocket, pulled out another Antabuse tablet, and swallowed it.

TWENTY-NINE

By 8:00 A.M. Clevenger was sitting at the conference table in the library of 11204 Beach Drive in Miami with Ken Rawlings and his two attorneys, Skip Wolfe and James Lowell, each in his midfifties. The press already had gathered outside.

"I can't begin to understand any of it," Rawlings told him. "I have no idea why Heather would be in Michigan. We're not particularly close to anyone there, certainly no one so far north. And her being killed—and in such grotesque circumstances. Understand, this was a fine woman. She had no enemies."

A fine woman. No enemies. Talk about measured praise. It didn't surprise Clevenger, given what he had heard from Shauna Groupmann, Patrice Hadley, and Scout Van Meyer, but he wanted to see whether he could get beyond it. "Will you be identifying the body?" he asked.

"Of course I will."

"Not everyone can bring themselves to," Clevenger said. "Especially given injuries like your wife's."

"I don't think we need to go . . ." Attorney Lowell began, in a voice like a radio announcer's. He looked like he had walked out of a Polo advertisement—wavy, closely cropped black hair, a dark blue pinstripe suit.

Rawlings held up a hand to stop him. "I've been to war," he told Clevenger. "Marines. Vietnam. I've seen things you can't even imagine."

But those things hadn't happened to the woman he loved, Clevenger thought. He wondered how Rawlings could miss the difference? Was it because the war had left him with impregnable psychological armor, or because he had no special love for his wife? "I hope you won't take offense," Clevenger said. "I ask this question of every spouse in a murder case." He paused. "Were the two of you happy?"

"Happy?" He shrugged. "How could we not be? We had absolutely everything. These should have been our best years."

Still delivered without a stammer, without a tear, Clevenger thought. And Rawlings sounded like a man convincing himself to feel what he thought he should be. *Happy? How could we not be?* Those were still questions, not answers.

Maritza walked into the room. She was wearing white pants, a tailored white blazer, and a mauve camisole. Her teeth were perfectly white, her hair perfectly straight, her nails perfectly manicured. She looked elegant, like the lady of the house.

"My assistant," Rawlings explained to Clevenger. "Maritza Cabral, meet Dr. Frank Clevenger. He's working with the FBI."

Clevenger stood up. "Pleased to meet you." He extended his hand. She shook it. "And I you."

Clevenger sat down.

"I'll be about an hour, but you can get me on my cell, if you need me," Maritza told Rawlings. She studied him. "You okay?"

Rawlings nodded.

Clevenger thought he saw something more than an employee's devotion in Maritza's eyes, but he couldn't be certain. Maybe it was just the fact that she was beautiful and spoke so warmly that made him wonder, or maybe it was the fact that Rawlings watched her leave the room.

"Can I ask where you went to school?" Clevenger asked him.

"Where I went to school?" Rawlings asked, coming back to the moment. "Phillips Andover, then Yale. Why?"

Yale. No surprise, anymore, and no coincidence. "Were you tapped for the Order of Skull and Bones?"

Rawlings glanced at Lowell. "If I had been, I wouldn't answer the question. Isn't that what the code would say?"

Clevenger glanced at Lowell's hands, saw he was wearing a signet ring with a Yale crest.

"What are you getting at, anyhow?" Rawlings asked.

"Each of the victims in this case was either a Bonesman, a close relative, or a spouse," Clevenger said. "Can you think of anyone who might have held a grudge against you for being in the order?"

"He didn't say he was," Attorney Wolfe broke in, in a surprisingly soft voice for a man who looked like a linebacker in a three-thousand-dollar Italian suit. He stared at Clevenger with unblinking eyes.

"I have Sutton's list back at my office," Clevenger said. "I figured you might save me the phone call."

"If you believe that list is accurate," Wolfe said.

Clevenger leaned forward and looked directly at Rawlings. "Your wife was just murdered by someone who may be connected to the order. Why wouldn't you give me every bit of information that could help me find her killer?"

Rawlings glanced at Lowell again. Then he stared back at Clevenger. "What a person 'wants' does not dictate how that person should behave. That's the nature of being part of something greater than yourself. I know there are needs and goals more important than mine—or yours—no matter how it might feel to either one of us at this moment. I've always understood that."

"Would your wife?" Clevenger asked.

"At least as much as I," Rawlings said. "That's just one of the reasons I'll miss her so."

"Keeping secrets here could cost lives," Clevenger said. His made eye contact with each man at the table.

"If someone is preying upon Bonesmen," Rawlings said. "I'm sure anyone in the order would wish you God's speed, but not at the expense of exposing his brothers."

That echoed what David Groupmann had had to say about Skull and Bones. The bonds between members overrode any other responsibility—to family, to the law, even to oneself.

A few seconds passed.

"Are we done then?" Rawlings asked, looking around the table.

Lowell smiled a synthetic smile. "Up to the doctor."

Maybe it was having two lawyers at the table, or maybe it was having raised Skull and Bones so directly or maybe Rawlings really did feel guilty about something, but Clevenger felt like he was deposing a suspect, not interviewing a bereaved family member. "No further questions," he said.

He was headed out, escorted by Lowell, when he noticed an architectural drawing lying on a table just inside the door to the library—Crosse's rendering of stables for the Rawlingses' Montana property. He stopped to look at it. The structure was infinitely more human, more alive than the Rawlings house. His eyes traveled from the curved corner brackets to the gambrel roof to the arched windows, then settled on the kaleidoscope of cut glass set into the center of the facade, just below the roofline. The use of glass in such a dramatic and creative way reminded him of the glass ceiling etched with falling leaves at the Van Myer Chicago mansion and of the two-story maze of beams ending in an etched glass panel at the Groupmanns' Pacific Heights estate. And all at once, the facts and intuitions stored in his conscious and unconscious minds began to align like tumblers on a lock. A wave of shivers ran down his spine.

"Can I help you with something?" Lowell asked, turning back toward him.

"You're building stables?" Clevenger asked aloud, still looking at the drawings.

"Excuse me?" Rawlings said, from his seat at the table.

"Stables," Clevenger said, glancing at him, then looking back at the drawings again.

"Yes, right. We were," Rawlings said. "Heather and I were planning to build on a parcel we own in Montana. The stables were to be part of it."

Clevenger's eyes scanned the drawing. He couldn't find the architect's name anywhere. "Who designed them?" he asked.

A few seconds passed in silence.

"Excuse me?" Rawlings said.

Clevenger looked over at him. "The stables. Who designed them?"

"A firm in Manhattan, I think," Rawlings said. "Graves, Dickinson, maybe. Heather was taking the lead on that. She left a copy of their first pass for me."

"I see," Clevenger said.

"Do you ride?" Wolfe asked from his seat next to Rawlings.

"Harleys, whenever I get the chance. That's about it."

"They eat less," Rawlings joked.

Just another little joke in the wake of another murder. Clevenger nodded. "Less trouble on the highway, too."

"Call me anytime," Rawlings said. "If you have a question, I'll certainly try to answer it."

"I'll keep that in mind," Clevenger said. He headed out.

THIRTY

As soon as he left Ken Rawlings and his attorneys, Clevenger reached North Anderson on his cell phone, in his car. He shared his gut feeling that one architect might have designed properties for three of the victims' families—the Groupmanns, Van Myers, and Rawlingses. But linking together their three properties immediately made him think of the other estate he had visited: the Hadleys' on Meadow Lane in Southampton. He remembered the remarkable palette of gray stone, shingles, slate, and lead-coated copper that seemed to turn the house into a charcoal drawing of itself. But he also remembered walking through the house, noting the transom glass at the top of every wall—the six-by-six-inch rows of windows, like transparent crown molding—that allowed sunlight to flow through the entire dwelling. The interplay of glass and light, the timeless and endless nature of each design element, was unmistakable. An etched-glass ceiling that was no ceiling, an etched-glass panel above a two-story maze of beams that never seemed to end, a glass kaleidoscope designed to invite sun or moon inside majestic stables, walls allowing light to flow over them, into and out of every room, infinitely. "It could be all of them," Clevenger said. "If not an architect or a decorator, maybe a builder."

"There aren't many construction firms building homes coast to coast. Architect sounds more likely."

"Rawlings said his wife hired whoever designed the stables. He wasn't in the loop. He thought it might have been a firm called Graves, Dickinson, in Manhattan."

"I'll check them out," Anderson said.

"I don't know if he's leveling with me. He wouldn't tell me whether he was Skull and Bones, and he didn't seem to want to tell me who did that drawing."

"You're the shrink, but maybe that means the two are linked."

"Huh?"

"Maybe both questions are really one question. Maybe the architect *is* a Bonesman, and that's how he networks. By referral, from brother to brother."

"Good thought. I'll call the Groupmanns and the others and try to find out who designed their places."

"I'm back in the office in five minutes. I'll check Sutton's list to see if Rawlings is on it. And I'll find out what I can about that firm."

"Great."

"When are you back?"

"I land about two-thirty."

"Any word on Billy?" Anderson asked.

"I haven't heard a thing. I assume he's detoxing okay. I'll go by Mass General later."

"Fair enough. See you in the office."

"Done."

They hung up.

Clevenger dialed Whitney McCormick. Her secretary put him through. He told her what he knew.

"I'll check whether we have any person of concern at Graves, Dickinson," she said. "What else can I do?"

"I suppose you could let the president in on what we know. I'm sure he has a way to get the word out to anyone who belongs to Skull and Bones."

"Interesting," she said. She grew especially serious. "Again, I want to be clear that *we* shouldn't be getting the word out publicly."

"About Bonesmen being targeted?"

"If they are being targeted. Don't forget: Six people at that level of wealth and influence may have more things in common than being in a club together. They could be in one hedge fund together. They could have fractional ownerships in the same jet. We still have a long way to go."

McCormick sounded like she was holding a press conference herself. "What's the political reality here?" Clevenger asked her. "Is the president uncomfortable being identified with the order?"

"He's never formally admitted being part of it. He said, 'No comment,' when he was asked about it on network television. I think the exact quote was something like: 'If it's supposed to be a secret, then I guess I have no comment.' People took whatever they took from that, but I don't know to this day whether he was tapped or not."

"And you'd rather not have anyone focus on it."

"I just don't see what good it does. It feeds the conspiracy theorists who run around claiming these guys run the world, which is obviously complete paranoia. But more ridiculous things have hurt politicians."

Maybe Clevenger was suffering from paranoia, too, but he wasn't absolutely certain there was no reality to the theory. "I'm not talking to any reporter about anything," he said, and left it at that.

"So, how's Billy?" she asked.

Anderson had asked, and now McCormick. It was probably time to check in on him. "I haven't talked with him today," Clevenger said. "I will."

"I hope he's doing alright."

"Thanks."

"Let's touch base later."

"You got it."

She hung up.

Clevenger slipped his phone into his pocket, but took it out again. He dialed Anderson.

"Long time, no talk," Anderson answered.

"One more name to check on Sutton's list," Clevenger said.

"Who?"

"A former U.S. congressman and Republican fund-raiser named Dennis McCormick."

"Whitney's dad?"

"Right."

"Was he Yale?"

"I never asked," Clevenger said.

"But she doesn't like talking Skull and Bones with you."

"Not one bit."

"Wouldn't be the first time we ended up going it alone on a case," Anderson said.

"No, it wouldn't."

"I'll let you know."

THIRTY-ONE

West Crosse sat in First Lady Elizabeth Buckley's office in the East Wing. He had been given Falcon status at the visitor's entrance, the same clearance given members of the Cabinet, allowing him to come and go as he pleased, with no prior notice and without being searched.

Liz Buckley, not yet fifty, Princeton educated, elegant and self-assured, sat on a brightly upholstered love seat opposite Crosse, who had taken a wing chair catty-corner to it. The walls of her office were covered with photographs of her and the president with heads of state, religious leaders, and groups of children around the world. "What I loved about your initial concept for the Museum of Freedom," she said, "is that it speaks directly to the possibilities for creative expression, for limitless imagination, when people are liberated from tyranny." She smiled a smile that was equally warm and self-assured. "I know you understand everything my husband has been working for."

"Yes, I do," Crosse said. He glanced at his drawing on the coffee table between them. It called for walls of glass, with reflecting pools extending beyond them. The works of art would hang on bronze panels or be placed on bronze shelves cut into the walls. The roof would be a crystal and bronze dome, with the constellations etched into it. All a visitor would see on entering the museum would be the

187

art itself, almost suspended in air, with nothing to stop the eye or the mind from traveling wherever it might. An endless horizon. At night, panels of the dome were built to slide away, creating an observatory. And at the touch of a button, a powerful telescope would rise into the exact center of the museum, pointing to the heavens. "You want people to live out their full potential," he said. "You want them to be truly free, no matter the cost."

"And no one knows better than these artists what the cost can be." She leaned forward slightly, energized by the vision. "A quarter of them lost family members when their countries were liberated by us."

Crosse's skin turned to gooseflesh. "I only hope my final design does your idea justice."

"I know it will," she said. "God willing." She sat back, fingered the strand of pearls at her neck.

She suddenly looked tired and vulnerable to Crosse, perhaps because he knew her burden: a retarded, unmarried, seventeen-year-old daughter pregnant with a retarded man's child—an affront to nature and an ever-growing threat to the president's standing in the country and in the world. "How is Blaire doing?" he asked, in the gentle, yet strong voice of a healer, a shaman.

The question was enough to spark a struggle between Buckley's inner self and her public persona. It played out on her face—a brave smile she couldn't quite hold, a sheen to her eyes as she fought back tears, then the resolute tightening of her jaw she was known for. "Warren told me you were very helpful to him when he shared what we're facing," she said. "I want to thank you for that."

"No need," he said. He waited a few seconds. "How is Blaire?" he asked, even more quietly.

Her eyes filled up. She swallowed hard. "She's happy," she said. "That's the saddest part." She wiped away a tear. "She has no understanding of what this really means to her, or the father of her child. And she certainly can't conceive of how it will impact everything Warren has worked so hard to achieve during the past three-and-a-half years."

"You don't anticipate a sympathetic reaction," Crosse said.

"In this town? They'll crucify him." She took a deep breath and let it out, steadied herself. "Don't forget, my husband has taken courageous stands against distributing condoms, against inappropriate sexual education, against abortion. It won't be what people say publicly that erodes his power to do good around the world. It's what will be said in private, the snickering in all the offices at the Capitol filled with 'pubic servants' who think nothing of two men marrying, but think religion is a dirty word."

"How are your sons handling it?" Crosse asked.

"Neither of them knows. James just took a job at Brown Brothers Harriman, and William just made partner at Simpson Thacher Bartlett. I don't see any reason to involve them, until it's absolutely necessary."

"When will that be?"

"When she's showing, I suppose." She shook her head. "It honestly doesn't seem real yet. It doesn't seem like something God would . . ." She closed her eyes. "It shouldn't say that. We can't know his ways."

Crosse disagreed. He believed God made his ways plain to man, but that man was often too frightened or too selfish to act in accordance with his will. President Kennedy, before he grew weak and came to doubt America's power to reshape the world, had put it well: "With a good conscience our only sure reward, with history the final judge of deeds, let us go forth to lead the land we love, asking His blessing and His help, but knowing that here on earth God's work must truly be our own."

Hadn't Jesus carried his Father's truth in his heart? Hadn't Abraham been willing to sacrifice Isaac after the voice of God instructed him to do so? Hadn't President Buckley done God's work here on earth, liberating whole peoples from oppression? And didn't Crosse himself know precisely what God expected of him? "Maybe he's listening more than you know," he told the first lady.

Buckley looked at him. "I'm not praying for this pregnancy to end," she said. But the way she turned her head, her gaze drifting toward the floor, said the opposite.

"Of course not," Crosse said.

She cleared her throat, took another deep breath, and abruptly stood up.

Crosse stood up.

"I know you need to take much more precise measurements of the existing space," she said. "Feel free to ask for help from me or my assistant Joyce."

"Thank you," Crosse said, extending his hand. They had had their talk, between the lines. The deal was done. She would sleep better that night, not knowing why, nor wanting to know. "I may need to come back a few times," he said, "to make certain my design will accomplish exactly what I intend it to."

She shook his hand. "Not a problem. Your clearance is complete. You won't be held up."

"And if I tend to wander about, it's only because my mind does. Please tell your staff to yank on my leash. I learn quickly." He smiled.

"Wander wherever you like," she said.

He looked into her eyes. "I want you to know I realize how much you and your husband have sacrificed for the public good," he said. "I'm truly honored to work with you. If I could design just one more structure in my life, this would be it."

THIRTY-TWO

By 3:55 P.M. Clevenger was sitting with North Anderson at the Boston Forensics offices in Chelsea.

Clevenger had already reached Scout Van Myer and Patrice Hadley and asked them who had designed their homes.

Van Myer hadn't been willing to tell him, citing a strict confidentiality agreement in the architect's contract, specifying liquidated damages of twenty-five million dollars for any material breach. "If I thought there were even a remote chance we were speaking of someone with the capacity to kill," he had said, "I'd obviously put the agreement in perspective. But I'm certain that's not the case."

Hadley had offered a similar ironclad endorsement of her architect, also citing the confidentiality provision in her contract. "Even if I wanted to tell you, I would be prevented," she said.

"They won't budge," Clevenger told Anderson. "I hinted they could be subpoenaed, and they politely referred me to their attorneys. I'm still trying to reach Shauna Groupmann, but I'd bet she turns me down, too—if she even knows who her husband hired to design their place."

"I can tell you from working on Nantucket that people usually toss those agreements in the trash the minute a better deal knocks on the door, let alone the Feds," Anderson said. "This feels more like a code of silence."

"Skull and Bones," Clevenger said.

"I checked Sutton's list," Anderson said. "Ken Rawlings is on it. And I called that architecture firm—Graves, Dickinson. No one there designed any stables for him. At least they won't admit they did. So it doesn't look like he leveled with you."

"Home run. Sounds like the architect could be our man."

"There's something else: Dennis McCormick is on Sutton's list, too."

Clevenger grimaced. He would have preferred to hear that McCormick hadn't made the list. He didn't want to start wondering whether he could trust Whitney. "I wanted to check him out, but I really don't think it's in Whitney's character to play politics with a murder investigation."

"Right." He smirked. "The FBI never plays politics. Tell that to Joe Salvati."

The FBI had framed Salvati and kept him in prison for three decades to protect one of their informants.

"I know Whitney," Clevenger said.

"No, you love her, which is a world of difference. It might mean you can't know her—yet. Your lens is still fuzzy. Could take five, ten years to clear." He paused. "Stop kidding yourself: She's a very good psychiatrist, a very good investigator, *and* a very good politician. And she's from a very powerful American family."

"You should start seeing patients."

"I just did."

Clevenger laughed. "Got that right." He nodded to himself, refocusing. "We better check Sutton's list to see how many Skull and Bones members ended up as architects. I'm hoping it's a small enough group to take a serious look at each person."

"I'll get on it," Anderson said.

"And I'll contact the first two victims' families in Connecticut and the parents of the twelve-year-old in Montana. Let's at least see whether they've built homes in the last several years."

"I should also check with the building departments in the cities and towns we're talking about," Anderson said. "Architectural plans have to be filed—with the architect's stamp."

"Great thought," Clevenger said.

Anderson stood up. "Occasionally I come through." He smiled. "Check on Billy yet?"

Clevenger shook his head. "Not yet. I will."

"Let me know how the champ's doing. I'll be on my cell."

"I'll call you."

Anderson turned and walked out.

Clevenger picked up the phone and dialed Mass General. He got put through to the locked detox unit, but the unit clerk there wouldn't tell him anything about Billy, citing hospital policy. "Can I speak with him?" he asked, knowing what the stock response would be.

"I can't confirm or deny whether he's here," she said.

"Sounds like everyone has a confidentiality agreement except me," Clevenger said. "I'll come by. Maybe he'll let me visit."

"Thank you for calling."

"Thank you." He hung up.

He drove over to Mass General and headed up to Phipps 4 North. He hit the buzzer at the door.

"May I help you?" a woman's voice said through the intercom.

"I'm here to visit Billy Bishop. I'm his father."

"Someone will be right with you."

Clevenger waited.

After a minute or so, the steel door clicked open and a middle-aged, overweight woman with bleach blond hair, carrying a clip-board and a ring of keys, stepped outside. She locked the door again, turned to him. "Dr. Clevenger?"

He extended his hand. "Nice to meet you."

She shook it. "Paula Nealy," she said. "I'm afraid you aren't on Mr. Bishop's visitors list," she said, "if he is or was ever here."

"If . . ."

"Federal regulations protect the identity of anyone in drug treat-ment. I'm sure you know the law."

"Of course." But he also knew the staff tended to be lax about the rules when there was no bad news to tell. He needed a quick way to find out whether Billy had left the place. He reached into his pocket, held out four twenty-dollar bills. "Family members can leave things for patients, right?" he asked. That was a little glitch in the confidentiality laws.

She looked at the money.

"Canteen money. Trust me, he'll want it." He held it out closer to her.

"I . . ."

Clevenger looked at her and saw the truth. Billy had signed himself out. "Thanks," he said. He turned around and headed down the hall. Before he got to the elevators, he spotted a house phone. He still wanted to be certain Billy had left. He walked over and picked up the receiver, dialed zero.

The operator answered.

"This is Dr. Clevenger," he said. "I need to page Dr. Jane Monroe."

"One minute."

A few minutes passed.

"Hello, it's Dr. Monroe," Monroe answered.

"Frank Clevenger. You helped my son Billy Bishop in the emer-gency room."

"Of course."

"I think he left the hospital. But I need to know."

"According to Federal law I . . ."

"I'm asking for one more favor, doc-to-doc. Help me out. My kid's in trouble."

A pause. "Hold on, okay?" She was back on the line in fifteen seconds. "He doesn't come up on the computer as an inpatient," she said. "And he would if he were here. Just remember, I didn't . . ."

"You hung up on me when I asked."

"Good luck with him," she said. "He really seemed like a good kid."

"He's a lot of different things."

"Like most of us. Let me know how he does."

"I will," Clevenger said. "Thanks."

They hung up.

Clevenger headed to the garage, got his truck, and started toward Chelsea. Part of him wanted to let Billy's walking out of the hospital equal his walking out on him, too—for good. He could go back to the loft, pack Billy's things, leave them in the stairwell, and get on with his life. He could start a real family. Maybe that was the best he could do for Billy, anyhow. Maybe there really wasn't any way to love him enough to kindle his love for himself. Maybe there were people in the world who were fatally flawed psychologically—with all their potential for good already beaten or abused or humiliated out of them—for whom ministering to their spirits was no better than holding vigil by the bedside of a patient on life support, praying for a miracle that will never come.

The trouble was it didn't feel that way—at least not to Clevenger, at least not yet. And if that kind of undying hope for others was a drug, too, another distraction from the fact that we were all ultimately alone, that some of us cannot be redeemed in this life, he just wasn't ready to put that drug down.

Since when did a prayer come with a guarantee?

He picked up his cell phone, dialed North Anderson.

"Whattcha got?" Anderson answered.

"Billy signed himself out of detox. I have to find him."

"You checked at home?"

"I'm headed there."

"Alright," Anderson said. "I'm on it."

"Unless you think we should let him be for a while."

"Leave that to John Lennon. The kid doesn't belong on the streets, period."

"I'll call you from the loft."

"Done."

They hung up.

Clevenger drove to the loft, ran up the four flights of stairs, and was about to open the door when his cell phone rang. Anderson. He answered it. "What's up?"

"Found him."

"That was quick."

"He's not exactly keeping a low profile," Anderson said.

"Meaning?"

"A cruiser spotted him. He's hanging on the steps outside the Royals' house at 22 Suffolk Street."

"Their 'house'?"

"They have a gutted brick row house down there. It's owned by Leo Berman."

Berman was a bookie, drug trafficker, and pimp who posed as owner of the Me and Me deli on Broadway, a stone's throw from Chelsea City Hall. Until the city started to get cleaned up by yuppies, gays, and a stack of state and federal indictments, most of the cops had been able to double their salary just by looking the other way. "The Royals run drugs for him?" Clevenger asked.

"Drugs, girls, whatever. I wouldn't be surprised if he was behind these extreme fighting bouts, too. Bad news all around."

Clevenger started down the stairs. "I'm going over there."

"We might as well."

"Thanks," Clevenger said.

"Enough with that," Anderson said. "You forgot to give me back my Glock."

"It's in my truck. I'll bring it."

"That was my point."

THIRTY-THREE

Clevenger and Anderson parked on Broadway and walked down
Suffolk Street, past brownstones and brick bowfronts waiting their
turn for gut rehabs, like ghosts of Chelsea's past, a city literally
risen from the ashes not once, but twice, lingering still near flash
point.

They could see a dozen shadowy figures in front of a house two
blocks away, tossing a football back and forth across the street,
pushing each other up and down the front steps, playing chicken
with a lone car speeding past.

"So what's the plan?" Anderson asked, when they had closed to
one block.

Three or four of the Royals, wearing their trademark skullcaps,
baggy jeans, and football jerseys, spotted them and started drifting
up the sidewalk.

"I really haven't given it a lot of thought," Clevenger said.

"Great. Me, neither."

"I just need enough time to talk Billy into getting the hell out of
here."

The Royals formed two rows of two on the sidewalk, an urban
gauntlet.

"Here goes nothing," Anderson said. He walked ahead of Clevenger so that they were single file. Then he kept walking, just in front of Clevenger, right between the Royals. "Evening, gentlemen," he said, with a nod.

"What the fuck, Nigger?" the biggest of them, black, about nineteen or twenty years old, called after Anderson, just as Clevenger stepped in front of him. He was wearing a thick silver chain with a snake with ruby eyes on it.

Clevenger turned around and faced him, turning his back to two of the Royals. "I'm looking for Billy Bishop," he said.

Anderson stopped walking, so that he was back-to-back with Clevenger, sandwiched between the four Royals.

"Who the fuck are you?" the big man asked Clevenger.

"His father."

"His old man's in jail" he said, leaning toward Clevenger. "Murder rap. So, take off."

"No problem," Anderson said. "We'll find him." He scuffed his shoes on the ground as he stepped forward, to let Clevenger know he was moving toward the house.

Clevenger turned to follow him, but something hit him hard, across the back of the head. His scalp, then neck felt wet and warm with blood. He managed to stay on his feet, swung around and smashed his forearm into the jaw of a Royal holding a length of pipe. The kid went down.

"He's got a knife," Anderson said, pointing at another one of them, lunging toward Clevenger.

Clevenger arched away as a blade flashed in front of his eyes.

Anderson whipped his pistol across that one's face.

The kid—maybe fourteen, maybe less—dropped the knife as he staggered back, blood pouring from his nose.

Anderson sensed someone coming up behind him, threw an elbow and found a soft spot. He turned around, saw the big Royal with the medallion doubled over. He aimed his gun at his head.

At least ten Royals had spilled from the front door of their town house.

"You done now, Mothafuck!" one shouted.

Another disembodied voice: "Outgunned, out-fuckin'-manned."

Clevenger drew his Glock, grabbed the bloodied kid, and held it to his head.

That didn't stop more Royals from streaming out of the house, down the sidewalk, but it kept them from closing to less than ten feet. They ringed Clevenger and Anderson, their voices soft and steady and fierce—the rattle of a rattlesnake.

"C'mon, man, let homeboy go."

"Suffolk, wrong place, wrong time, Dude. You *know* better than be here."

"Cap these two fuckers 'fore they do Gas and Steel, man."

"Die 'em."

But no one took another step. Even in a Chelsea gang, where death was no stranger, life remained precious.

"Where is Billy Bishop?" Clevenger asked no one in particular.

Anderson grabbed the big Royal by his thick rope chain, pressed his .44 Magnum to his jaw. "Answer the fucking question, or I'll off you and a few of your friends in self-defense."

The big Royal looked up at Anderson and spit at him.

Anderson jammed the gun into his mouth.

Clevenger looked at Anderson, saw his jaw churning. "North," he said quietly. "Don't. He isn't worth it."

Anderson didn't answer, didn't blink, didn't move his finger off the trigger. "Where's Billy?" he asked, through clenched teeth. He pulled the gun out of the big Royal's mouth.

"Fuck you."

Anderson pulled his arm back, ready to smash the gun across his face.

"I'm right here," Billy said, from behind Clevenger.

Anderson stopped.

Clevenger turned and saw Billy pull back the hood of his sweat-shirt, then pull a bandanna away from his face.

"What do you want?" Billy asked.

"My truck's on Broadway," Clevenger said. He noticed Billy's pupils were pinpoints, even in the moonlight. He was high, proba-bly on heroin. "Walk up the street. Let's go home."

"I live here," Billy said.

Nods and murmurs from other Royals. A couple of them near Billy held out their hands.

Billy slapped them five.

"Bullshit you do," Clevenger said.

Anderson had his gun trained on the big Royal, again, while his eyes tracked back and forth from him to the others, like he was try-ing to figure out how long the stalemate could hold.

Clevenger nodded toward Broadway. "C'mon," he told Billy. "Let's get out of here."

"How about you get out of here?" Billy said. "This is my family. You're nothing to me."

Hoots and high fives from the Royals.

Clevenger looked at Billy and saw him looking back at him in a different way than he ever had before—as though the two of them were strangers. No anger, no fear, no contempt. A sterile, dispas-sionate gaze. And that hit Clevenger much harder than the length of pipe that had opened a gash on his head. He lowered his gun, nearly dropped it.

Anderson saw what was happening. He pushed the big Royal away from him, grabbed Clevenger and dragged him out of the circle, pointing his gun at one Royal, then another, to keep them from rushing him. "Let's live to fight another day," he whispered to Clevenger, grabbing his belt and pulling him backward.

Clevenger started walking toward Broadway under his own steam.

The Royals stopped following them after about a block.

"Royal blood thicker than yours, Daddy!" one of them shouted, his voice echoing down the street.

Raucous laughter.

A chorus of taunts: "Big fucking gun, man, no fucking balls."

"Love youuuu, Papa Doc."

Clevenger pushed his gun back into the waistband of his pants.

"What now?" Anderson asked.

"I don't know. Maybe that's the end of it. Maybe I have to be okay with that."

"I can tell you right now: You tried harder, for longer, than almost anybody would."

"What do I get, a medal?" Clevenger asked.

Anderson shook his head. "Raising a family is a whole different kind of war. Nobody ever thanks you for your service."

That turned a key inside Clevenger. Because it reminded him again that his fight for Billy's soul wasn't one battle or two or ten. It *was* a war. And the good news and the bad news was there was no way to be defeated. It could go on and on and on. That was the beauty and terror of being a parent or a priest or a peacemaker in the first place. The only way to lose was to surrender—either your will or your humanity or both. "I want you to call in one more favor from John Rosario," he told Anderson.

"You want him to keep an eye on Billy?"

"No. I want him to arrest him. He's using heroin. Ten-to-one he'll get him for possession."

Anderson nodded slowly. "They get him for that, he goes away. No bail this time. Could be six months, maybe a year, before his case is even heard."

"People come through worse," Clevenger said. "The point is to come through. I don't know if he lasts on the street." He paused. "And I don't know what he turns into if he does."

Anderson took out his cell phone. He dialed Chelsea police headquarters. It started to ring. "Last chance," Anderson said to Clevenger. "You sure?"

An operator answered.

"Of course not," Clevenger said. "What do you think?"

Anderson stared into Clevenger's eyes several seconds.

"Hello?" the operator asked.

Anderson brought the phone to his lips. "I need to get in touch with John Rosario," he said. He listened a few seconds. "Yeah. Tell him it's an emergency."

THIRTY-FOUR

West Crosse had spent three hours gathering measurements of the East Wing he knew he would never use. At 11:10 A.M. he started toward the first family's private residence on the second floor of the main building, taking a less-traveled route he had memorized from classified plans of the White House given him by the president. Ten minutes later he stood outside Blaire Buckley's bedroom. He knocked softly on her door.

No response.

He tried the door. Unlocked. He opened it, walked inside, closed it behind him.

Although Blaire was seventeen, her room was indistinguishable from a seven- or eight-year-old's. A lacy, pink comforter on the bed. A stuffed bear, a stuffed giraffe, and several dolls propped against the pillows. A light-up Barbie vanity. Two jump ropes and a hopscotch mat. Board games stacked in a corner. A bookcase filled with children's books.

Crosse walked over to the bookcase, pulled out one of the volumes: *Judy Moody Predicts the Future.* Another: *Judy Moody Was in a Mood, Not a Good Mood.* Another, this one a picture book: *A Lion at Bedtime.*

He walked over to a tall chest of drawers, saw Blaire's ribbon hair ties, rhinestone rings, and plastic bracelets, glittery barrettes, a dozen lip glosses, neatly arranged in baskets on top. Next to them was a stack of *Highlights* magazines, written for children in grade school. Behind them was a photograph of Blaire on a swing, overweight, with dull eyes, being pushed by her father, the president of the United States.

A wave of disgust washed over Crosse. How could it be that an organism with the intellect of a gifted primate could cause such chaos and pain in the life of the leader of the free world? How could a being without the mental acumen to read at half her grade level be permitted the freedom to take a lover and carry a child? How could anyone miss the fact that her DNA was itself deeply flawed, that to pretend she was fully human was to make a mockery of the miraculous potential of man?

Blaire's existence was no different from any other architectural disaster. Poorly designed footings can take down a building. A poorly designed building can foul an entire cityscape. But in this case, the potential losses were exponentially greater. The president could fall. The prestige of America could be damaged. The cause of world freedom could be set back.

History had its own structure, as vulnerable to a fault of design as any other.

Blaire Buckley was no different in her destructive potential than a terrorist.

Crosse recalled one of the first great American voices with whom he had strongly identified. He had read and reread the writings of Supreme Court Justice Oliver Wendell Holmes, Jr., a devout Christian and eugenicist who advocated the sterilization of defective women. In one famous case, upon ordering a hysterectomy be performed on Carrie Buck, a mentally retarded, seventeen-year-old woman whose mother and child were also retarded, he wrote, "It is better for the world, if instead of waiting to execute degenerate off-spring for crime or to let them starve for their imbecility, society can prevent those who are manifestly unfit from continuing their kind . . . Three generations of imbeciles are enough."

At Holmes's side as he wrote his decision was his trusted assistant and confidant, Harvey Hollister Bundy, a brilliant Bonesman who also served as special assistant to Secretary of War Henry Lewis Stimson. Stimson, himself Skull and Bones, was instrumental in the decision to drop nuclear bombs on Hiroshima and Nagasaki during World War II, demolishing an evil empire that would have destroyed world freedom.

It would always be left to men of action and men of God to put in place those designs necessary to perfect human experience and liberate men to live more complete lives. Because, as Kennedy said: "Here on earth God's work must truly be our own."

In this world, Bonesmen would always do infinitely more than their share. It was in their genes and their souls, their biological and spiritual destiny.

Crosse heard footsteps coming toward the door. He made no attempt to hide. He had carte blanche to wander the house. In the same way that his clients always neglected to mention his name to the police, they explained away even his most suspicious behaviors. They would be his unconscious accomplices to the end.

And the end was near.

The doorknob turned, the door opened, and Blaire Buckley herself walked in.

She had grown taller than in Crosse's photos and had put on a good deal of weight. She wore jeans and an oversized Britney Spears T-shirt that did little to conceal her oversized breasts.

She took three steps, saw Crosse, and stood still, a deer in headlights.

"Hello, Blaire," he said. "I'm sorry if I frightened you. My name is West. I'm a friend of your parents. I'm helping your mom design her museum."

"She said it was okay for you to come up here?"

"Sure. Do you want to call her and check?"

"No. It's okay. What do you want?"

Crosse smiled at her directness, born of neuronal circuitry with little complexity and less resistance. She had a question, she asked it. She was hungry, she ate. She wanted sex, she had it. "I heard the good news from your parents," he said, "about your baby."

She tried to fight off a smile, but couldn't, showing her slightly crooked, slightly yellowed teeth. Her hand drifted to her fat belly. "Eden," she said.

"Eden?"

"My baby. Do you like her name?"

Maybe for a normal child of a normal mother, Crosse thought to himself. "You know you're carrying a girl?" he asked.

She nodded.

It was too early for her doctor to know. "I guess you can just tell," he said.

"Uh-huh."

"And you want the baby?"

"Want her?" she asked, incredulously. "I can't wait. I want to be a mom really, really bad. More than anything."

"You're not worried whether the baby—little Eden—could be . . . slow, mentally—the way you are?"

She shook her head. "Not as long as she's happy like I am."

She didn't even seem hurt by what he had said. She didn't seem to have the capacity for hurt, or fear, let alone reason. He couldn't resist examining her in more depth. "What makes you happy, Blaire?"

She smiled, again, blushed. "Harry, for one thing."

"Is he the father?"

"Uh-huh. He's my boyfriend."

"Does he work? Will he be able to support Eden?"

"Yup."

"What does he do?"

"He puts things together for a company. Parts to things."

"At a sheltered workshop? He works with other people like him—and you?"

"Pens," she said. "He puts together pens and key chains."

Asked and answered, Crosse thought. "What else makes you happy?"

She looked down at her T-shirt. "Britney."

More sex, with a little background music. Very elevated. He laughed out loud.

Blaire laughed, too. "Isn't she totally cool?"

He slowly stopped laughing, then stopped smiling. "Do you believe in God, Blaire?"

"Definitely."

"Do you think God wanted you to be with Harry and get pregnant?"

"He must have, since I did."

Dog logic, Crosse thought. If it itches, scratch. Eat your chow until the bowl is empty. It was the best she could do. But human beings with normal brains could do more. They could feel impulses—sexual urges, greed, fear—and control them for a greater good. He kept at it. "Do you think having a baby might make things difficult for your father?"

She shook her head, again. "He'll be a good grandfather. He'll like it a lot."

Crosse smiled. He let a few seconds go by. "Would you like to meet Britney?" he asked.

"Meet her? How?"

"I'm designing her new house."

"You *know* Britney Spears?" She leaned forward into her excitement, as though her emotions were literally hardwired into her musculature, with no intervening thought process between stimulus and response.

"Yes, I do. And she's coming to see me here in Washington two days from now. Why don't you come meet her?"

"I don't know if my parents . . ."

He held up a finger, shook his head. "It has to be our secret. She can't let anyone know she's in town. You just have to figure out a way to meet me, two nights from today. Nine o'clock. The Mayflower Hotel. We'll be in the Presidential Suite."

"I'll get there, somehow," she said.

"If you do, remember to bring something for her to autograph."

She giggled with excitement. "I got out to see Harry before when I wasn't supposed to."

"Apparently," Crosse said.

"I know I shouldn't have," she said. "Everybody was all worried, out looking for me. But it was worth it, you know? Because Eden is special. She's really going to be somebody. I can feel it."

THIRTY-FIVE

Clevenger had gotten a call from North Anderson at 1:40 A.M. that John Rosario had arrested Billy for possession of narcotics. He'd kept him locked up at the Chelsea station a couple of hours, then transferred him to the Nashua Street Jail in Boston, where he was being held without bail. His public defender had steered clear of the Middleton Jail because of the beating Billy had taken there. And he had made it clear to everyone that his client was not taking visitors.

Clevenger knew the guards at Nashua Street. They could let him in to see Billy "by mistake." But the truth was he wasn't ready to see him again—not behind bars. He wasn't ready to field another barrage of questions from him, limited to whether he would get him a high-powered attorney or try to convince a judge to reinstate his bail. And he definitely wasn't ready for the kind of empty stare Billy had leveled at him on Suffolk Street.

Instead, he had gone to the office at 4:30 A.M., thrown himself into his work, trying to bury what was dead and dying inside him in the hunt for a killer, as he had so many times before. He pored over the FBI and local police files on each of the killings, read everything he could on Skull and Bones off the Web, combed Sutton's list of members.

211

The list continued to amaze him: Henry R. Luce, founder of Time-Life; Dean Witter, investment banker; Russell Davenport, editor of *Fortune* magazine; Harold Stanley, founder of Morgan Stanley investment bank; Supreme Court Justice Potter Stewart; Dino Pionzoi, CIA Deputy Director; Richard Gow, president of Zapata Oil; Representative Jonathan Bingham; Senator John Chaffee; John Lilley and Winston Lord, both ambassadors to China.

Loyalty to the order was its creed. Stories of devotion abounded. One son of a Bonesman recalled watching his father bathe for the first time and seeing that he wore his Skull and Bones pin through the skin of his chest.

When thoughts of Billy broke Clevenger's concentration, he found himself thinking about taking a drink, so he took another Antabuse tablet. He knew the majority of twelve-steppers sneered at the drug, called it a crutch, but having stumbled and fallen badly more times than he cared to think about, a crutch seemed like an idea whose time had come.

By 1:00 P.M. he was sitting with Anderson in his office at Boston Forensics, trying hard to stay awake and stay focused.

"I called the victims' families from Connecticut," Clevenger said. "Each of them built a new estate—one nine years ago, one seven years ago. And the Hastings family in Montana built a retreat on Parrot Cay in Turks and Caicos. But none of them would tell me who drew up the plans. They're all under confidentiality agreements."

"More important, they're all Skull and Bones," Anderson said. He paused. "I checked with the building departments in Southampton, San Francisco, Chicago, and Miami. Each set of plans was stamped by a different architect. Two men, two women."

"And . . ." Clevenger said.

"None of them are listed with the American Institute of Building

Design or anyone else. No phone directory listings. Nothing. They don't exist."

"Don't they have to show ID or anything when the plans are filed?"

"Usually they're filed by the general contractors, sometimes by the property owners themselves—whoever pulls the building permit. And nothing says a contractor ever has to meet the architect."

"What about the Sutton list? Did you look into how many architects are on it?"

"That could be our ticket. I hired two researchers. So far, they've only found eight architects. Chasing them down is the second half of my day."

"Let's split them up," Clevenger said.

"Fair enough," Anderson said. He took a piece of paper out of a folder. "Roger Grains, Manhattan. Johnson Alexander, Philadelphia. West Crosse, also Manhattan. John Bradford, London. Farleigh Smith, right here in Boston. Dennis Jay, Dallas, Texas. Paul Midland, Los Angeles. And last, but not least, Christopher Heinz, D.C. You take the first half, I take the second?"

"Done."

He ripped the paper in half, handed the top to Clevenger. "The only one we couldn't get a current address on was Crosse. I'm saying Manhattan because he worked for several years at a firm there. Jones, Alison Design. But no one I talked to seemed to know where he landed after he left there. I can't find him in any current database or directory, either."

"That's interesting."

"I thought so, too."

"I'll start with him," Clevenger said. "If the researchers feed us new names, we can split those up, too. If we end up with too many, we get a P.I."

"I'll call Aaron Kaplan, tell him he's on deck. He can be a pain in the ass, sometimes, but he's relentless."

"I'll take that combination any day."

"I'm starting with Smith since he's local," Anderson said. "But then I want to check on this Dennis Jay in Texas."

"Why him?" Clevenger asked.

"They love the capital punishment thing out there. They executed Karla Faye Tucker, that woman who was reborn in prison, remember? The pope appealed for mercy."

"I'm not sure I follow," Clevenger said.

"Simple: If I were a killer, I'd want to be around killing," Anderson said. "Maybe I wouldn't know it up here"—he pointed to his head—"but I would in here." He laid a hand over his heart.

THIRTY-SIX

Clevenger was boarding the 4:00 P.M. US Air Shuttle to La-
Guardia when his phone rang. It was Whitney McCormick.
"Hey," he answered.

"Where are you?" she asked. She sounded worried.

He suddenly realized how deeply his faith in her had been
shaken by knowing her father was a Bonesman. Maybe he was
half-paranoid, falling headfirst into a crazy conspiracy theory, but
he just couldn't bring himself to tell her that he had called Laine
Jones, senior partner at Jones, Alison Design, and was headed for
Manhattan.

Jones had given him an honorable response to his request for information about West Crosse. He wanted to be sure Clevenger was
actually who he said he was before commenting on a former employee. He was willing to meet for a drink at the Pierre Hotel on
Fifth Avenue at 6:30 P.M.

Luckily, Clevenger thinking about a drink after swallowing an
Antabuse tablet translated into thinking about dropping dead or
getting so sick that he wished he were. Imagine being choked
within an inch of your life—for a couple hours. There was an old
saying in psychiatry: Nobody ever has two Antabuse reactions. Either you die or you learn.

"Frank, did you hear me?" McCormick asked.

"I'm in Boston," he answered, and left it at that.

"Visiting Billy?"

"No," he said. "A lot's happened. He's not in detox."

"I know. That's why I'm calling."

"You know?"

"I know more than you do right now, actually."

She sounded like a doctor about to deliver bad news. "Whitney," Clevenger said. "What the hell is going on?"

"There are a bunch of indictments coming down in Massachusetts today. The Royals, that gang Billy hangs out with, are getting rounded up. So is another gang called Night Game, out of Lynn and Somerville. Heroin distribution. Billy's name is on the list."

Clevenger lowered himself slowly into an aisle seat on the plane. "What?" he asked.

"They know he's already in custody at the Nashua Street Jail, but he's going to be indicted on federal charges now, too." She let out a long breath. "Why didn't you tell me he got arrested?"

"It happened so fast, I . . ."

"Truth."

He rubbed his eyes. "I don't know. I think I wanted to keep us separate from all that, somehow."

"I keep telling you it's all right. You have to do what you have to do for him. We're another story."

But the two stories seemed linked, always had. "How many counts?"

She hesitated.

"Just tell me."

"Nine."

"Fuck." Clevenger felt himself getting lightheaded. Nine indictments for drug distribution could bring twenty years in federal prison.

"If he cooperates and helps identify people farther up the food chain, it changes the calculus. I know that's not a lot for him to hold onto right now—or you—but it would help."

The calculus. Even though the Supreme Court had finally over-turned the sadistic and rigid federal sentencing guidelines that doled out decades in prison like penny candy, plenty of judges still used the same system to sentence drug offenders. Under that system, defendants got a certain number of points for breaking each law. Judges simply added them up, subtracted points for defendants ratting out their suppliers, then moved their fingers a couple columns over, and read off how many years the accused—including first-time, nonviolent offenders—would spend in prison. Nothing Solomonic about it. Might as well have an ATM machine doling out justice.

"I don't know if Billy will cooperate," Clevenger told Mc-Cormick. "I feel like I don't know him at all anymore."

"The DEA sent a press release to the *Globe* and *Herald*," she said. "With Billy's public profile—the adoption and everything, all the press around that—you know they're gonna focus on him."

"No way around that."

"He really needs a lawyer now. And he really needs you."

"We'll see what he wants."

"I wish there was something I could do. I feel awful."

She sounded like she meant it. "I'm glad I know what's happening," he said. "And I'm glad I heard it from you."

"Do you want me to fly in tonight?"

"I thought you were seeing someone."

"You shouldn't have to go through this alone."

That didn't exactly answer the question. And, for some reason,

Clevenger didn't like the idea of Whitney offering to visit the minute it looked like Billy would be visiting a federal penitentiary. "I need a little while to get my head around this," he said.

"No problem," she said, tightly.

"It's just . . ."

"I totally understand. Honestly. It isn't my place. It's not like I'm his mother or anything."

He felt like he was out of words.

"Call me with anything, any time, okay? Whether it's the case, or Billy, or whatever."

"I will." It struck him again that he hadn't told her a thing about West Crosse or the other architects or that he was headed to see Laine Jones.

"Take care," she said.

"You, too." He hung up.

THIRTY-SEVEN

Laine Jones was a tall, imperially slim man about fifty, with curly hair the color of graphite, hazel eyes flecked with gold, and a broad forehead that promised high intelligence. He had a habit of looking at you longer than you expected after he spoke, as if to catch your true reaction to what he had said. And yet his gaze was not unsettling. To the contrary, it gave you the sense he valued authenticity, and that you could trust him.

He wore khakis, a white shirt, and worn Docksiders, no socks. He didn't need to dress for success. He was already the architect of choice for a client list that read like *Who's Who in America.*

"I'm satisfied you are who you say you are," he said, after looking at Clevenger's medical license and forensic examiner's badge. His voice was precise, yet gentle. He motioned for the waiter. "Tell me why you're so interested in West Crosse."

"He was tapped for Skull and Bones at Yale," Clevenger said. "We think the killings may relate to that order."

Jones's eyes never left him. "Is he a suspect?

"No," Clevenger said quickly. "He's one of many people we're trying to exclude as suspects."

"Semantics," Jones said, with a smile.

The waiter arrived. "What might I get you?" he asked.

"A glass of merlot, please," Jones said. "The ninety-seven Three Nuns."

"Coffee, please," Clevenger said. "The two-thousand-and-five, black."

Jones laughed.

"Thank you, gentlemen," the waiter said, and left.

"So, what can you tell me about Crosse?" Clevenger asked Jones.

"A genius," Jones said. "He came to work with us shortly after he graduated architecture school and stayed until about five years ago. He was the best I've ever seen, or expect to see."

"Present company excepted, of course."

"No. He was better than I was."

"What made him so good?" Clevenger asked.

"He knew how to use space to create life. Very few people do."

"Meaning?"

Jones laid his hands on the table. "What is this?"

"A table."

"Keep going."

"Wooden," Clevenger said. "Rectangular. About two feet by three, about three inches thick."

"It is wood," Jones said. "It is of those dimensions. But, of course, there's much more to it than that."

"Okay . . ." Clevenger said.

"It helps us be human."

"Human . . . How do you figure?"

"For starters, it separates us enough to feel comfortable, but doesn't keep us too far apart. Am I right?"

"I think I can buy that."

"Well, that didn't just happen. Someone had to decide that. Shorter might work for romance, but certainly not for business.

Longer and wider would help if we had a stack of documents to review, but this isn't a place designed to encourage that kind of work. It encourages conversation." He ran his fingertips over the wood. "The dark stain implies a certain gravitas. It says this is a space for serious discussion, totally in keeping with a landmark hotel."

"Quite a table," Clevenger said.

Jones held up a finger. "But there's more. The way it sits in the room—far enough away from others to let us talk, but not so far that we feel isolated." He nodded toward the main aisle through the restaurant. "There's plenty of room to walk up to us, should someone care to, but a flow to the space that allows strangers to pass without feeling compelled to acknowledge us at all. Someone we knew could even pretend not to see us, and get away with it. And those were someone's decisions, too." He looked up. "The ceiling—marvelously high, but also densely illustrated. It draws the eye skyward. We can think lofty thoughts, but the deep colors and domed shape hold us, ground us. We feel elevated, but steady." He stopped, looked at Clevenger. "You'll note I haven't felt the need to shout or to whisper. I have no fear of you missing my words, nor that they will be overheard. The acoustics work. And I mean that in the most active sense of the word. They do real *work*. They encourage dialogue, rather than silence. And someone—"

"Decided that, too. I'm with you."

Jones nodded. "Good. Then you understand a little of what architecture can achieve and what West Crosse had already mastered on a much grander scale—making space come alive and nourish the life within it."

"You must have been very disappointed when he left the firm," Clevenger said.

"No," Jones said. "I wasn't disappointed at all. I fired him."

"Why?"

The waiter delivered Jones's wine and Clevenger's coffee. They thanked him.

"You don't drink?" Jones asked.

"Not today," Clevenger said.

"Ah. You're sober."

"Not very long, but, yes."

"Congratulations." He touched the rim of his wineglass. "I'm sorry I ordered this."

"It's fine. One thing about alcoholics: We're very self-centered people. We never worry about what other people are drinking, only what we can. And I can't—at all. Period."

Jones sipped his wine. He pursed his lips, shook his head.

"Not good?" Clevenger asked.

"Fantastic." He motioned the waiter. "But I don't want it."

"I told you . . ."

"I don't buy that line of bullshit for one second. If this stuff is poison to you, it has no place at our table. Period."

The waiter came by.

"I've changed my mind," Jones told him. "If you could take this away, I'm going to switch to coffee, too. Milk on the side, for me."

"Very good," the waiter said. He took the wine away.

Now Clevenger was the one quietly studying Jones, looking for a hint of insincerity, finding none.

"Where were we?" Jones asked.

"Crosse. You fired him."

"Right. You asked why. I'll tell you straight out: I fired him because he was an artist."

"Now, you've lost me," Clevenger said.

The waiter dropped off Jones's coffee.

He sipped it. "An artist or a poet can be uncompromising. They own the canvas or the page. But an architect is always a coauthor.

222

The needs of the client have to be honored. That includes their fears, quirks, frugality, all of it."

"He pushed them too hard?"

"He wrestled them to the ground. He wasn't satisfied to create anything less than pristine space with the potential to revolutionize the way they lived or worked. He was so sure his designs could transform their very existence that he believed they should spend whatever it took to build them. The universe would repay them that much, and more. He drove some into bankruptcy, others to divorce. One eccentric client of ours who wanted a retreat ended up embezzling money to complete a stone fortress West designed out in Rye, complete with a moat. He ended up in jail. There was a couple who actually put their infant twin sons up for adoption after West designed a home in which they could be passionate with one another again. It was a one-bedroom loft." He took another sip of coffee. "You can play the tortured artist in this business—the purist—to a point. When you start torturing clients, you're going too far."

Clevenger pictured the magnificent homes he had visited, with magical, beckoning entryways, libraries that invited reflection, glass ceilings and transoms that let the mind travel like light, soaring views. And he recalled, too, the lack of sorrow shown by those whose lives had been rearranged—redesigned—by murder. "Was he right, though?" he asked Jones.

"Right? About what?"

"His plans," Clevenger said. "Did he come to know his clients so well that what he designed for them actually did have the power to free them, even if they sometimes couldn't see it?"

"For some." He nodded, thinking to himself. "I might say all of them—if not for one thing."

"What?"

"They were human."

Clevenger kept listening.

"You can completely rehab a building or perfect an architectural drawing," Jones continued. "At least you can come close. But people are a lot tougher to redesign. You have to understand where they're coming from—their histories and hopes and fears—not just where they should end up. Sometimes they can get there, sometimes it's asking too much, or maybe not the right time to ask at all. I'm sure you understand all that, as a psychiatrist."

Clevenger thought of Billy. "I know it as a psychiatrist and I know it as a . . ." He almost said "father," but he wasn't sure he could claim that mantle, anymore, not with the way Billy had looked at him on Suffolk Street, not with him looking at decades in federal prison. "As a human being."

"West couldn't accept it," Jones said. "He couldn't accept it at home."

"At home?"

"It's not a pretty picture." He paused. "He left his wife—Lauren—after she got sick. About seven years ago."

"Sick?"

"Breast cancer."

"Did she survive?"

"Oh, yes. She went through hell, but she made it. She's a very brave woman."

"When did he leave her?"

"That's the most interesting part. He stood by her during the mastectomy, the chemo, all that. What he couldn't stand was the physical imperfection the disease left in its wake. He was fairly open to me about it. Lauren had reconstructive surgery—three times—but he was never satisfied with the result. He obsessed over it."

"Did they have children?'

"No. She was quite young when he left—twenty-eight. She's still a model, with a degree in philosophy from Yale, to boot."

"Did she remarry?"

Jones nodded. "Shortly after he left the firm."

"And did he?"

"Never to my knowledge, I haven't seen him or heard from him, but I doubt he'd risk it again."

"He took it hard—her remarrying?"

"No." Jones smiled. "That's not what I meant at all. I don't think he'd risk being blindsided again by nature or biology or whatever. He married a model with perfect breasts, then found out she needed one removed, and that no surgeon alive could completely restore what God intended. He needed more control over events than that. A lot more."

"Do you know where I can find Lauren?"

"I certainly do." He winked.

Clevenger looked at him askance. "What?"

"Meet me at nine at my apartment. Five-sixty-two Park. We should be done with dinner. Kids should be asleep."

"Excuse me?"

"I'm the one who married her, Frank. Four-and-a-half years, two kids, never a regret." He paused, looked Clevenger in the eyes. "You asked whether West knew his clients so well that his designs really could change them for the better, even if they didn't see it at first."

"Right."

"In a strange way, I think he knew Lauren and I would end up together. I wonder whether a lot of what he told me about her—her bravery during her illness, her intelligence—was designed to intrigue me. The way he described sex with her, how intuitive she was, how close to perfect her body was, even after the surgeries . . .

I've questioned whether my firing him was really my idea, or his—whether he was ready to disappear and wanted all the loose ends tied."

"You think he was that good an architect?" Clevenger said wryly.

"He was *the* architect. If that had been enough for him, if he wasn't looking to be God, he could have been one of the greatest of all time."

THIRTY-EIGHT

With all the ugliness swirling around him, Clevenger found it difficult not to stare at Lauren Jones. She was an oasis of beauty, five-foot-nine, a dancer's lithe body, straight blond hair, bright blue eyes, flawless skin, high cheekbones, full lips. She was barefoot, in jeans worn through at one knee and a black leotard that showed ample cleavage. But all that was just the beginning. The gentleness in her gaze, her graceful neck, the way she held her head slightly to one side as she listened, conveyed a level of curiosity, intelligence, and kindness that was disarming. Even her voice was special—self-assured, yet slightly plaintive, with a hint of seduction, as though she might need a shoulder to cry on now and then, and that there was at least a chance she would be looking for *your* shoulder.

She, her husband, and Clevenger were seated in the study of the Jones's five-thousand-square-foot apartment on Park Avenue, a dramatic space with high-gloss, deep red walls, a gold and red carpet, and works of art by Matisse, Picasso, and big-name newcomers like Julian Schnabel and Brian Farrell. The floor was darkly stained oak planks, six inches wide, with a border of inlaid bronze stars.

Lauren had just described her ex-husband West Crosse's crusade to restore her anatomy after her mastectomy, taking her to top plastic surgeons in Manhattan, then Paris, then Milan. "I felt lucky enough to be alive," she said. "I couldn't have cared less whether I looked exactly the way I did before. But I knew West. He wasn't going to be able to accept any memory of what we had been through together—certainly not any physical reminder of it. And I wanted to help him get past it, the way he helped me when I was sick."

What we had been through together . . . the way he helped me . . . She was still giving him plenty of credit. "Why couldn't he get past it?" Clevenger asked.

"I think he had his fill of ugliness growing up," she said.

"How so?" Clevenger asked.

"His father," she said.

Fathers and sons. The sins of one generation seeping into another. Clevenger knew it at the core of his being, but listening now reminded him yet again: "There is no original evil in the world. Everyone is just recycling pain."

"What about his father?" he asked Lauren.

"He contracted polio when West was seven. He was crippled by it."

"He never got out of a wheelchair," Laine Jones said. "It brought the family to its knees, financially. Not-enough-to-eat poor."

"It was more than the money, though," Lauren said.

Clevenger listened.

"His father changed," she went on. "He felt helpless, and he tried to show how powerful he still was by controlling everything and everyone around him. West was an only child. He grew up afraid to turn on a light switch or turn up the heat or go to the refrigerator without permission. His father approved his clothing every morning before school—until he was sixteen. And he drank. When he did, he beat West's mother."

"West couldn't protect her," Clevenger said.

"Her, or himself," Lauren said. "This disease came, ruined his father, ruined the family, and there was absolutely nothing he could do about it. He begged his mom to take him and leave, but she wouldn't. So they both kept suffering. West always felt he could have achieved much more in life if she had only had the courage to move on."

"How did he put it?" Laine Jones asked his wife. "I can't remember exactly." He looked at Clevenger. "It was quite morbid, really very disturbed."

If Clevenger had wondered why Laine Jones had been so forthcoming with him, why he had brought him home so quickly to meet his wife, now he knew. Jones liked the idea that Crosse might be a monster. He wanted Lauren to hear that her ex was a suspected serial killer—probably because he wasn't quite sure she had ever stopped loving West.

Maybe she hadn't. Maybe Crosse's design for Laine and Lauren Jones had a critical flaw: Laine Jones just wasn't West Crosse.

"He only said it once," she said defensively. "I didn't respond well."

"You can tell me. I've heard just about everything," Clevenger said.

She still hesitated.

"Tell him," Jones urged. "It's important. We're talking about seven murders."

"He said . . ." She stopped, shrugged, then tilted her head in the miraculous way she could. "He said his mother and he lived with a corpse she never had the guts to bury."

That was interesting, given that the killer never buried his victims. "And how did you respond?" Clevenger asked.

"I told him he needed to see a psychiatrist," she said with a smile.

"Sounds like it's time," Clevenger said. "How do I find him?"

"We have no idea," Lauren said.

Clevenger kept looking at her.

"He disappeared," Laine said. "He had a few very committed clients who tried tracking him down. None succeeded, to my knowledge."

Clevenger's eyes traveled momentarily to Lauren's breasts. He made himself look up, into her eyes. "Just out of curiosity, was your third surgery your last?" he asked her.

"Excuse me?" she asked.

"I wondered whether you had another surgery after things didn't work out with your first husband. Or were you still feeling lucky to be alive?"

"How does that have anything to do . . . ?" Laine started.

You really don't want the answer to that question, Clevenger was thinking to himself—as Jones stopped asking it.

Something cold and rageful came into Lauren Jones's eyes for the briefest moment, a fleeting sign that she was indeed human, not a goddess, that she was subject to tides of emotion like the rest of us. "I had two more surgeries," she said. "I guess the shock of facing my mortality wore off. I had the emotional reserves to think about my body again."

"Nothing abnormal about that," Laine Jones said.

"Not at all," Clevenger said. "Were you able to have the work done here in the States?" he asked Lauren.

"Argentina," she said. "Buenos Aires."

"Did the two of you make a trip of it?" Clevenger asked. "It's so beautiful there. I've been twice. I stayed at El Porteno both times—that hotel that was a factory."

"It is amazing, isn't it?" Lauren Jones asked. "Phillippe Starck was the architect. I would love for Laine to see it." She glanced lovingly at him. "I went alone. Not exactly the kind of thing you want to do as a couple."

Unless, Clevenger thought, she were still coupled with West Crosse. She had traveled with him to surgeons in Paris and Milan.

"Next time," Laine said.

"Who was the surgeon in Buenos Aires, by the way?" Clevenger asked Lauren. "I have a friend who would really appreciate the referral."

She hesitated again.

"Vega, wasn't it?" Laine asked.

"Of course," she said. She shook her head. "Maybe *I* need a psychiatrist. My memory isn't what it used to be. Enrique Vega."

"I think he's generally considered the top plastics man in the world," Laine said. "I checked him out with doctors around here. One of them put it pretty clearly: *After you see Enrique, there's no one to see but God.*"

"Did he do that comment justice?" Clevenger asked. "I don't mean to pry."

Lauren smiled and looked over at Laine.

"Perfect," he said. "Man's a genius." He winked. "I'm forever in his debt."

THIRTY-NINE

Clevenger called North Anderson as soon as he was out of his meeting with Laine and Lauren Jones. It was 10:55 P.M.

"How did it go today?" Anderson asked him.

"All I have so far are hunches. But this guy Crosse certainly loved rearranging people's lives. I'm going by Jones, Alison Design in the morning to look at some of the plans he drew up when he worked there, see if they look anything like the Groupmann estate or the others."

"The guy in Boston—Smith—wouldn't tell me a thing. I got thirty seconds with him in his office. But then his lawyer called and told me he'd be sending me copies of his travel documents. I've got 'em. Private plane reservations, American Express receipts, even affidavits from two pilots and the manager of a hotel in Istanbul. Smith was working a project there most of last year, including long periods before and after bodies were found."

"You still tackling Texas next? Dennis Jay?"

"I made a call. He's away, too. London. These guys travel plenty. I'll move on to Philly."

"I could use help with one thing on Crosse."

"Shoot."

"I met his ex-wife, Lauren. She married Crosse's former partner, Laine Jones."

"Keeping it in the family."

For some reason, that made Clevenger think of the note the president had received from the killer:

One country at a time or one family at a time,
Our work serves one God.

"It's convenient, that's for sure," he told Anderson. "Her name is Lauren Jones now. She told me she was a patient of a plastic surgeon in Buenos Aires named Enrique Vega. He supposedly performed reconstructive surgery on her breast after she had a mastectomy. I'd like to know if that's true."

"I'll get on it," Anderson said.

"You may run into confidentiality issues."

"I'll have my wife call, give the name Lauren Jones, and ask to book a follow-up. If they've never heard of her, we've got our answer."

"Whatever it takes."

"We could have the FBI contact Interpol. I'm sure they could pull her medical record, one way or another."

"If Crosse is our man, I want to move the ball far enough down field that Whitney has to pick it up and run with it. Otherwise, I'm worried you're right: Politics could get in the way."

"Fair enough. It's you and me, brother."

"Always seems to end up that way," Clevenger said. He thought of something else. "If you can send my cell phone a bunch of photos from the crime scenes—especially Chase Van Myer—I might be able to use them."

"You need to give somebody a little religion?"

"Put it this way: When you're as beautiful as Lauren Jones, it could be hard to imagine how ugly murder can really be. Seeing is believing."

FORTY

Clevenger finished off his second cup of coffee and looked out the window of the pastry shop. From his seat he could see the door to the Jones's apartment building at 562 Park Avenue. He ordered a third cup.

Laine Jones had suggested he meet him at 8:00 A.M. at Jones, Alison Design, about twenty blocks away, at 222 Madison Avenue. He promised to have several sets of West Crosse's architectural drawings for Clevenger to peruse.

Ten minutes later he saw Jones walk out the door and disappear into the back seat of a black sedan. It drove off.

He stood up, paid the bill, and walked over to 562 Park.

"May I help you?" the doorman asked.

"I'm here to see Lauren Jones," he said.

"Who shall I say is calling?"

"Dr. Clevenger."

The doorman picked up a phone mounted to the wall, dialed. Someone picked up.

"A Dr. Clevenger to see you, Mrs. Jones." He listened, then held the phone to his chest. "Mr. Jones just left. He thought you were meeting at the office."

"I'm headed there," Clevenger said. "I wanted to stop by and see Lauren first—just for a few minutes, if she has the time."

The doorman relayed the message into the phone, listened again, hung up. "Apartment 17E," he said. "Elevators just inside."

Clevenger's cell phone rang. He looked at the screen. North Anderson. "Thank you," he told the doorman. He answered the phone as he walked toward the elevator. "What's up?"

"Very nice people in Argentina. My wife got through to Enrique Vega, personally. Talk about big medicine. Google this guy, you find out he's plastic surgeon to the stars. But he's a real human being. He apologized to her up and down, but said he just couldn't recall ever treating any Lauren Jones. She told him she sometimes goes by her maiden name, Lauren Crosse. Still didn't ring a bell. He even put her on hold and asked his secretary whether he could be forgetting a patient. Not the case."

"Pretty much what I figured."

"Which means?"

The doorman looked like he was getting antsy watching Clevenger standing at the elevators.

"Let me call you back on that," he told Anderson.

"Done."

They hung up.

Clevenger took the elevator from the lobby to the seventeenth floor, walked down the long hallway to 17E. He knocked on the door.

A few moments later, Lauren Jones opened it. She was wearing a white silk and terry-cloth robe. But she didn't look like she had just rolled out of bed. Her hair was perfect. She was wearing mascara, a pearl necklace, and diamond studs in her ears. "What a surprise," she said. "Come in." She walked toward the kitchen. "You can wait for me in the living room, if that's alright."

"Of course." Clevenger walked into the living room, really more of a library, with a fireplace at either end, yellow-orange high-gloss walls, animal-skin rugs, and a six-foot by twelve-foot painting of two elk fighting, their horns locked. Silver-framed photographs and books filled deep shelves along one wall.

"Can I get you anything?" she called to him.

"No, thank you. I'm fine." He looked at the photographs— stunning black-and-white shots of Lauren walking alone on the beach, Lauren playing with her three-year-old daughter and four-year-old son in Central Park, Lauren and Laine dancing at two black-tie events, the entire picture-perfect family together on a sailboat. They looked like originals of the photographs that come with frames when you buy them—something unreal about them, staged.

She walked in with a cup of tea, sat down on one side of a deeply cushioned, red velvet couch with big throw pillows embroidered with gold family crests. "Please," she said, nodding toward the other side.

Clevenger sat down.

"You wanted to see me before meeting with my husband." Her tone of voice was no less strong, or kind, or needy than it had been the night before.

Clevenger literally had to look away a moment to steady himself. Her beauty was mesmerizing. "That's right," he said.

"Why?"

He looked back at her, saw that the neck of her robe had gaped open enough to show more of her chest than before. He could see the top of one perfect, light-brown nipple. She was a Greek statue come alive. "Because I think the truth always comes at a price," he said. "And I don't see any reason you should pay more than you have to. Your husband never has to know what we say here."

She squinted at him. "Excuse me?"

"I really only do one thing in the world. I listen to stories. I listen for whether they make sense. And when I listened to you, I never heard why you ended it with West Crosse. I understand why he left the firm. I understand why he left the area, even why he went into seclusion. But I don't see why he would ever leave you."

"I told you. I wasn't perfect, anymore."

"But you never stopped trying, did you? Almost as though you still wanted to please him. And look at you now."

"You would need to look a lot closer. After two babies, it's all smoke and mirrors."

False modesty. Clevenger looked down, nodded to himself. It was time. He looked into her eyes. "It's true that Enrique Vega is one of the world's best cosmetic surgeons," he said. "But you were never treated by him, were you?"

She didn't respond.

"I think you probably went to Buenos Aires. I think you probably stayed at El Porteno. Because those things could be checked. Laine could check."

"You know what? You're crossing the line." She started to get up. "I think you should leave."

"Give me thirty seconds."

"Why the hell should I?"

That flash of anger again. She changed from a goddess to a woman. It only made her more compelling. "Because you're a good person and you're smart. In your heart, you don't want to play any part in people being murdered. And you know the man you love might have crossed the line from genius to insanity."

She kept her eyes averted, but sat down.

"You went to Buenos Aires and had your surgery. But Vega didn't perform it." He paused. "West Crosse did."

"You're the one who's insane," she said, pulling her robe tightly closed.

"He may have left behind partners and clients who couldn't keep pace with his intellect and passion, but he never abandoned you. You wanted to be perfect again, and he wanted that for you, too. Because then he could love you again. Only then. When no surgeon could achieve it, he mastered the art himself."

She looked at him, said nothing.

He took out his cell phone. "I have a few pictures to show you. Enrique Vega may be great. West Crosse is beyond great. He's the master. Take a look." He turned on the phone, pulled up a photograph of Chase Van Myer, her eye sockets dissected. He held it out to Lauren.

Her face registered disbelief, then horror and sorrow.

He pressed the arrow key on his phone, brought up another image of Van Myer, naked, bound into a seat at Frank Gehry's Pritzker Pavilion.

Lauren closed her eyes.

"There's more. Much more."

She swallowed hard, looked back at the screen.

Clevenger cycled through photos of Jeffrey Groupmann's meticulously dissected spine, Ron Hadley's heart, Gary Hastings's kidney."

Her face registered confusion.

"The kidney," Clevenger said. "Perfectly dissected." He paused, pressed the key, again, bringing up a photo of Hastings in a Little League uniform six months before his death. "It's the kidney of an twelve-year-old boy." He pressed the key yet again, brought up a photograph of Heather Rawlings, naked, nailed to a cross, then a close-up of her neck meticulously dissected. "He's better than any pathologist or surgeon I've ever seen."

A tear escaped Lauren's eye, ran down her cheek. She wiped it away.

Clevenger scrolled back to the image of Hastings. He left it glowing on the screen between them, as though the boy were bearing witness to the moment. "You know where he is, Lauren. Tell me. Because if you don't, and if he's the one doing this, more people are going to die, just like this boy died. And if that wouldn't make you feel a lot less than perfect, no one on earth can help you. Then you really would need to see God."

FORTY-ONE

Clevenger dialed North Anderson from the street outside 562 Park.

"Hey, Frank," Anderson answered.

He flagged down a cab. "Where are you right now?"

"Logan. I've got about twenty minutes before my flight to Philly."

"Change of plans. Hold on." He climbed into the cab. "Madison and Thirty-eighth, please," he told the driver. He spoke into the phone again: "Let's both head to D.C."

"Why? What's happening?"

"I just got through talking to Lauren Jones. West Crosse is registered at the Mayflower Hotel, under the name William Russell.

"William Russell? Wasn't that the guy who ran Skull and Bones at the beginning?"

"Founded it. Eighteen-thirty-two. You remember. He supposedly made his fortune smuggling opium from Turkey to China."

"So what's Crosse doing in D.C., under a pseudonym— especially that one?" Anderson asked.

"Good question. Jones was supposed to meet him there tonight. He told her he wanted to see her, because he wouldn't be able to for a long time."

"As a forensic psychiatrist friend of mine would say: 'That can't be good.' "

"Doesn't sound it. I'm headed over to Jones, Alison now to look at some of the plans Crosse drew. I figure if you fly down and try to at least spot him, follow him if you can, we could be that much farther down the road"

"I'm walking to the ticket counter as we speak."

"And if you can get to a computer, his photo might be on-line, somewhere."

"I can pull up the Web on this phone."

"Good deal."

"Your gut tells you this is our man?" Anderson asked.

"I've been saving the punch line: He reconstructed his ex-wife's breast after she had a mastectomy. Lauren Jones."

"He . . . *what?*"

"He remade her. She says the two plastic surgeons who worked on her didn't even come close to what he achieved. He has a library of anatomy and surgery books as big as most medical schools."

"Ready to bring Whitney aboard?"

Clevenger knew the facts of the case merited it. So why did he still feel hesitant? Why go it alone when he could bring the resources of the FBI to bear? Did he really believe that allegiance to Skull and Bones would transcend Whitney's allegiance to her job, to the rule of law? "I will—in person," he said. "I'll call her before I leave for D.C. and see if she can meet me in the city."

"See you there," Anderson said.

"Call me when you get to the Mayflower."

"Will do."

They hung up.

Two minutes later, Clevenger's cab pulled up in front of 222 Madison.

He paid the driver and headed up to Jones, Alison Design, on the twenty-third floor. The receptionist escorted him to the conference room.

Laine Jones was waiting for him.

"Morning, Frank," he said. He extended his hand.

Clevenger shook it.

"All set for you," he said. He nodded toward the conference table, covered with six sets of architectural drawings. "I picked projects that span West's tenure here," he said. "His style shifted a bit—use of materials and what have you—but I think the central themes of his work stayed very consistent."

Clevenger walked slowly around the table, studying the plans, flipping pages. And his confidence that he was looking at the work of the man who had killed Jeffrey Groupmann and Chase Van Meyer and the others grew. Every square inch of the drawings was covered with extensive notes on color, the wood and stone and metal to be procured, specific guidelines on construction. And in every design was the magical use of space and light that Clevenger had seen in Pacific Heights, Southampton, and Chicago. Etched-glass ceilings, crisscrossing beams soaring skyward, endless runs of transom glass.

More than anything, though, what the plans showed was Crosse's sensitivity to the life stories of his clients. A car collector would have a garage in which his cars were stored on ramps built into the interior side walls, conserving floor space. A remarried couple trying to maintain their independence while sharing their lives would move into a nine-thousand-square-foot home that was really three homes: five rooms for her on one side, five for him on the other, ten shared, in between. A playwright would have an amphitheater with a retractable roof and an ebony stage inlaid with a Mark Twain quote in bronze lettering: "All art is a lie that tells the truth."

But Crosse had apparently moved far beyond the use of space to honor life stories. He was designing the life stories themselves.

Clevenger noticed a small cross penciled in the upper right-hand corner of each page. "Did he mean the cross as a religious symbol here?" he asked Jones. "Or does it have some significance architecturally I don't know about?"

"It doesn't have any special meaning within the field. West put that on every page of every set of plans he drew while he was here," Jones said. "For a long time we took it as shorthand, in place of his initials or last name. But then he started speaking quite openly about his devotion to God. By the end, it had become a real problem."

"How so?"

"I certainly didn't want to get in the way of him worshipping whatever he wanted to. But there was an evangelical quality to it. It made people very uncomfortable."

"They felt he wanted to convert them, save them?"

"All that, but even more, that he still needed saving himself, that he was using God the way some people use alcohol or drugs—as an escape."

"From?" Clevenger asked.

"Well, that's really your territory. I'd say his entire past. His father's polio. That wheelchair. Growing up poor. All the rage and helplessness he felt. Most people around here didn't know anything about his childhood, but I think they sensed real chaos under the surface. I think they were worried the religious stuff ultimately wouldn't be enough to keep it in check, that he could lose it and become violent."

Clevenger realized he was being sold a story about why Crosse might be the killer, and that Jones had a vested interest in his buying it. But that didn't make it untrue. "Why do you think you kept him around so long?" he asked.

"Honestly?" Jones smiled, but only for an instant. "The company was young." He nodded at the drawings on the table. "I needed those," he said. He looked at Clevenger. "And I wanted Lauren."

246

FORTY-TWO

West Crosse had chartered a Citation X to take him back to Thunder Bay. He landed at 9:05 A.M. The plane would wait there for his return trip at 5:00 P.M.

He had a limousine take him home. He wanted to spend several hours in his studio completing more detailed sketches of the Museum of Freedom to deliver to Elizabeth Buckley in the morning.

But he had more to do before returning to Washington. His plans for the Buckleys went far beyond an addition to the East Wing. He would free the first family from the terror of their broken child and increase the president's power to liberate people around the world.

Crosse had not voted in the five years since he left Jones, Alison Design, left New York, left behind all useless compromise and all half-truths, and committed himself fully and irrevocably to God's vision. Now he sat at his desk and filled out the New York State Voter Registration form, writing in the address of a studio apartment in Greenwich Village he had rented five weeks before, and changing his party affiliation from Republican to Democrat. He sealed the envelope, stamped it, set it aside.

He turned on the computer in his office and pulled up the Web site of Bradley Jay, the most liberal of radio talk show hosts, clicked on the Feedback button and typed out a message:

How can a president and first lady possibly fathom the suffering of those who have lost sons and daughters in war when they have never suffered the loss of a child themselves? The party of Abraham Lincoln, who knew the grief of losing not one, but two sons, was once mine. But no longer.

—West Crosse

He called up Web sites for Jack Forbes, President's Buckley's opponent in the last election, for the Democratic National Committee, the *New York Times*, a dozen other liberal newspapers, MoveOn.org, Common Cause, the ACLU. He sent the same message to each.

He turned off the computer, took an engraved sheet of stationery from his desk drawer, and wrote out the same message in flowing script. He penned a tiny cross in the corner of the page. Then he folded it, tucked it in an envelope, and addressed it to President Warren Buckley at the White House.

He turned off the computer, stood up from his desk, and walked down a winding stone corridor to a two-story library, its domed glass ceiling etched with an outstretched hand. The hand of God.

An entire wall of bookshelves was filled, floor to ceiling, with anatomy and surgery texts.

He pulled down *Grant's Atlas of Anatomy*, Ronan O'Rahilly's *Basic Human Anatomy*, Ben Pansky's *Gross Anatomy*, Naomi Nicholi's *Obstetric and Gynecologic Surgery*, and Randolph Maloney's *Principles and Practice of Vascular Surgery*. He laid them on a mahogany library table ten feet long, engraved with the Yale University crest beside the emblem of Skull and Bones—a skull and crossbones atop the number 322, reflecting the year 1832, when the Yale chapter was founded, along with it being the second such chapter in an international network.

He sat down to study.

He started with *Grant's Atlas,* opened to chapter 3, the Perineum and Pelvis. He turned to Diagram 3-11, the female pelvis, in median section.

God's greatness was everywhere visible—in the ovaries designed to marry egg and sperm, the uterus designed to cradle new life and deliver it into the world. And the perversion of that greatness by Blaire Buckley, unwed, herself genetically unfit, nauseated him.

What he would create the next night would look horrifying to others. Monstrous. He knew this. Yet to him, it would be beautiful beyond all words. Because he would create it in the name of the Lord, and in the cause freedom, taking no personal pride in its perfection, all glory to God.

FORTY-THREE

Clevenger landed at Reagan International in Washington at 2:30 P.M. He checked his cell phone as he was walking out of the terminal and saw he had missed four calls—one from North Anderson and three with blocked caller IDs.

He dialed voice mail. He had three messages. The first was Anderson's, telling him he had arrived in Washington and made it over to the Mayflower Hotel. He'd been able to pull up a photo of Crosse on the Web, but hadn't spotted him yet.

The second message was from Whitney McCormick, suggesting she meet Clevenger at 4:00 P.M. at *1789,* an exclusive Georgetown restaurant tucked away on a quiet block of Thirty-sixth Street.

The third message made him stop dead in the middle of the corridor. He felt someone bump him from behind, turned, and muttered an apology. Then he just stood there several seconds, listening to Billy's voice, unable to focus on his words.

He walked to the side of the wide corridor and hit Replay.

"It's Billy," Billy Bishop said. "I got out. The lawyer they gave me was pretty good. The drugs—or whatever—were in that house and on a couple other guys, not me. They can't yank my probation until they prove something called 'constructive possession' when I go to trial. I don't want to go back with those guys, but I can't find my keys to the loft. So if you're around, give me a call, okay?"

He'd lost his keys. Clevenger shook his head, wishing he and Billy were like other fathers and sons who could make a big deal out of lost keys. What a gift it would be to be able to scream at one another over something that mundane. They had much bigger problems. Billy was still all about legal wrangling and street smarts. He liked his lawyer just fine because he'd sprung him from jail. Now he needed a place to crash. Who knew why? Maybe the DEA hadn't left any Royals on the street. Or maybe they were all running scared, worried which of them would flip and make a deal with prosecutors to nail the others.

He dialed Billy back.

He answered after five rings. "Hey."

"I got your message," Clevenger said.

"Are you around? I'm just hanging around downtown right now."

There was no anxiety in his voice. No remorse. Something had to give. "No, I'm away."

"Oh," Billy said. "Does North still have a key?"

"He's away, too," Clevenger said. He closed his eyes, forced the words out. "Even if I were there, I wouldn't let you in."

Silence.

"I won't let you come back home until you check yourself into detox and complete a rehab program."

"I don't need detox. I'm clean."

Clevenger opened his eyes. "Give me a fucking break, will you? You expect me to take your word for that?" He took a deep breath and let it out. "I'm making it easy: Go back to Mass General and get yourself readmitted. If you do all right there, you can come home."

"And if I don't, I can't?" Billy asked. "Like, ever?"

Clevenger felt his throat getting tight.

"I was totally out of line on Suffolk Street, I know, but I didn't mean any of that," Billy said.

Clevenger pictured Billy's cold stare, remembered his words: "This is my family. You're nothing to me."

"Maybe you meant it, maybe you didn't," he said. "That doesn't matter right now. Right now you have to—"

"It matters if you think I'm a liar," Billy said, righteous indignation creeping into his voice.

It was time for a dose of reality. "Of course you are."

"No more than anybody else. Everybody lies."

Everybody lies. It sounded like Billy might be about to rehash the hypocrisy of Clevenger drinking while he was leaning on him to stay sober. Or maybe it was Billy's genuine worldview as the biological son of a man imprisoned for murder and a mother who was no better. The questions a psychiatrist would ask were clear to Clevenger: *Who is 'everybody'? Who lied to you? Let's go back, one by one, as far as you can remember.*

But Billy wasn't Clevenger's patient, and the moment seemed to scream out for limits, not hand-holding. "Forget 'everybody,'" Clevenger said. "Worry about yourself. You have a son you're no father to. You have a second chance in life you don't have the balls to take. You run away like a ten-year-old to a gang of losers and pump yourself up with drugs because you're scared to feel anything— about yourself or anyone else." He was trembling. "I love you, Billy. As God is my witness, I do. But you're turning into a liar and a coward, and it's getting pretty late in the game to turn that around. Maybe it's too late. I don't know. I know one thing: The way out is *in,* toward your pain—detox, then rehab, then therapy. First step, go to Mass General. That's the deal, take it, or leave it."

The phone went dead.

"Billy?"

Silence.

"You there?"

Nothing.

Clevenger dialed him back. No answer. He waited for the beep. "Call me, and I'll let the E.R. at Mass General know you're on your way," he said. "I don't care what time it is. It can be now, or two in the morning." He paused. "Just call." He hung up.

FORTY-FOUR

"*It's not my decision* alone, obviously," Whitney McCormick said, seated at an out-of-the-way table at *1789,* with Clevenger. "But, personally, I don't think it's enough to move on. To investigate further, put resources on it, sure. But an arrest? No way."

"We've got an architect designing victims' homes who happens to be a part-time surgeon," Clevenger said. "How is that not enough?"

McCormick sipped her coffee. "We don't know for sure he designed those homes, Frank. They look like the work of this West Crosse to you, but you're not an architect. And the fact that his ex-wife and her new husband say he has a collection of surgery books and operated on her is beyond bizarre, but we don't even know if it's true. You said yourself this Laine Jones seemed to be trying pretty hard to get you interested in Crosse as a suspect."

"Crosse is in D.C. under a pseudonym. North confirmed it. He's registered at the Mayflower."

"It's still a free country. You can't be thrown in jail because you want to pay cash and use an assumed name." She smiled. "Unless I'm wrong, you and I did that a dozen times at the Ritz in Boston."

Clevenger sat back a bit in his seat, looked at McCormick. "How about the Skull and Bones connection?"

"What about it?"

"He's using the name of the founder of the order."

"Can we look at this like scientists for a second?"

"Alright . . ."

"We have someone who may or may not have designed the victims' homes. We have an author—Sutton—who lists Crosse as Skull and Bones, alongside members of the victims' families. Now, that list might or might not be accurate. But even if it is, I've told you before: You're talking about America's leading families. They invest together, educate their children together, buy vacation retreats together. Even if Crosse is Skull and Bones, even if he designed their homes, that doesn't equal probable cause for an arrest warrant."

"You could bring him in for questioning."

"We might barely meet the threshold for that. I could ask."

"You could . . ."

"I will ask. But here's my real point: We'll get more mileage out of watching him. Let's find out who he's visiting here, who he knows, maybe where he heads next. Then maybe we have enough for a search warrant for his hotel room."

Clevenger nodded to himself. "I'm good with that." He kept looking at her.

"Doesn't sound like you are."

He wasn't sure he wanted to tell her what was on his mind.

"C'mon," she said.

He shrugged.

"What?"

A few seconds passed.

"Say it," she said, rolling her eyes.

"Your father is Skull and Bones. He's on the Sutton list, too. So maybe you can't see this objectively."

"You're joking. I'd let a killer go because of some rumor my dad belongs to a college fraternity? That's absurd."

It did sound absurd when she said it. He didn't respond.

She leaned forward slightly in her seat. "My father is a Yale grad and former congressman who donates heavily to Republican candidates around the country, including President Buckley. Of course he's on the list. They say he's been to Roswell, too, seen the aliens in formaldehyde out there. And who knows? I guess it's possible he kept his secret society a secret from me his whole life. But if he is Skull and Bones, I wish he had at least pulled a few strings for me. I got wait-listed at Yale, then rejected." She winked. "Maybe they were just trying to throw me off the scent.

"You want to have Crosse followed, for starters, that's fine. It feels anemic to me, but it's your investigation."

She looked at him askance. "What's going on here? Is Billy alright?"

"This has nothing to do with him," Clevenger said. "Why are you bringing him up?"

"Can I be honest?"

"I hope so." He felt his words increase the tension between them, even as he spoke them.

"I think you're burnt out and you're being sloppy."

"What?"

"You've got a favorite horse in this race and you want to bet everything on him. You don't want to look at the field. But what if you're wrong? What if Crosse isn't our man? What if one of his clients is the killer, or a draftsman who worked with him years back, or his former partner—this Laine Jones? He's an architect, too, after all. How mad is he that Crosse took business from him? How about the ex-wife, Lauren. How mad is she that Crosse gave her to another man?"

Clevenger rubbed his eyes, looked up at the ceiling, back at McCormick. He nodded. "You're right. I've got a little tunnel vision going here."

She sat back in her seat.

"They let Billy out again," Clevenger said.

"They *what?*"

"The judge didn't believe constructive possession was a slam dunk for the government. So she wouldn't violate him on his probation. They have to prove their case at trial."

"So where is he now?"

Clevenger shrugged.

"You don't know?"

"He wanted to crash at the loft. I told him he had to head to detox and a rehab program first. He hung up on me. I haven't heard from him since."

"Did you call him?"

He nodded.

"Well, it's about time, anyhow."

"About time?"

"That you drew a line in the sand. Either he gets free of that crap or he doesn't. It's his decision."

"Yeah," Clevenger said. "That's what worries me."

FORTY-FIVE

When he was within a couple of blocks of the Mayflower Hotel Clevenger got a call from Anderson. "What's up?" he answered.

"Where are you?" Anderson asked, quietly.

"In a cab, headed to the hotel. How about you?"

"In the lobby, fifty feet from Crosse."

"What's he doing?"

"Sitting at the bar, alone."

"I'll be there in under a minute."

"Good deal."

Clevenger walked into the hotel. Anderson was seated in a leather wing chair near the fireplace, reading *USA Today*. He walked up to him. "Is he still there?" he asked, without looking at the bar.

"Reading the newspaper, on his second scotch. Laphroig. Good choice."

"Not for me," Clevenger said. "Not anymore." He reached into his pocket, took out a loose Antabuse tablet. Funny how his mind and his disease had conspired to make him forget it was there—until now. He popped the pill into his mouth, swallowed it. Then he glanced at Crosse, dressed in jeans and a white untucked shirt, black cowboy boots. "Nothing special, huh? Looks like your average movie star."

Anderson smiled. "What did Whitney have to say?"

"She's going to have him followed. I called her after I hung up with you and told her he was here."

"They're not gonna pick him up?"

Clevenger shook his head.

"Why not?" Anderson asked.

"She doesn't think there's enough evidence to get a warrant."

"Give me a break. Have her take another look at the Patriot Act."

"She made a decent case for waiting."

Anderson shrugged that off.

"Let's keep an eye on him ourselves," Clevenger said. "On the off chance she doesn't come through."

"We might end up sitting here a while. He likes to drink."

"I was with Lauren Jones this morning when she left him a message that she wouldn't be meeting him tonight. He can't be happy about that."

"Not a man who plans the way he does," Anderson said.

Several seconds passed.

"I get that the FBI is keeping its distance," Anderson said. "Why are we?"

"Why are we . . . ?"

"Hanging back." He shook his head. "I mean, something's not right here. Either Whitney's maneuvered you into working this case *their* way, or Billy's got you distracted, or there's something I don't know about. But sitting here like this isn't your style. It's not *our* style."

Clevenger stared at him.

"The Frank Clevenger I know would be at the bar with this lunatic, with or without a drink, crawling inside his head."

"Maybe."

"*Maybe?* I don't remember taking a back seat to the Feds on the Highway Killer, or John Snow. Do you? We *drove* those buses."

Clevenger knew Anderson was right. But he wasn't sure what the difference was this time? Was Whitney truly setting the pace? Had his trouble with Billy spiraled so far out of control that he couldn't take control of anything? Or had drinking until a few days ago taken away his edge?

He glanced over at Crosse again. Maybe there really was synchronicity in the universe. Maybe stepping up to the plate on the case and taking a step forward in his sobriety both meant sitting at that bar with Crosse, focused wholly on the work he had chosen to do in this world. "I remember both cases exactly the way you do," he told Anderson.

He walked over to the bar, sat down two stools away from Crosse. He glanced at the newspaper Crosse was reading, saw a two-page spread on the invasion of Iran, with a large photograph of an Iranian man screaming, carrying his dead daughter in his arms. He remembered the note the killer had sent to the president: "Keep faith. One country at a time or one family at a time, Our work serves one God."

The bartender walked over. "What can I get you?"

"Soda water, lime," Clevenger said.

The bartender pulled out his soda gun, filled a glass, dropped a lime into it, and placed it on a napkin in front of Clevenger.

Crosse motioned for a third scotch.

Clevenger sipped his soda water, nodded at the newspaper. "Is it all that bad?" he asked Crosse.

Crosse looked over at him.

Clevenger nodded at the page again. "The war."

Crosse's eyes shone. "You wouldn't think it was bad news if you lived under the regime in Iran—the ayatollah and a bunch of unelected, bloodthirsty mullahs. You'd want a Blackhawk to fly you out of the Dark Ages, too."

Clevenger smiled. "Maybe. Maybe I would. I'd certainly want to know how the lights got turned out. Just in case there was a way to turn them back on." He nodded at the photograph again. "Other than all the killing."

Crosse's third scotch arrived. He sipped it. "You figure we ought to negotiate with these people. Well, let me help you out here: You can't talk people into abandoning a theocracy lifted straight out of the Koran. We're not talking about thinking beings. We're talking about robots following a recipe for world domination thousands of years old."

"They're not human?"

"For all intents and purposes, no." He took a deep breath, then chuckled to himself as he let it out. "We're taking each other pretty deep, pretty fast, my friend" He held out his hand. "Will Russell."

"Frank Newman."

Crosse took a long swallow of scotch. "What do you do, Frank?"

Clevenger downed some of his soda water. "I'm a psychiatrist."

"A *psychiatrist*. Ah, well. You should have said so up front. That explains it."

"Explains . . . ?"

"You believe men can be changed, healed—by talking to them."

"I think that depends who's doing the talking, and whether he's just as committed to listening."

"Psychotherapy for terrorists? Is that your prescription?"

"I guess I don't believe children grow up wanting to be killers—not a single one of them," Clevenger said. "To want power that much—power over life and death—you have to have felt utterly powerless. Something has to destroy a person before he decides to destroy others." He let that comment linger a few seconds. "I wouldn't be satisfied until I knew exactly what that something was. Otherwise, I might end up declaring victory, only to find out in twenty or thirty years that I'd really lost big, because I'd left the real pathology to infect another generation."

"Get into their pasts, come up with a psychodynamic theory to explain why they have a habit of knocking down office buildings, and blowing themselves up in public places. Maybe they weren't breast-fed or properly toilet trained."

Clevenger smiled. "What do you do, Will?"

"I lobby."

"For?"

"Freedom. Let's leave it at that."

"Not a problem. Where's home?"

"Manhattan. And, you?"

"Boston."

"A Boston psychiatrist," Crosse said. "That's a very fine thing to be. My father saw a psychiatrist for a bit."

"Did it help?" Clevenger asked.

"Not at all." He sipped his scotch.

"Sorry to hear that."

"You know what the Bhagavad Gita says—the holiest of Hindu texts?"

"I'm not sure I do."

" 'Sorrow is sheer delusion.' "

"Meaning?"

"Grief paralyzes people," Crosse said. "Weak people. It prevents needed action. And here's a little more from the Gita, if you can stand it: 'You have no cause to grieve for any being. Know what your duty is and do it without hesitation.' "

Clevenger looked into Crosse's eyes, but only for a moment. Because what he saw there was some cousin of what he had seen in

Billy, colder and more hollow, but related, and it made him literally shiver. He picked up his glass, stared into it. "How about grieving for yourself?" he asked. "Or do you think that's worthless, too."

"Me? I've never known a single moment of sorrow." He downed the last of his third scotch, looked off at nothing and recited more holy text: " 'Blessed are warriors who are given the chance of a battle like this, which calls them to do what is right and opens the gates of heaven.' "

FORTY-SIX

Clevenger had checked into the Mayflower, down the hall from Crosse. He had just finished another round of calls to victims' families urging them to reveal who had designed their homes. He'd had no luck. His cell phone rang. It was Anderson. He picked up.

"Crosse just walked into the White House," Anderson said.

"The White House . . . I thought you had him at St. John's Episcopal."

"He was there just under two hours. He drove straight to 1600 Pennsylvania Avenue. White-glove service at the visitor's entrance. Took his car, the whole nine yards."

"I'm getting Whitney on the phone—now." He hung up, dialed her cell.

"Frank?" she answered.

He started to pace. "Crosse is at the White House."

"I know," she said. "He went to church first. I promised you we'd watch him."

"And?"

"And we'll handle it, like I said. It's extremely unlikely he's the killer. He has no criminal record. He's well known to the president and the first lady. He's certainly not at their home under false pretenses. He's designing an addition to the East Wing."

265

"You're talking about the competition for that Museum of Freedom or Liberty, or whatever? I thought the winner's name was Ethni . . . something, out of Philly. They had a front-page piece on her in *USA Today*. She's black."

"You already know he likes to use pseudonyms. I guess he also has at least one stand-in. He shuns publicity."

"The killer wrote to the White House," Clevenger said. "Now we've got West Crosse inside."

"Which doesn't have me panicked. Why send a note to the president when you can chat with him over coffee? We're talking that kind of relationship. He's got Cabinet-level clearance. If you really want to know what worries me, it's that somebody else out there is about to leave another anatomy lesson lying around. How about we focus on that?"

"Why not bring him in for questioning? What's the harm?"

"What's the harm in dragging one of nation's top two or three architects who happens to be a personal friend of the president in for an interrogation by the FBI Behavioral Sciences Unit? Oh, I don't know. Can you think of anything?"

"I sat with this guy. I looked him in the eyes. He's dead inside. He has it in him to kill."

"Like a lot of people," McCormick said. "That doesn't mean he ever has." She paused. "Look, here's the bottom line: It's out of your hands. It's out of mine. I know for a fact the Secret Service is going to check and double-check whether he's any threat. I'm told that comes directly from the president's chief of staff."

"You're told."

"Right. I know you think I'm part of a vast conspiracy to rule the world, Frank, but I really just have a job down here. I don't run the place. I report to the director. And he doesn't take me into his confidence on every matter." She let out a long breath. "You need to develop other leads. Crosse doesn't look like our man."

Clevenger sat on the edge of the bed. Maybe she was right, he thought. Maybe he really was being myopic. But then why did it seem like everything pointed to Crosse? How could his instincts be failing him so badly? Could he have mistaken the mysteries inherent in a secret society for the real mystery he was trying to solve? Had he misread their code of silence as evidence of a conspiracy when it was nothing more than tradition? "If you say the Secret Service is on this, I'll take a step back. I'm not trying to tell you how to do your job."

"Of course you are," she said. "You can't help yourself."

"I guess not."

"And I'm not asking you to take a step back. It's the opposite. I just don't want to get distracted."

Maybe it was time, Clevenger thought, to visit David Groupmann again or Laine and Lauren Jones. But neither of those two paths felt like the one that would lead to the killer. And if he stopped working off what felt right to him, off his gut, he knew he would be lost. He decided to call North Anderson and suggest he head back to the office in Chelsea, use the resources there to take a more serious look at Jeffrey Groupmann's skyscraper project in San Francisco. That building had connected at least two of the families of murder victims.

"Have dinner with me tonight," McCormick said, her tone suddenly much warmer. "We'll figure out where we go from here."

"With the investigation?"

She hesitated. "With everything." Another pause. "Come by my place at, say, eight?"

He didn't know where the investigation was going. He didn't

know where Billy was headed. And those things might not have caused the empty feeling in his stomach if it hadn't been for the fact that he didn't have booze. The booze had filled him up when nothing else could. "Sounds good," he said.

FORTY-SEVEN

Finally back at the hotel, West Crosse called the bell desk and asked whether his steamer trunk had arrived via Federal Express. He had shipped it from Thunder Bay, just before flying to D.C. It was waiting for him.

The bellman delivered it to his room ten minutes later.

Crosse rolled the trunk to the bedside, opened it, and knelt beside it. He carefully arranged his scalpels, clamps, and sterling silver nails on the sliding stainless steel tray he had built into the upper compartment. He filled a hypodermic syringe with succinylcholine. He checked to make sure his vial of chloroform was intact, with the white cloth that would cover Blaire Buckley's nose and mouth floating safely inside.

He stood up and pulled off the bedclothes. He unfolded a new plastic sheet and placed it atop the mattress. Then he made the bed again.

He removed Nicholi's *Obstetric and Gynecologic Surgery* from a drawer in the steamer trunk, walked to the study, and opened it on the gracious, claw-foot mahogany desk there.

His plans were more ambitious than ever. He would expose the glorious architecture of one body, while removing every trace of another. He would leave Blaire Buckley's remains to inspire public sympathy for her father, while minimizing any chance an autopsy would reveal she had been pregnant when she died. There were layers to be thinned, minute structures to be excised. No trace would remain of the ill-conceived child Buckley had had the gall to name Eden.

When his work was complete, Buckley would, in a real way, be more normal than ever—relieved of her pathologic brain function, relieved of the moral responsibility for passing on her damaged genes, relieved of her unwitting role in the undoing of her great father.

He thrilled at the backdrop for his effort. The Mayflower Hotel was an architectural triumph, designed in the early 1920s by Warren and Westmore, New York architects who also worked on Grand Central Terminal. Magnificent gilt rams—proud, beautiful, fearless—stood guard on the frieze in the hotel lobby.

Often called the "second best address in Washington, D.C.," the Mayflower had hosted President Calvin Coolidge's inaugural ball and Charles Lindbergh's celebration after crossing the Atlantic.

And Coolidge had worked closely with master Bonesman Henry Lewis Stimson, the personification of the Skull and Bones order.

Crosse sat down at the desk and began to study. He had less than five hours before his moment of truth, the greatest contribution to liberty he would make in his life, the one he hoped to be remembered for, for all time.

FORTY-EIGHT

Clevenger tried calling Billy before heading over to Whitney Mc-Cormick's apartment at the Watergate. He got no answer. He tried again. No answer again. He decided to leave a message. "Hey, Billy," he said, "I don't know where you are right now, but I wanted you to know I'm thinking about you." He paused. "I'm just hoping you decide to try Mass General again. Try it for one day. See how it feels. Not the locked unit, the open one. And . . . call me, already, will you? Alright . . . I love you." He hung up. He looked at the phone. And he realized he had been talking to no one but himself, trying to soothe himself. Billy hadn't called him and might never call.

He took a taxi to the Watergate, walked into the elegant lobby.

The doorman called up to McCormick's apartment for him, then pointed the way to the elevators.

He found apartment 1812, knocked on the door.

"One minute," Whitney called out.

She opened the door ten seconds later. She was barefoot, in jeans and a tight, black Juicy Couture T-shirt stenciled with the word LIBERATOR. She looked as radiant as the day he had first met her. "Thanks for having me," he said.

"Did I?" she asked coyly. "I can hardly remember."

He laughed.

"C'mon in."

He walked in, saw she had the table set, candles burning. "Very impressive," he said.

She disappeared into the kitchen. "You know I never cook. I'm counting on the table to distract you."

He looked out the window at the majestic Potomac River, always moving, always constant. "I'm just glad to be here," he said. He turned and saw her smile to herself as she stirred something on the stove.

Maybe life could be as simple and beautiful as that smile, he thought. Maybe it was, for some people. He turned and looked back out at the river.

FORTY-NINE

• 9:00 P.M.

A knock. West Crosse opened the door to his hotel room a few inches. Blaire Buckley stood in the hallway, beaming in a Britney Spears Onyx Hotel Tour baseball cap and T-shirt, her belly spilling over tight, hip hugger jeans, obscuring the buckle of her polished, metal and rhinestone belt. She wore three long, silver necklaces, a large cross dangling from each. "Is she here?" she asked, trying to peek into the room.

"Did anyone follow you?" Crosse asked.

"No way. I left with the caterers, in their van. They always help me get out."

"They dropped you off at the hotel?"

She rolled her eyes. "Down the street. I'm not stupid."

Crosse smiled. "Britney should be here in ten minutes." He opened the door and stepped aside.

She walked in.

He closed and double locked the door behind her.

The suite was magical. White rose petals and myrtle covered every inch of the floor. A hundred white votive candles burned. Handel's *Messiah* played just above a whisper.

"Way cool," Blaire said. "You did all this, for Britney?"

"No," Crosse said, coming up behind her. "For you."

273

FIFTY

Clevenger's cell phone rang. He reached over McCormick, picked it up off the nightstand and checked the caller ID. *555-726-2000.* Mass General Hospital. "Thank God," he whispered. He answered it. "Billy?"

"Dr. Clevenger?" a woman asked.

"Yes."

"This is Jane Monroe at the General."

Monroe was the emergency room physician Clevenger had met on Billy's last trip there said. He cleared his throat. "It's great to hear your voice," he said. "You have Billy there?"

"Yes," she said.

He felt the weight he had been shouldering begin to lift. "I was hoping he would come in. I promised him he could detox on the open unit this time."

Silence, then, "He isn't here for detox."

Her voice was soft and kind and cut Clevenger to the core. "I'm sorry. What do you mean?"

"He . . ."

She paused not more than two seconds, but that was long enough for Clevenger's eyes to fill.

"He overdosed," she said.

"Oh, God, no." He stood up, started pacing.

McCormick raised herself onto one elbow, squinted at him. "What's wrong?"

"He isn't responsive right now, but he is stable," Monroe said.

"Is it about Billy?" Whitney asked. "Is he alright?"

"Heroin? Coke? I mean, did he have a stroke, or . . . ?" Clevenger asked.

"Oxycontin," she said. "He doesn't seem to have had a stroke." She let the other shoe drop. "But he is on a respirator."

Clevenger felt something hard against his knees and realized he was kneeling. "Is he going to die?"

"I don't know," Monroe said.

"Is he going to die?"

"He's in the ICU," she said. "His heart is holding out. His blood gases are steady. And they've seen this before. Way too many times. They know exactly what to do. He's getting the best care at the best hospital in the world."

Snake oil. He'd tried the same balm on parents and husbands and wives dozens of times. Right now, Monroe was a salesman with absolutely nothing to sell. "I'm not in Boston," was all he could think to say. His voice cracked.

McCormick put her arms around him.

He leaned back against her.

"How long will it take you to get here?"

That question literally doubled him over. Because it obviously mattered whether it was an hour or two or three, or half a day. "The first shuttle is . . ."

"I'll get the helicopter," McCormick said. "There's a helipad on the roof." She stood up, started over to her phone.

"I can be there in two, three hours," he said.

"Great. I'll be here."

"Thank you. And, please, call me if . . ."

"If he wakes up and wants to talk to you, I'll try you," she said.

That wasn't what he had meant and he was sure she knew. "Thank you," he said.

FIFTY-ONE

West Crosse pulled his Range Rover into the driveway of the visitor's entrance at the White House. He knew by the time he came to a stop at the door that his license plate had already been run against a database on the computer inside. A series of cameras equipped for night vision had captured his image and transmitted it to the security desk. At any point, sharpshooters could have blown out his tires or put a bullet in his head.

A guard armed with an Uzi approached his window.

He lowered it.

"May I help you, Mr. Crosse?"

"Yes, I have a trunk in the back full of samples of granite and wood for the museum. I need to bring it to the First Lady's office, as close to the new site as I can get it. Some of the pieces are very heavy."

"You're at work awfully early," the guard said.

"Not for me. This is when I'm most productive. No interference."

He smiled. "I'm with you on that."

Crosse parked and stood outside the car as the security guard ran a chemical probe over the Louis Vuitton steamer trunk, checking for explosives.

"Protocol," the guard said. "You understand."

"Of course," Crosse said.

He finished checking. "All set." He helped Crosse pull the trunk out of the car.

"I'll be okay from here," Crosse said.

"Very good."

Crosse wheeled the trunk inside, down the regal corridors of power, to the first lady's office. He pulled it to the curved wall of windows looking onto the site of the future Museum of Liberty, exactly where he had stood the first time he contemplated its design.

He fully expected the museum would still be built according to his plans. What he had done, after all, was no insult to freedom, but his greatest act in defense of it.

He was unarmed. His clearance was so high that he probably could have carried a gun into the White House, but he knew he would not need one in order to sacrifice himself to his cause. He could not walk into the Buckley White House, do what he was about to do, and walk out again. He knew his client very well.

He took off his overcoat and boots, leaving him barefoot, in a new, clean white linen tunic. He knelt beside the steamer trunk, unlatched it and opened it.

He smiled.

Blaire Buckley lay wrapped in a sheet inside, the magnificent organs that had nearly birthed resistance to her father's great leadership neatly dissected, every trace of Eden gone, as if it had never existed.

He reached down and picked her up in his arms, closed the trunk, and lay her atop it. Then he knelt in front of her, and prayed to God, who had given his life and his death such glorious meaning:

THE ARCHITECT

Our Father, who art in heaven, hallowed be thy name.
Thy Kingdom come, thy will be done, on earth as it is in heaven.

He stood up and gazed out the windows.

He knew he would not need to wait long. Within ten minutes, security cameras would focus on him and on Blaire, and Secret Service agents would begin racing toward the room.

It took just over four minutes for them to arrive.

He heard footsteps and turned around to see two men in dark blue suits emerge from different doorways, pistols drawn. Three more followed them, carrying Uzis. He watched their magnificently trained eyes collecting data, saw their perfect detachment—even from this moment—in which the President's daughter lay perfectly dissected before them.

For an instant, he thought he saw the President himself watching from a distance. But perhaps he just wished that it were so.

He moved his feet apart and raised his empty hands out to his sides, replicating precisely the stance of da Vinci's divine human form. The Golden Section. And as the first bullet struck his chest, his heart swelled with pride that he had designed his last moments on the earth so flawlessly, that the architecture of his existence reflected the will of Almighty God and that eternal life would be his.

FIFTY-TWO

Our great romances and triumphs and conquests ultimately do nothing to bind us together, one to another. It is in defeat and tragedy that our souls show through, and we are known.

A person may tell you about a glorious achievement in business, about being promoted or being hired for a dream job, and be saying nothing at all about his core self. But have that person speak to the sinking feeling of once being laid off, the anxiety of scrounging for tuition money and coming up short, the terror of losing a business or a home, and you are on your way to having a real bond, a real friend.

A woman may speak glowingly about finishing a marathon, or building a dream home, or having a child admitted to college, and yet be telling you nothing. But have her tell you about her panic at getting older, about the slow erosion of her body, or the lingering grief of a miscarriage years ago, or her waning passion for the man she still loves, and you may realize that we are, truly, more alike than different in our needs and fears—and much more alone than we need to be.

But perhaps nowhere can we see each other more clearly than in an intensive care unit, under the cold fluorescent lights, exhausted by our vigils, surrounded by tubing running into and out of our bodies and those of loved ones, listening to the constant beeping of cardiac monitors. Because in an intensive care unit, your job doesn't matter, the new addition to your house doesn't matter, your religion and political party and even sexual orientation are irrelevant. The things that define you and those who love you are simply whether you will live or not and whether you are suffering or not.

There are no strangers and no enemies in the ICU.

Clevenger walked into cubicle 8D and sat down next to Billy's bed. He had been there for over six hours, walking in and out of the room, standing, sitting, watching.

North Anderson had come and gone three times, and would be back again. And again.

Just listen, and the ICU will even tell you whether a man is your friend.

Billy was still comatose, a tube down his throat to deliver oxygen, IVs running into each arm. A new tattoo of a crown was emblazoned across his chest.

Yet even Billy had something to say, and Clevenger heard it.

A tear ran down Clevenger's face. He took Billy's hand and leaned close to him. "Don't worry, buddy," he whispered in his ear. "I won't leave you. I'll never give up on you. We'll make it through together, out of here and wherever you need to go in life. Okay? We'll just figure it out together."

He sat up and looked at his son, and all at once he felt the incredible force the best part of Billy had had to fight against, those early and brittle chapters of abandonment and fear and loss. A violent father. No real mother. A nineteen-year-old Billy Bishop might be in the ICU, but a nine-year-old, already shattered Billy Bishop had taken the overdose that put him there.

Clevenger thought of a favorite passage of his, by author Robert Pirsig:

I don't know what kind of future is coming up from behind.
But the past, spread out before us, dominates everything in sight.

"Dr. Clevenger," Jane Monroe said from behind him.

He turned around. "It's Frank."

"Frank," she said, with a smile. "Someone's here to see you. She's in the family waiting area."

He walked out to the waiting area.

Whitney McCormick was standing just outside, looking very pale and tired.

He walked up to her. "You didn't need to . . ."

She shook her head. "You were right," she said. "You were right about Crosse."

"What? Why do you say that?"

"He brought the body of the president's daughter—the retarded one, Blaire—to the the White House a little over six hours ago. Her abdomen. . . ." She stopped herself.

"Their daughter?" More than ever, he understood. "My God. Is he in custody? Tell me he didn't get away."

She looked at him and said nothing.

What he heard in that silence made him slowly take a step back. He looked into McCormick's eyes, through a tiny window onto her soul, and saw . . . nothing. He saw the same emptiness he had seen in Billy's eyes on Suffolk Street and in West Crosse's eyes at the Mayflower Hotel bar. "I don't think I understand," he said.

She spoke even more quietly. "You don't kill the president's daughter and get taken into custody—not *this* president." She shrugged. "The official reports will say he had a gun and fired first." She looked through him. "That's between you, and me. Period. No North Anderson this time."

285

Clevenger squinted at her. "You're saying they killed him?"

"There wasn't any question of guilt here," she said. "He had a whole mini operatory set up at the hotel. The last thing anybody needs is some long, drawn-out trial with Mark Geragas and Barry Scheck arguing an insanity defense or whether or not his surgical gloves fit." She paused. "I should have listened to you. You had the thing solved for us."

"They didn't arrest him because it was easier to . . . eliminate him? Isn't that what *he* was doing with his victims?"

"Maybe that's the poetic justice here." She winked. "Case closed."

Clevenger felt a cold sweat break out at the back of his neck.

McCormick looked over his shoulder, toward the ICU. "How's Billy?" she asked.

He turned around and walked back inside.

FIFTY-THREE

Gary Field, the president's chief of staff, phoned Clevenger three days later and invited him to the White House. The president and the first lady, he said, wanted to thank him for his service and ask him for his help.

Now Clevenger sat across from president Warren Buckley and Elizabeth Buckley in the Oval Office. "I'm sorry for your loss," he said.

"Thank you," the president said. "I know the grit you showed hunting down our daughter's killer. And I know if you'd had your way, we'd have gotten him before he got Blaire."

The first lady smiled and nodded.

The president sounded like a kid playing Cowboys and Indians. *You got my guy, but my other guy got you, except not until...* His wife looked like a windup doll. No apparent grief.

"I wish we could have found out why he did what he did," Clevenger said.

"Hated me, hated the party," the president said. "You probably saw the garbage he spewed to the newspapers, just before he killed our girl."

That garbage, together with the tragic death of his daughter, had driven Buckley's approval rating to seventy-one percent, the

287

highest point of his presidency. And that was before her funeral service, set to be broadcast nationally the next day. "Yes, I did," Clevenger said. "I'm just not sure that explains anything. After all, normal people don't kill to make a point."

The president smiled tightly.

"And thank God for that," the first lady said.

"Doesn't really matter what was in his head when he cut people up," the president said. " 'Cause he won't be doing it again. Ever."

The first lady smiled and nodded.

"That's one way to look at it," Clevenger said.

" 'Course, a trial would have been the best result, for Elizabeth, my sons, and me."

"I thought you didn't much care to find out anything more about him."

"I don't," he said. "But I wasn't here when he pulled that gun and made the Secret Service cancel his ticket. I would have liked to be at his execution and say good-bye to him, personally."

"And I would have been right there beside him," the first lady said.

"I understand," Clevenger said.

The president grinned and winked, then seemed to catch himself and put on a blank mask of a face. "I want you to think about signing on with us here," he said.

"Signing on? In what sense?"

"Let's figure that out in the next week or so. Maybe something high up at the FBI. Maybe CIA. They need psychiatrists now more than ever. Get the truth out of people. You could make a real contribution to our country."

"I don't think this is the time," Clevenger said.

"Why not?" the president asked.

"I don't mean timing, historically," Clevenger said. "I mean personally. My son just got out of the ICU. He overdosed on Oxy-contin. And he has legal problems. Drug charges. He needs me."

"Well, maybe there's a pardon in his future," the President said. "I can't promise, but I can look at the case on its merits."

"Thank you," Clevenger said.

"Our prayers will be with both of you," the first lady said. She glanced at her husband.

"Remember," the president said, "the cause of freedom needs more good men than ever."